WHEN THE DEVIL BIRD CRIES

A BERNADETTE CALLAHAN DETECTIVE NOVEL

LYLE NICHOLSON

Book Editing and Design;

EbookEditingPro http://ebookeditingpro.com

Book cover design by www.Damonza.com

ISBN ebook, 978-0-9959781-5-7

ISBN print, 978-0-9959781-6-4

❀ Created with Vellum

This book is dedicated to the memory of Bill Loving.
His wife, Ada, graciously lent me Bill to return to the cigar lounge
and become an important character in this book. I met Bill and
Ada many years ago on the Silversea Cruise ship. Our meeting
became years of friendship, with Bill passing on too soon.
I thought, it only right to bring Bill back to life in this book,
perhaps in name only. He was after all, a Texan, and we spent
many an evening in the cigar lounge on the ship, while he listened
to my stories. His pipe puffed lazy smoke rings towards the
ceiling.

CONTENTS

1

THE LONG BAR, RAFFLES HOTEL, SINGAPORE

THOMAS ADDINGTON SIPPED his gin and tonic while watching the young blonde at the end of the bar drinking her Singapore Sling. She looked late twenties, perfect skin, and those looks that only glamor magazines portrayed, but you never see in public.

Thomas hoped his gin would give him the courage to approach her. He was a moderately good-looking man in his early thirties, with a decent head of dark hair coifed in the latest style, pale green eyes, and blemish free skin. With his group of mates back in London, he was never the draw with the ladies, but he could often talk himself into a relationship for the night.

That was his plan this evening. London, England and his girlfriend, Camilla Farnham, were a world away from here. His occupation as an investment analyst for one of England's largest banks left him with a need for excitement.

Casual hook-ups in bars from Singapore to Berlin and New York were his compensation for his boring life. He analyzed numbers all day and attended dreary concerts and poetry readings with Camilla back in London.

Thomas swirled his gin, taking one last gulp before he made his way toward the beautiful blonde. He'd been turned down many times, but his track record of scoring one-night stands was excellent. As an analyst, he knew his success increased with constant advances.

The bar was getting louder. A table of German tourists were laughing at the prices of the expensive drinks and throwing peanut shells on the floor, Raffles Bar being the only place in Singapore you could litter without a two thousand dollar fine.

Thomas understood German, and he looked away from the group as he focused on his target. He timed it perfectly. An elderly Chinese couple vacated their seats just as he arrived. He slid onto the barstool next to her. He could feel her heat, smell her perfume. This beauty already fascinated him.

"Do you like Singapore Slings?" Thomas asked. He waved to the barman to get his attention, trying to avoid her beauty.

She turned her head, as if noticing his presence for the first time. Her look was one of assessment, first at his face, then letting her eyes drop from his chest to his lap, then back up again. A smile edged her lips; he'd passed some kind of evaluation. He felt elated.

"They taste fruity and herbal, but the drink is growing on me," she said.

Thomas turned to face her. "Did you know, this is the very bar that invented the drink back in the early nineteen hundreds?"

She flashed a smile with perfect white teeth. "I don't think so. You seem like an intelligent man, what's the story behind it?"

"Ah," Thomas said, "the good people of Singapore needed to hide their afternoon drinking habits, and they frowned upon ladies drinking. Thus, a Gin Sling became a Singapore Sling. May I buy you another?"

She pushed her empty glass forward. "That would be wonderful. Does this mean you'll be sleeping with me tonight?"

"Ah, that would be—"

"Beyond your wildest dreams?"

"Well... yes," Thomas said with a broad smile as he extended his hand. "Thomas Addington, a pleasure to make your acquaintance."

"I'm sure it will be, Thomas," the blonde said.

Thomas moved slightly forward as the bartender brought them fresh drinks. "And you are?"

"Who would you like me to be?"

"I'm not sure I catch your meaning."

The blonde sipped her fresh cocktail and turned fully towards him. "We only have tonight, what does it matter who I am or my actual name? I could be any name you like. Do you have a favorite?"

Thomas chuckled. No woman had ever been this bold or this beautiful. "How about Cassandra?"

The blonde winked, placing her hand on his leg, squeezing hard. "Cassandra it is."

Thomas placed his hand on hers. He loved this; he couldn't believe how much she aroused him. "You know," he said, giving her hand a soft caress, "I'm here for a few days, we could make this into more than one night..."

Cassandra sipped her drink, her eyes going wide. "Sorry,

Thomas, I can only indulge you for one night. I'm boarding a ship tomorrow."

Thomas gazed into her eyes. They were perfectly matched almond with flecks of gray. "Ah, on a world tour, are we?"

She took her hand off his leg, placing it around her drink. "Yes and no. I'm a crew member on a very luxurious cruise ship that sets sail tomorrow afternoon."

"What's the ship?" Thomas asked.

"Can't tell you. But it has only two hundred passengers, and they're mostly all millionaires."

Thomas took a sip of his gin. "Sounds boring, I work for a bank managing the portfolios of millionaires. They can be tiresome. What are you doing on the ship?

"The most important job of all," she replied. She took a long sip of her drink. "I'm not into conversation, Thomas. I have a long three-month stretch coming up where there's no fraternizing allowed with crew or passengers. I need some action tonight. You up for it?"

Thomas pushed his drink aside and motioned for the bill. "I'm your man, Cassandra."

The bill arrived, Thomas paid with his credit card, something he almost never did as he'd have to reconcile this later with his company. They walked out of the Raffles Hotel into the heat and humidity of Singapore's night.

Taxis seemed scarce. Thomas waved at a few in vain. Cassandra was getting restless. He waved harder at the cabs.

"How about a rickshaw?" Cassandra asked.

"They aren't quick," Thomas replied. He stood there looking somewhat lost.

Cassandra placed her hand on his chest. "I'm in no hurry. Look, I'm going to make love to you all night long. A brief ride in a rickshaw will be nice."

Thomas' chest swelled. "Yes, well then, let's grab a rickshaw." He took her hand, leading her to a small bicycle-powered rickshaw with a slim young Asian driver. The driver put down his cell phone. "Where to?" was all he asked in a thick Malay accent.

"The Carlton Hotel," Thomas replied.

Cassandra snuggled up beside him, her lips brushed his cheek. "Well, I didn't know you were staying at the Ritz-Carlton."

Thomas squirmed a bit, "No, actually, it's just the Carlton. My company policy, you see..."

"Never mind, we'll be just fine. I'm sure you can order some champagne when I get thirsty."

"Why yes," Thomas said. He wondered how he'd manage that. A charge like that would be disastrous to his room account back in London. He'd have to slip the room server cash. Hoping he had enough.

The driver stood up on the pedals and they moved into traffic. They were only a twenty-minute ride away. Thomas settled in, letting the warmth of Cassandra melt away his anxiety of the expense account. His girlfriend Camilla, was half a world away and forgotten.

"We need to stop here," Cassandra said.

"What for?" Thomas asked as she directed the driver to park in front of a small shop.

"I need something for tonight," she said with a wink.

Thomas ran his hand over her thigh. "I hope it's sensual and smells wonderful."

"It's a toothbrush, you silly," Cassandra said, running out of the rickshaw.

"I could order one for you at the hotel..." Thomas said as she disappeared into the crowded store.

The rickshaw driver went back to his phone, Thomas

did the same. He looked at his FB site, checking on his friends. He didn't see the black Mercedes pull up behind him, nor the two men in black suits walk into the store.

He finally looked up from his phone. It had been ten minutes. How long did it take to get a toothbrush? He looked into the store. The crowd had dispersed, and only the shopkeeper stood at the till watching a television show.

Thomas ran into the store. He yelled to the little Chinese man behind the counter. "The young blonde. Where is she?"

The Chinese man looked up at Thomas. "She gone. Go with her two men."

Thomas rushed outside. There was no sign of her. He looked up and down the street—nothing.

"Did you see the girl I was with?" Thomas asked the rickshaw driver. "Did you see her leave the store?"

"I see nothing," the rickshaw driver replied. "You want to go now?"

"I don't know, the girl I was with... I don't know what happened to her." Thomas replied weakly.

The rickshaw driver shrugged his shoulders, looking back at his cell phone.

Thomas felt stuck. What should he do? Was the girl taken by someone? Was he scammed somehow? He reached into his back pocket and removed his wallet. It was still there. He was missing nothing. How could he report this strange encounter with a woman when he didn't know her name?

A light rain began to fall. The rickshaw driver raised the passenger canopy, "You go now?"

"Yes," Thomas replied. "I go now." He got into the rickshaw and slumped into the seat. He had a bad feeling in the pit of his stomach. He knew he should call the police, but his own self-preservation of his so-called good name made him powerless to act.

He finally did something. He did a quick search on his phone of the Singapore Police Department. Using a burner email that he used for his various hookups with ladies with a Gmail address that would only lead back to a Google IP address, he dashed off a quick email. Under the heading of a suspicious observation, he stated the store's location and that he'd seen what may have been the kidnapping of a young lady.

He sighed, hit send, and put the phone away. "Thomas, old boy, you'll get yourself into deep trouble one day," he muttered to himself.

2

Hawker Alley, Singapore

BERNADETTE CALLAHAN FELT something strange as she walked down the row of food stalls with her husband Chris. They'd arrived the day before in Singapore on a flight from Calgary, Canada with stops in Vancouver and Seoul, Korea. Jet lag was wearing on her, but the sights of Singapore were more important than trying to recover lost sleep.

She had a feeling of eyes on her. That they were being followed. She looked up at the many cameras that watched the streets. Could that be it, she wondered?

"How are you feeling about our trip so far?" Chris asked. He was a big man, late thirties, with an impressive build of muscles from his dedication to the gym. He stood out amongst the Asian crowd for his height, curly black hair, and olive complexion. Chris was Greek and Israeli heritage, with a calm disposition that complemented Bernadette's fiery nature.

Bernadette squeezed his hand. "For a girl who has never been much outside of North America, this is cool." She was five foot eight with a look of a woman who gravitated between the gym and her love of food. Bernadette was a mix of Native Cree and Irish. Her hair was red and her skin was a bronze with freckles. Her green eyes missed not one food stall as they made their way down the long alley looking for dinner.

"How's some Pad Thai sound?" Chris asked, looking over the menu of one stall.

"I'm thinking spicier. Something that goes with a good jug of Singapore beer," Bernadette said.

"You didn't get enough beer on the plane?"

Bernadette laughed. "I loved the Tiger beer they served on the plane. I just need a nice spicy four alarm curry to go with it."

"Great, the food here costs next to nothing, a jug of beer costs a small fortune."

"They're trying to keep the population from drinking themselves to death with high prices," Bernadette said.

"Yeah, with that and the two thousand dollar littering fines, they're doing pretty well," Chris said.

Bernadette stopped in front of a food stall. The food listed had several dishes with three to four chili signs, denoting super-spicy food. She let her gaze turn behind them as she scanned the food.

When she saw a little man duck into a crowd, her senses went into overload. That was not a coincidence.

"You okay?" Chris asked.

"I had this feeling we were being watched. Just now I saw a guy duck into a crowd."

"Where should I be looking?" Chris asked. Bernadette was one hell of a detective with the Royal Canadian

Mounted Police in Canada. Her instincts were accurate. "You think we've a pickpocket tailing us?"

Bernadette gazed at the menu to make like everything was normal. "We aren't the usual marks for pickpockets. We don't have cameras, I don't have a purse, and both of us are carrying our money in our front pockets. And you're as big as a house compared to the people here. You'd think they'd mark someone else."

Chris looked around them. A group of elderly tourists walked by happily displaying expensive cameras, jewelry, and large handbags. "I have to agree, we're poor targets for theft—especially when this place is loaded with them."

"Let's order and see what happens," Bernadette said. She ordered a spicy pork dish and Chris chose something with only a two-chilli sign as he wanted to feel his tongue later. They found a picnic table and sat down with two Tiger beers as they couldn't find a vendor selling it by the jug.

"Damn, this is spicy," Bernadette said, then took a drink of beer and wiped her brow with a Kleenex.

"You wanted hot. That's what you got," Chris said. "You see anything behind us?"

Bernadette lowered her head and put the Kleenex to her eyes and looked to the side. "Yeah, he's trying hard to be invisible behind a group of tourists. He's wearing a yellow shirt and holding a bag. Oh, no wait, he just disappeared behind a beer sign."

"Hard to believe someone could be that bad. Are you sure it's not some local guy hiding from his wife?"

"When was the last time my instincts were wrong?" Bernadette asked, taking another big spoonful of curry and rice.

"Okay, I'll tell you but only if you invoke the privilege of non-incrimination. Because I'm not about to hang myself."

"You're free. No recriminations. Go for it," Bernadette said.

"Well..." Chris began carefully, "There is this trip we're on. This is an all-expenses paid, first class cruise on a two hundred passenger ship, and we have no idea who paid for it. Doesn't that classify as going off the grid, instinct wise?"

"I thought we discussed this. It's fine. This was a gift at our wedding. There are no strings attached to the gift, and none of the convicts I put behind bars would have the money to purchase this. Besides, it could have been one of your new-found relatives in Europe."

"So, your instincts told you what? As long as you don't know who paid for this trip, it's okay to do it?" Chris asked with a smile. He knew he had her in a corner on this one.

"No, smart ass, my instincts told me the only way to find out who paid for our cruise was to go on it and find out," Bernadette said with a wink.

Chris leaned in closely to Bernadette. "So far we've been on a first-class flight from Canada and staying at the Ritz-Carlton. I'd say we've done okay for two middle income Canadians on a dream trip we're not paying for—"

"Don't move your head."

"Why, what's up?"

"Our man is on the move. He's meeting up with some-one," Bernadette said.

"See, I told you. Nothing to worry about. The guy is here to meet someone."

"Yeah, you're right. The someone in the yellow shirt just handed the bag off to a guy in a white shirt. Now *he's* now watching us. It's a handoff. Looks like we have a new tail."

Chris finished his beer and gathered up the empty plates to dispose of them. "Look, I doubt if he'll follow us once we leave here."

They joined the crowd in the market, winding slowly down Hawker Alley toward the main street. Bernadette stopped once to fix her shoe and looked casually back. She couldn't see him.

"I told you, you're imagining things," Chris said.

They found a bicycle rickshaw for the return to the hotel. The rickshaw moved slowly through the night with car horns honking and the streets full of people getting ready for late nights of Singapore. They rolled up to the Ritz.

"You go on inside. I'll be right behind you," Bernadette said, stepping out onto the sidewalk.

Chris shook his head in resignation. He knew she'd be looking to see if they were followed. He walked into the hotel without looking behind him.

Bernadette stopped short, then slid in behind a pillar. She watched as a motorized rickshaw came to a stop several hundred yards away. The man in the white shirt carrying the bag got out and made his way towards the hotel. She smiled.

INSPECTOR LEE WOKE to the sound of his phone ringing beside him. His watch read 5 a.m. Early morning phone calls meant homicides; his staff never called this early otherwise.

"Inspector Lee," he mumbled, waiting for the inevitable.

"Inspector, Corporal Chen here. We have a fatality at the Clarke Quay."

"Details."

"A young woman, Caucasian, maybe twenty years old. The street cleaners found her in the river. She is naked. No ID, no signs of struggle."

"Has the medical examiner arrived?"

"She will be here shortly."

"Any media there?"

"None. We've cordoned off the area," Chen said.

"Good, I'll be there in twenty minutes," Lee said.

He called his driver. It was Friday. Inspector Simon Lee was forty-one years old but looked younger. He had jet black hair, soft brown eyes and a tall frame. He always walked with a purpose, never slouching in the shoulders, with his head erect. You'd think he'd been in the military, but you'd be wrong. He'd been a police officer since he left school. That was his life.

He'd married at age thirty, late in the eyes of his mother, and after his wife had given birth to a son, she'd died. That had affected Lee. He didn't know who he loved more, his wife or his son. Now, he had no choice. His son was his major concern. The boy was eleven, growing up in a world that confused him with the absence of his mother.

Lee sent a text to his housekeeper, Imran, a twenty-one-year-old single mother who lived with her grandmother and her aunt's family. Imran was used to being on call for Lee. Many times, she brought her daughter to play with his son.

Lee dressed quickly, then made his way to the elevator. He lived on the twenty-fifth floor of one of the many expensive high-rises in Singapore. His income as an inspector was good, but not good enough to afford his own car.

He felt the warm morning air. It would be unbearable later in the day. The weather in Singapore was the same for the month of June, hot with showers in the afternoon or evening. The locals lived with it and carried an umbrella.

A white Toyota arrived at the curb. Lee got into the front. He went over his cell phone messages to see what had transpired in the evening. There was a report of a woman being taken from a store on Middle Road. He'd ask the evening shift sergeant about it later.

Clarke Quay at this time of the morning lay quiet. It did not open until 11 a.m. Singapore's bars and nightclubs stayed open until 4 a.m. The area and river seemed to breathe a sigh of relief in the morning stillness.

A body under a tarp lay on the side of the river. Chen stood beside it with the medical examiner kneeling by the body.

Lee said hello to Dr. Permata. Today, she was wearing a bright blue Hijab. She was a slight, delicate woman in her late forties. Lee found her fascinating; they'd had dinner together once. There was a mutual interest there, but her Muslim background and his Buddhist would never have made it into the actual world.

"Is it a drowning?" Lee asked.

Dr. Permata looked up from the body. "I can't tell until I do an autopsy. If she drowned, I'll find hemorrhaging in the sinuses and airways."

Lee liked that about her, so concise. Never a conjecture, only fact. "No abrasions or signs of struggle?"

"I cannot see on visual examination. I will find much more in my lab, however, there is little rigor mortis set in. I have determined only six degrees of heat loss to the body temperature. And I've taken into account the water temperature of the canal. I estimate the time of death at midnight."

"Thank you, doctor, most helpful as usual," Lee said. He turned to Chen. "Were there any witnesses we can interview?"

Chen looked at his notebook. "So far we have nothing. This area is far from the nightlife of Clarke Quay. That never stops until four thirty."

"Yes, I see that," Lee said. "This area is just far enough away from the activity; did you find any clothes the deceased might have thrown off?"

"No, Inspector, we did a complete search of the area. We found nothing."

Lee ran his hand over his forehead. This was looking like murder. He disliked the thought. Singapore had one of the lowest crime rates in the developed world. He hated to have this arrive on his shift.

"Take a picture of the deceased and send it to our

surveillance team. Have them review pictures of the entire city immediately," Lee said.

"Yes, inspector," Chen replied. He hurried to the body, took a picture of the dead girl's face, and sent it off.

"I need to speak to the sergeant who received the report of a girl being taken away last night," Lee said.

The next four hours were the basics of police procedures working backwards from the last known lead. Someone reported a girl being escorted from a shop by two men on Middle Road at 10 p.m. The police noted a rickshaw was outside the store. They scanned every surveillance camera going back in time for the evening until they saw her with a man in a camera outside the Raffles Hotel getting into a rickshaw.

Lee looked at the picture of the dead blonde victim and the blonde in the street surveillance photos. There were a lot of similarities. The same hair color and style, the height matched, but not once did she look up at a camera. Finally, he had to let his gut and instincts tell him this had to be the same girl.

"We need to find the man she was with last night," Lee said.

The police descended on the hotel to interview all the staff of the hotel, pulling some of them from bed to do so. No one complained once told the gravity of the crime.

The barman of the long bar remembered the beautiful woman speaking to a man. He pulled up his credit card receipts. The police also found the rickshaw driver. He remembered the evening, the disappearing girl, and the man who left without her. He'd dropped him at the Carlton Hotel.

Inspector Lee stood outside room 2211 on the twenty-second floor of the Carlton Hotel with Constable Chen and three police officers. The hotel manager was at his side. They knocked on the door.

Thomas Addington came to the door, and the color drained from his face when he saw the police. "Oh, dear God," was all he could say.

"Do you think this is okay to wear for our first day of cruising?" Bernadette asked as she pulled on a yellow print dress.

Chris looked up from buttoning his shirt. "You look outstanding, girl. How did you afford that? Did we win the lottery?"

Bernadette laughed. "No, I went into Calgary last week and splurged at one of those consignment shops. It's amazing what the rich people get rid of."

"Well, you look like you'll fit right in," Chris said. He finished buttoning his blue shirt he'd matched with some casual tan cotton pants. No matter what he wore, his muscles stood out. His size seventeen and half neck barely squeezed into his collar.

"Do I look okay?" Chris asked.

Bernadette walked over to him and let herself fold into his enormous arms. "Honey, you look incredible in anything."

"You don't think we look like two law enforcement officers trying to schlep their way into the rich and famous?"

"We have a two-week cruise on a fabulous ship, let's just enjoy it and not worry about it," Bernadette said.

The doorbell of their room sounded. As the bellman took their luggage, Chris frowned. He could have hauled everything down, but Bernadette insisted they enjoy the first-class treatment. Their trip to the ship included a limo. They might as well experience it all.

The journey to the cruise ship terminal took only fifteen minutes. They felt like kids going on an adventure.

Big ships docked end-to-end formed an imposing wall of steel at the terminal. The limo cruised by the huge *Carnival Spirit, Celebrity Solstice*, and the *Diamond Princess*. All these ships carried over six thousand passengers and looked like small cities. The limo made its way past them to a separate area reserved for smaller cruise ships. There, sitting on its own in a low gleaming profile, the elegant *Orion Voyager* claimed the prize for being the sleekest looking ship amongst the giants gathered around it.

The ship was a brilliant white with four rows of sparkling glass balconies. It was small compared to others in the harbor, but it looked like an overblown yacht. Only one hundred staterooms, all outside cabins, and each with its appointment of opulent comfort. That's what the brochure had said, and that is exactly what it looked like.

As the limo parked beside the pier, two porters hustled to take their bags. A ship's agent scanned their tickets, and they followed a man who introduced himself as their welcome agent. They had their temperature and health cards checked, then presented with their ship's passes.

They walked onto the ship, did a quick security check, had their passports scanned, and were met by a young man in a white uniform.

"My name is Marcus Smith," he said, bowing. "I'll be your butler for the duration of the cruise. I will unpack your luggage for you if you wish." He was small in stature, brown skinned with dark hair. His hands looked elegant in white gloves.

"No, that will be fine, Marcus," Bernadette said. "We can

unpack ourselves." She cast a sideways glance at Chris. There was no way she wanted another man handling her clothes.

"Very well, the champagne reception is this way. I will meet you afterwards and escort you to your room."

He motioned for them to continue down a corridor lined with serving staff dressed in fine uniforms holding platters of champagne and canapés.

Bernadette walked down the line, picking up a glass of champagne and a shrimp on toast with a napkin, and proceeded towards the reception area where they met the ship's crew. They wore impressive white uniforms, giving fist bumps with their white gloves. At their center stood the captain, a tall man with piercing dark eyes and just enough gray hair to make him look distinguished and elegant. He introduced himself as Captain Nicolas Prodromou. He had a slight Greek accent that Chris didn't recognize. They moved on down the line until Bernadette stopped in front of a female security officer.

"Cynthia McCabe, what the hell! I haven't seen you since basic training," Bernadette said to the female officer standing ramrod straight and holding a glass of water. Cynthia was mid-thirties, the same height as Bernadette, with blue eyes and mid-length blonde hair tied in a tight ponytail.

Cynthia looked stunned. "Wow—Bernie, of all the cadets to make it out of the RCMP, I never thought I'd run into you."

Bernadette wanted to give her a good old-fashioned Canadian embrace, but the place seemed stuffy, and Cynthia was working. She gave her a double fist bump before turning to Chris.

"Chris, this is Cynthia. We did basic training in Regina

together, I helped her pass firearms training and taught her how not be a pussy in combat."

Cynthia suppressed a laugh. "Nice to meet you, Chris. Bernie's right on both counts. But I taught her how to write a proper citation and type. Her handwriting equated to hieroglyphics. Actually, if she'd gone into medicine, she'd have been fine, but not so much in the legal system."

Chris smiled, "Yes, I'm still trying to decipher her notes to me. It's nice to meet you."

"How did you end up here? I didn't know you left the force?" Bernadette said.

"It's a long story that would take a few beers, but the short version is I tired of my life in Canada. I loved police work, but not the small towns they posted me to. I wanted to see the world..." She leaned forward and whispered, "...and not have to pay for it."

"Sounds like a cool gig," Bernadette said.

A security officer walked up to Cynthia, touched her shoulder, and spoke close to her ear.

"I have to go. Seems we have the Singapore police at the pier. They have a question regarding one of our passengers," Cynthia said. "We'll catch up later."

Cynthia joined the other security officer who had just briefed the captain. They left together to the frown of a well-dressed lady who was regaling the officers with her previous voyages.

"That seems serious," Bernadette said.

"Well, I'd like to see our room, maybe stretch out on our own private deck and get some rest before dinner," Chris said. He paused for a moment. "Are you going to check the situation with the Singapore Police?"

Bernadette placed her empty champagne glass on a

table. "I think I'll take a quick walk about the ship. I'll see you in the room shortly."

"Always the detective," Chris said. "Enjoy yourself." He kissed her and went to find Marcus.

Bernadette made her way down to the deck where they'd embarked. Cynthia was there with the captain and the other officer. A tall, thin policeman with the name tag of Lee was speaking to them. She stood off to the side and behind a lifeboat to hear them.

"I must know if any of your crew is missing. We have a murder victim who claimed she was to board a ship today before she was killed. This is the only ship that matches the description she gave our witness." Lee said.

"And I'm telling you, Inspector Lee, none of our crew are missing," Cynthia said.

"What about passengers? Any missing, any not show up?" Lee asked.

"Again, no, we do a complete scan of every crew and passenger's ship pass. We have one hundred percent accounted for," Cynthia said. "I'm, sorry, but perhaps your victim was telling a story, perhaps too much alcohol."

Lee looked from the captain to Cynthia and down to the picture he held in his hands. "You have never seen this woman before?"

"No, Inspector Lee. I've already told you, we've never seen her, and our ship is getting ready to set sail," Cynthia said.

Lee shook his head; he had a muted conversation with his officers, then turned and bowed to Cynthia and the ship's officers. "Thank you. I'll be leaving now."

Bernadette watched them leave. The inspector bounded down the gangplank and into a waiting car. She saw the car speed away and was about to turn away when she spotted something.

The little man in the white shirt, who had followed her in the market and then to their hotel, was on the pier, standing behind a large box. The ship's horn sounded. Lines were being cast off. They were getting under way.

4

BERNADETTE FOUND her own way to their cabin. It was on the highest level, with only eight penthouse suites. Everything about the ship showed its opulent charm. Original paintings hung on the walls, and sculptures secured to pedestals showed the guests just what kind of taste this cruise ship had.

She had no formal art training, couldn't tell Picasso from a Stan Lee comic book, so little of it impressed her. Passing her ship's card in the door, she entered the room that took her breath away.

It was big, as in massive. The brochure had said it was 900 square feet, and it felt bigger because the outside teakwood deck was over 220 square feet. A dining room with six chairs and a crystal chandelier showcased itself just off the hallway. A living room with a sofa and two comfortable armchairs was front and center, with a wet bar amply supplied with several bottles of alcohol.

Bernadette walked to the wet bar, saw two bottles of fine fifteen-year-old single malt scotch, a bottle of Courvoisier and a bottle of Absolut vodka. A bottle of Dom Perignon champagne sat chilling in an ice bucket along with a platter of canapés.

She saw Chris on the deck, his shoes off, a Heineken in hand with his ear buds in, rocking his head gently to music. Grabbing a beer from the fridge, she walked out to join him.

He looked up as she sat down beside him. "Did you figure what the mystery was of the Singapore Police?"

She sipped her beer and looked out into the ocean. "Yeah, and now it's got me wondering what's going on."

Chris took his ear buds out. "What's that?"

"The condensed version is a murdered woman claimed to be a member of the ship's crew. The ship claims no one is missing."

"So, what's the problem?"

"I saw our mysterious man in the white shirt. He was watching the ship leave," Bernadette said. She sipped her beer and looked far into the horizon.

"And that means what?"

"I have a mystery to solve, and I'm going to check my laptop for the latest news from Singapore," Bernadette said.

Chris sat up. "Before you get too involved in solving the world's crime, we received an invitation for dinner at the captain's table for eight tonight."

"Great, I have time to do some web surfing," Bernadette said as she pulled her laptop out of her travel bag. She'd brought her thirteen-inch MacBook Air with her as an iPad sometimes didn't have the connection capability she needed. And there were still some cases back in her home-town of Red Deer, Alberta she wanted to work on while away.

She'd seen a website called Singapore Strait Times in English when they were in the hotel. She turned on her laptop, logged into the ship's WIFI—it was free and always available because of a satellite dish—and found the site. The *Orion Voyager* claimed their latest technology would keep passengers always in touch with the world. Bernadette was about to see if their claims were real.

She looked for the heading of court and crimes, clicked, and found no information as yet. If Singapore Police used the same system as Canada, they blocked newspapers from crucial information.

Her next site was Twitter, Instagram and bloggers. They were the ones who heard things before anyone else. It was usually so wrong it was almost comical, but sometimes they had the hint of what was going on.

She hit a search for the dead blonde, Singapore. There were twenty-two hits. The rumor mill was alive. It was something the police could never control during an investigation. The one on Twitter stated "naked body of young blonde girl found in a canal near Clarke Quay. A witness claims she missed her ship."

There was a picture taken of the site of the body's discovery. Cell phone cameras must have been active once the police cars and coroner's van came out. Someone with a telephoto lens posted the body bag being lifted into a van.

Someone had posted a photo of the girl getting into a rickshaw outside the Long Bar of the Raffles Hotel. They had cropped the picture from a selfie. There were two heads on both sides, but in the background was the young girl. How someone had figured this was the girl and posted it was remarkable. But such was the world of phone cameras and the internet.

She made a file on her laptop and put some of the most relevant items into it. Closing the laptop, she looked around at Chris. He seemed to have fallen asleep on the deck. The jet lag had probably hit him again. Jet lag and the champagne pulled at her eyelids, but she needed to wander the ship. She grabbed her ship pass card and walked out of the room.

The ship was moving; she felt the sway beneath her feet. Her ship experiences were the ferry to Vancouver Island from Horseshoe Bay and small fishing and sail boats. This was going to take some getting used to.

She let herself adapt to the wider stance she needed at first to stop from going from side to side and bouncing off the walls of the corridor. She found the stairs and made her way to the seventh deck. She smelled smoke.

She stopped. "What the hell... that smells like cigar smoke," she muttered to herself, more to confirm her suspicions and ease her concerns. She followed her nose to a large double oak door in the center of the passageway. A brass etched sign proclaimed Cigar Lounge.

Bernadette loved the smell of cigars; her grandfather had smoked them when she was a little girl. Every so often, when the mood was right, the stars aligned and there was a fabulous cigar available, she'd puff on one, never inhale, but just let the incredible smoke roll around her mouth and expel it into a long stream. That, paired with a cognac, was a magical experience.

She pushed the door open. The room smelled like old wood, leather, and cigars. A man wearing a dark suit greeted her with a smile.

"Welcome, madam, I am Ernesto. Would you like to come in for a fine cigar and a cognac?" he asked.

"No, not at the moment, but I've always loved the smell of cigars," Bernadette replied. She felt like a schoolgirl, caught out in an area she shouldn't be in.

"Please, come in, come in. I will show you around," Ernesto said.

Bernadette made a tentative step inside the room. The chairs were leather, the walls a rich wood paneling. Soft jazz played in the background. This was her kind of place. It felt super comfortable.

"I will show you our fine selection of cigars," Ernesto said as he motioned for her to join him in front of a small room with a glass door. He opened the door, and she walked inside. The humidity and fine tobacco smell floated into her nostrils and brought her back to days on the river with her grandfather.

Her native Cree grandparents had raised her on a reservation in northern Canada. On lazy summer afternoons when she was off school, she went down to the big river to fish for sturgeon. Her grandfather often pulled out a fine Cuban cigar that he'd received as a gift as a fishing guide. The aroma would waft up in the forest, the river, and everything would collide into a small capsule of what was good in the world.

Ernesto opened a small wooden box. "I just received these this morning, the last box of Cohiba Behike 52 in Singapore. And this is a very fine Cohiba Espendidos, half the price but a lovely choice."

Bernadette looked at the Espendidos. It was the very one her grandfather smoked with great pleasure. She picked it up, rolled the cigar between her thumb and forefinger to feel its freshness, then sniffed it. She felt her senses go back in time.

"May I ask how much this cigar is?"

"The Behike 52 are 112.00 USD and the Espendidos are 47.50, we bill all cigars to the room, the regular cognacs are all included," Ernesto said with another smile.

"Thank you, Ernesto, I may indulge in one of these later on the voyage." She turned and walked out of the room. She let the smell linger not just in her senses but in her memory.

She continued her tour of the ship. The brochure she'd read on the website had given her most of the details of this new luxury ship. The ship's website billed it as 'Where Luxury meets Discovery.' The ship did not have large swimming pools and common lounge areas. All the rooms had ample balconies for guests to enjoy themselves at their leisure. A helicopter was on board for guests to go flight seeing, a small submarine to explore the depths and zodiacs, kayaks and paddle boards to check any hidden bay or reef the *Orion* took the guests into.

Bernadette ventured down the stairs to the main deck. The ship boasted four lounge bars. One was just for scotch, one a brew pub with craft beers, a wine bar and a cocktail bar where guests could mingle and do the time-honored tradition of singing karaoke. To Bernadette's experience, the drunker you got, the better you sounded. She checked out the main dining room that required elegant dress in the evening, a bistro style Italian restaurant, a sushi bar, then saw the directions to the aft deck with the casual grill for breakfast and lunch.

She knew she might get fat on this ship. Her detective partner, Evanston, had told her most guests gained seven pounds on a cruise. Bernadette was just hoping to fit into the dresses she purchased by the end of the cruise.

Guests and crew members walked by her, all smiling and nodding as they passed. Bernadette nodded back at each of them and knew in the back of her mind what she was looking for. A young blonde matching the description of the girl she'd seen on the Instagram post.

She asked herself why she wouldn't let it go? But the answer was obvious. If there had been only one incident, perhaps just the dead girl claiming to be a crew member, that might be it. But the two men shadowing them, that clawed at her intuition and wouldn't let go.

Turning around to head back to her room, she saw two young blonde ladies in white uniforms walk by her. They smiled and nodded at her. Her mind ticked off more possibilities. She would need a conversation with her security officer friend, Cynthia, to work on some of her suspicions.

5

BERNADETTE ARRIVED BACK at the room to find another bottle of champagne on the table with a fresh plate of canapés. Chris came into the living room putting the finishing touches on his tuxedo.

"You going to get ready for our dinner soon?" Chris asked.

Bernadette poured herself a small glass of champagne and picked up a canapé. "Sure, but there's lots of time."

"It's seven forty-five," Chris said.

"What! I have to get ready." Bernadette shot out of her shoes and ran to the bedroom. They had a full walk-in closet, that made finding her clothes a simple task. She'd brought one black dress and a few others that she could mix and match shawls and pashminas with. It also limited her selection of jewelry. Chris couldn't afford to buy expensive baubles on his salary, and she didn't want them.

She slipped into her new black dress. It had an off the shoulder neckline that showed way more cleavage than she was used to. She put on her silver Navajo necklace with turquoise stones, hoping it was adequate for the rich crowd.

Passing a brush through her hair and putting on some lipstick, she called it done.

The high heels were a problem. She wore boots as a detective, athletic shoes for working out, and in her full red serge of the Royal Canadian Mounted Police she wore tall riding boots. The three-inch heels would be interesting. She put them on and walked into the living room.

Chris looked up from trying to wrangle the tie onto his neck, "Damn, Bernie, you look amazing. Maybe we should stay in tonight."

"Easy, big guy," Bernadette said, helping him with his tie.

Chris raised his chin as she expertly tied his tux bowtie. "How come you know how to tie one of these?

"There was a formal ball for the RCMP every year, and I always got invited for being in the top of my team for investigations. I also hated the clip-on ones, and..." Bernadette said as she finished the tie, "it's no harder than cinching a saddle on a horse."

They left the room and walked to the elevator. There was no way Bernadette was about to navigate several flights of stairs in the three-inch heels that made her feel like she was on stilts.

Music met them the moment the elevator doors opened. Voices, elevated and loosened by alcohol, produced a wall of sound that competed with the string quartet that was playing near the waterfall.

They made their way through the crowd to the *Voyager* dining room. The room was gold and white with accents of blue. Bernadette thought it was a cross between an arctic expedition and a mountain climb. The tables and chairs were solid white, as were the table settings.

The maître d met them at the front of the restaurant. He was wearing a white tux with the name tag of Augusto. His hair and his eyebrows were slicked back. His eyes, dark and furtive, missed nothing. He did a quick visual examination of Bernadette and Chris, judged them worthy of his establishment, and bowed ever so slightly.

"May I have your names, please?" Augusto said with a flourish that was almost a purr.

"Bernadette Callahan and Chris Christakos," Bernadette said.

Augusto didn't need to check his guest list, he memorized it. "Welcome, madame et monsieur, please allow me to escort you to the captain's table. All the other guests have arrived."

Augusto stood beside Bernadette and offered his arm, Bernadette took it. Chris raised only a slight eyebrow to this procedure. Augusto took Bernadette towards the table with Chris following.

Augusto stopped at the table. "May I introduce Madame Callahan and Monsieur Christakos." He directed Bernadette to a chair, pulled it out, then glided the chair under her as she sat down. He did the same for Chris.

They sat next to Captain Prodromou and his first officer, Felicia Torres, who looked striking in her white uniform. She was a petite lady in her late thirties with close cropped black hair, olive skin and dark eyes. Her name badge stated she was from Lisbon, Portugal.

"Allow me to introduce this fine table," Captain Prodromou said. "To my right is Nigel and Lucinda Braithwaite, George and Ashley Compton, and Fred and Elizabeth Redstone."

They all nodded at them. There were some pleasantries exchanged while the waiters poured wine and brought menus.

Bernadette did her quick assessment of the table. Nigel

was much older than Lucinda. He looked in his late seventies while Lucinda was barely pushing forty. She wore an elegant sequined dress with major cleavage. An enormous diamond rappelled down the twin peaks of what looked like enhanced breasts. Her hair was a color of blonde not seen on the planet for years. Her lips would make Mick Jagger envious. And her skin was a perfect bronze tone. Bernadette had once seen that tone sprayed on by an undertaker.

George looked to be the same age as Nigel and his wife, Ashely, was about the same age and design as Lucinda. Same cleavage, major diamonds with the exception she might have been a few years younger. The two ladies' accents were a southern twang and drawl, while Nigel and George's were more refined, but southern, nonetheless. The Redstones sounded Midwest to Californian.

The two blondes were sipping large martini's while George and Nigel nursed glasses of wine. The blondes looked slightly drunk.

The Redstones seemed somewhat normal. They looked to be in their seventies and in good athletic shape. Elizabeth wore a plain black dress with a string of pearls that went well with her simple brunette hair style. She smiled across at Bernadette.

"Is this your first voyage with us," Captain Prodromou said to Bernadette and Chris.

"Our first voyage anywhere, actually," Chris said.

"You'll just have to get out there, won't you," Lucinda said placing her hand on Nigel's. "My sweetie has taken me on eleven world cruises."

Nigel smiled at her and lowered his eyes to his menu. "It's only been seven, Lucinda. You took the others with your former husband."

Lucinda rolled her eyes. "Oh my, that's right. Silly of

me." She leaned forward and looked at Ashley. "Hard to keep them straight."

Ashley smiled, nodded her head, and glanced at her husband, George. He ignored the conversation. She drained her martini glass, waving her hand at the waiter for a refill.

Bernadette noticed a bond between Lucinda and Ashley. She looked down at her menu and decided on the steak, rare. This table's conversation was going to get interesting.

"I take it you are Greek?" the captain asked as the soup was delivered.

"Yes, both my parents came from Athens, but I've discovered recently that my family originated in Israel," Chris said as he submerged his spoon in the tomato soup that had a swirl of cream in it. A small artfully decorated crouton floated in the cream, daring the diner to destroy its beauty.

The captain beamed. "Ah, the Mediterranean is a wonderful melting pot of cultures. I found out recently that although I'm Cypriot Greek, my ancestors come from Turkey, Lebanon and Israel." He raised his glass of wine to Chris. "Here's a toast to the wonders of our ancestors."

"Well," Ashley said with her eyes locked on Chris, "You're kind of exotic then."

Chris shrugged, "I don't think my ancestry is that special..."

"Ashley means y'all are handsome and well put together," Lucinda said. She picked up her glass and flicked her eyes over Bernadette to see if it got a rise out of her.

Bernadette felt Chris's foot under the table. It was his 'don't get involved in this' message. There was little chance she was going to let this ride. She'd bide her time. She jammed her spike heel into Chris' foot to let him know she had it handled.

The captain jumped into the conversation, turning it to

the wonders of *Orion Voyager* and the many exciting things they could do on the ship. He then gave some extensive lists of the ports of call and what they'd be able to do.

The soup was cleared to be replaced by salads. The waiter arrived with a silver tray of salad dressings and served each diner professionally from the right, his white gloved hands deftly dressing each diner's salad to their taste.

Bernadette fixed her gaze on the captain, while watching Ashley in her peripheral vision. The woman was staring brazenly at Chris. Bernadette felt her temperature rising. She took in a deep breath and exhaled slowly.

Elizabeth could see the situation building. She turned to Bernadette. "Did you make any plans for the excursions in the ports we stop in?"

"No, actually, we thought we might just wander around, try some local food and get a beer. We're both casual, not much into crowds," Bernadette said.

"All the tours are small. I'd be happy if you joined us on our first port. There's an amazing temple in Kuala Lumpur I think you'd like. There's a good hike up to it, and I understand there's a local food market nearby," Elizabeth said.

Bernadette felt cornered. "Sure, why not. We can always take off after. Sounds good."

Lucinda leaned across the table, letting her cleavage almost drop into her salad. "Well, bless your heart. That's wonderful y'all coming along. Your Chris can help our men up the steps."

Bernadette looked across the table. Her glare said it all. George looked uncomfortable in his seat and he cast a look at Nigel. Both their wives were obviously drunk.

"What do you do back home?" Nigel asked, trying to throw some polite banter into the conversation. He looked annoyed at his wife's remarks.

"My husband was in law enforcement with the RCMP. He just changed to Wildlife Management, and I'm a detective in the serious crimes division."

"Oh my, Paul Bunyan and Ms. Dick Tracy, I love it," Lucinda said, slurring her words. Nigel tapped his hand on her arm. She looked over at him, narrowing her eyes. "You probably deal with a lot of dead people in your line of work?

"Yes, the dead, the nearly dead and dead beats—sometimes they look and sound the same," Bernadette said.

Nigel stood up. "I'm sorry, but Lucinda is quite tired. The trip from San Francisco was rather long. We thank you captain for a wonderful evening." He looked at Bernadette and Chris. "Very nice to have met you both."

Lucinda was about to say something. The glare she got from Nigel was enough. She took his hand and walked away from the table. George stood up and made similar remarks and took Ashely. She grinned at Bernadette as she walked away.

Elizabeth and Fred moved themselves across from Bernadette and Chris. "Sorry for the ladies, they don't play well with others. The problem with the two of them is when they get together, they seem to feed off each other. They'll be fine and nice as pie tomorrow."

"I take it you go way back with the others?" Bernadette asked. She let the waiter take her salad plate away. The main course arrived. Her steak looked delicious.

"Fred and I have been business partners with George and Nigel for years. We knew their previous wives. Nigel lost his wife to cancer ten years ago and then after several years of loneliness found Lucinda. George divorced his wife, Agnes, a very dear friend of mine, soon after Nigel found Lucinda. I don't know if it was a contest to see who could find the blonde bimbo the fastest, but that's what it seems."

"You don't pull any punches with your words," Bernadette said. As she cut into her beef, it oozed blood and her mouth watered.

Elizabeth laughed and sipped her wine. "You know, we built one hell of a company together in the electronics business. We did it by getting to the point in conversation. I hope we didn't scare you off from joining us on some expeditions. I could use some distance from the two atomic blondes."

Bernadette nodded her head. "Sure, Elizabeth, we're on. If the blondes become a problem, I have some good old-fashioned take down methods from my police manual."

Elizabeth turned to Fred. "I think the blondes will have met their match in Bernadette."

The dinner finished with more small talk—the captain and Chris discussed Greek culture and food, then they compared the seafood cuisine of Portugal and Greece with Felica until they parted at ten.

Bernadette and Chris returned to their stateroom to find turndown service with a selection of chocolates on the pillow and more champagne. Chris took two Pellegrino from the minibar and ventured onto the deck.

The ship sliced its way through calm seas with a blanket of stars overhead. The air felt warm and humid. They were on their way to Kuala Lumpur with an entire day at sea afterwards.

Chris had taken off his tux, thrown on shorts and a t-shirt, and Bernadette had done the same. They found one big lounge chair to fold into each other's arms as they watched the waves go by.

Some dolphins shot by in a pod, then veered off into the distance. A few flying fish broke the surface, then disappeared.

"Was that the strangest dinner you've ever had?" Chris asked.

"I felt like I was in an interview room with multiple suspects," Bernadette replied.

"Are the rich that weird?" Chris asked, putting his arm over Bernadette.

Bernadette put her head on Chris's chest, "Those were."

"Yeah, and those blondes were a piece of work."

Bernadette looked up at Chris. "Do you need me to help erase their vision from your memory?"

"I'd be more than happy to have you do that."

Bernadette got up from the lounger. "Follow me big guy, I have a bed ready for your memory removal."

Chris got up, kissed her, and walked with her towards the bedroom. She grabbed his butt and pushed him towards the bedroom. "I have to shut down my laptop."

He smiled at her; he knew what she was up to.

Bernadette quickly logged into her laptop, then did a quick search of Singapore news. The crime reporter had given the name of Inspector Lee and some comments. She saved it to a file and headed for bed.

6

BERNADETTE ROLLED out of bed at six. Her inner time clock still wouldn't let her sleep in. Chris was already up. He'd changed into his workout clothes. He welcomed her with a kiss on the cheek and a cup of coffee.

They had a house rule, no big hugs and kisses until after two cups of coffee. The balcony door was wide open, and the warm sea air wafted in, making the room feel like a sauna.

"What time do we dock in Port Kelang?" Bernadette asked, taking her first sip of coffee that Chris had loaded with two sugars and cream.

"I'm sure it's at 0900. I'm going to hit the gym for a quick workout then order us breakfast from room service. You good with that?"

Bernadette took another sip of her coffee, closed her eyes, and let the warm liquid slide down her throat. "Hmm, now this is good coffee. The rich folks know how to live. Yes, I'm fine with breakfast in the room, and I'll join you for a workout in about five minutes. Oh, and saunter slowly out of the room in those shorts."

Chris smiled, walked to the door, and stopped.

"Stop by again, sailor," Bernadette said with a wink.

He shook his head and closed the door.

Bernadette pulled up her laptop again. She found the news item on the dead girl in Singapore, then looked up Inspector Lee at the Singapore Police Headquarters. She wanted to call him to ask him some questions, but she needed to speak with Cynthia first.

She drained her coffee cup, threw on some workout clothes, ran her fingers through her hair, and headed down to the gym.

The gym was over two thousand square feet with modern workout equipment. A five thousand square foot spa was beside the gym. It offered to suck any fat from your body that your futile attempts at exercise failed to. The spa sign displayed a free half hour special to get guests hooked on 'cool sculpting.'

Bernadette grabbed a towel and a bottle of water at the entrance and walked into the gym. Chris was already busy doing some bicep curls, his massive arms flexing and retracting in slow motion. He did nothing quickly in the gym. His routine could be two hours of arms, shoulders and chest for a day, and the next could be legs and glutes. His normal weightlifting was ten hours a week. His bulging muscles showed the effects of the dedication.

She found a bike to ride for a warmup, as the rolling of the ship was not conducive to running on the treadmill. There was a large window to watch the waves. She set the bike to level four and pounded the pedals.

From the mirror on the side, she could watch Chris. He was always poetry in motion around the gym. Men and women noticed him and asked him for tips on getting a body like his. His answer was always the same: dedication to the workouts.

The door opened revealing Lucinda and Ashley wearing tight workout wear, set off by earrings and makeup.

Bernadette smiled. To her, anyone who came into a gym wearing makeup was there to show off, not to sweat. She turned her bike up to level six and did sprints.

Lucinda tapped Ashley on the shoulder and pointed out Chris on the bench doing his hammer curls.

The women shared a giggle and walked in front of Chris. They bent over to eye level. They were giving him an eye full of cleavage. Bernadette watched from the mirror and let her anger simmer.

"Hey, Chris, you look amazing with fewer clothes on," Lucinda said.

"My goodness, he sure does," Ashley said. "I thought he looked good in a tux last night, but my oh my, this is some major hunk of man."

Chris dropped his weights on the floor and grabbed his towel. "Thanks ladies, but I'm here to work out, not for a show. I'm sure you want to get to your workouts."

Lucinda leaned closer. "You know, sweetie, Ashley and I were thinking of a workout you might want to do with us—"

"And just what would that be?" Bernadette asked from behind them. She'd got off the bike. She'd seen enough.

Ashley sniggered. "Oh, Lucinda, the hovering wife... Sorry, Bernadette, we were just joking. You know, having some fun with your gorgeous husband. I'm sure he gets it all the time."

"Yes, he used to back in his police days. He called it slut talk."

Lucinda laughed. "Oh my, you sure have a mouth on

you." She turned to Ashley. "We best make ourselves scarce before this detective puts some moves on us."

They sauntered away, making sure their hips bounced and swayed as they walked.

"Yeah, I can think of a few moves I'd like to put on them," Bernadette said as she watched them walk away.

"Easy, there, girl. You're a black belt in karate, remember. You could do those two pieces of fluff an injury with a hip throw," Chris said with a chuckle. "You'd probably flatten some of their cosmetic enhancements."

They finished their workouts and headed back to their suite for showers. After a quick breakfast in their room, they changed into the clothes for the excursion in Kuala Lumpur.

Bernadette put on long pants with a long sleeve shirt and a sun hat. She found some sensible shoes with a good tread.

Chris came out of the shower and looked at her. "You look like you're going on a safari. I thought you'd be wearing shorts and a sleeveless top."

"I read the excursion's notes. We're going to the Batu Caves that honors the statue of Lord Murugun, the Hindu god of war. It's the most important temple to Hindus outside of India. As a sign of respect, they ask women not to wear shorts or miniskirts."

"Good to know, I have some lightweight pants and a long sleeve shirt to wear. I'm glad you told me."

"The restrictions are for women. You can wear shorts as long as they're not the shortest ones in your closet."

"Hey, I'm wearing pants if you are," Chris said with a smile.

.   .   .

THEY MADE their way to the disembarkation level of the ship and joined the line of passengers. Everyone had to go through the security to have their pass scanned. They did the same on the return, so the ship could account for all passengers.

Elizabeth Redstone had told Bernadette to meet them on the dock where a private bus would take them to the site. Bernadette saw Elizabeth waving at them in front of a silver Mercedes mini-bus.

"It looks like the terrible twin blondes aren't there," Bernadette said with hope in her voice.

They heard some shouts from behind and turned. Lucinda and Ashely were bounding down the dock, dressed in shorts and tank tops. They flopped as fast as they could in their flip-flops, while their cascade of jewelry bounced and clanged on their bodies.

"I think someone didn't get the memo on the dress code," Chris said.

Their tour guide was a young Malaysian girl named Nayla. She waited patiently until they came to the bus, then told them they would have to wear a sari at the temple site. Both women shrieked their disgust at the news.

George finally stepped in. "Girls, we're in a foreign country with different customs. I suggest you both go with it or you can stay on the ship. I imagine the beauty salon and spa is open on the ship. You could spend your time there while we're away.

"I checked this morning. It's closed while in port," Lucinda protested.

"Well, then," Nigel said, "get on the bus and wear the damn sari." He looked fed up.

They filed onto the bus. Bernadette and Chris took seats at the back to be as far as possible from the complaining women. Elizabeth sat close to them, raised her eyebrows in a sign of acknowledgement of their plight, then turned and mouthed another "sorry."

Bernadette leaned close to Chris. "You know how I told you there's nothing worse than having to visit the coroner during a murder investigation to look at a victim?"

"You're saying these two are worse than that?"

"At least the victim doesn't speak," Bernadette said. She slouched back in her seat and looked out the window.

Azim, the Malay driver, put the van into gear and made their way into traffic. Nayla, their guide, introduced herself and the driver, and gave them some local history. They wouldn't be there for at least an hour. The good thing was Nayla drowned out the two blondes.

Bernadette already had a plan of distancing themselves once they arrived at the temple. Her detective partner back in Canada, Evanston, had told her to be wary of crazy travelers on the cruise. She'd found them.

7

INSPECTOR LEE SAT in a room with Constable Chen and three other policemen. He stared at a file in front of him. There was little inside except the pictures from the scene and the medical examiner's report.

"I received the medical examiner's report," Lee said. "There was no sign of a struggle, no abrasions on the body or signs of sexual activity to the deceased. Her blood alcohol level was elevated, which is consistent with the reports of several drinks at the Long Bar in Raffles Hotel." He traced his finger to the bottom of the page. "There were trace amounts of phenobarbital in her system." He placed the file down on his desk and looked at Chen. "Did the techs get any hits on facial recognition?"

"No, Inspector," Chen said. He was in his mid-twenties; his family was one of the oldest in Singapore and well linked to the top brass in the police force. Lee knew he would proceed fast up the ranks of the force. He was to mentor him, but it bothered him—his family connections made him an '*anointed one*.'

"What have we checked so far?" Lee asked.

Chen looked up from his notes. "We searched the CCTV of all the travelers through the airport." He adjusted his glasses and placed his hands on the table as if he'd handed Lee an important piece of information.

"From how many days ago?" Lee asked, trying not to be too obvious to the other constables in the room.

"We ran it for the past three days," Chen admitted.

"And if the deceased came through the airport before that?" Lee asked in a dry tone.

"Ah, yes, I see, Inspector Lee," Chen said with a slight bow of his head. "I will expand the search."

"Did you have the tech scan all the videos from the bus station? Thousands arrive here from Kalua Lumpur every day. There's also private car hire. Did you send her picture to these companies?"

"No, Inspector Lee."

"What of all the hotels? Someone must have a missing guest in the city," Lee said.

"Yes, Inspector Lee, I will act on this immediately," Chen said.

"While you're at it, take a team back to the Raffles Hotel. A cab or a rickshaw must have dropped her off there. We know she wasn't a guest there. If you work back from there and canvas every hotel within a twenty-block radius, you might find they have a missing guest," Lee said.

Chen's eyes went wide. "Every hotel?"

"Yes, Chen, every hotel," Lee said. "The police have become lazy with surveillance cameras, Facebook and Instagram. Good police work is using your instincts and chasing down leads. Sitting in front of a computer all day will only make your bottom grow bigger. Now, take your team and go."

Chen pulled himself up from this chair. He was already

a substantially bigger man than he'd been when he left the police academy. He moved out the door towards the hallway and disappeared.

Lee sat back at the table and opened the file. The girl's face was beautiful, even in death. He wondered who could do such a thing and why. This did not seem a crime of passion or convenience. If it was the same girl who'd been abducted by two men at the store on Middle Road, then this murder was part of something bigger. Lee had interviewed the Englishman, Thomas Addington, for several hours. Lee thought that perhaps Addington was at the bar to lead the blonde girl away, then hand her off to the two men, making it look like he was an innocent. The Englishman had cried, pounded the table and wet himself in proclaiming his non-involvement. It was Lee's superior, an Englishman himself, who released Addington.

Now Lee had nothing. The case was growing old with no suspects. The first forty-eight hours were crucial. They were in day two and the trail was growing cold. So was the corpse of the blonde girl in the morgue.

8

BERNADETTE WATCHED the scenery of Kuala Lumpur roll by while the blondes talked loudly of the shops they should visit after this temple thing was over. Their husbands, George and Nigel, seemed to have tuned them out. They engaged in a quiet conversation that seemed serious. They hardly noticed their wives were being drama queens.

The mini-bus rolled up to the front of the site. It was huge, people were roaming everywhere. Tour buses were parking and picking up or dropping passengers off, with vendors walking after every group of tourists as if they'd become attached by an umbilical cord.

The driver opened the door, Nayla gave instructions for everyone to stay close to her and follow her off onto the pavement. A wave of heat and humidity met them.

The hot air felt like walking into a sauna. Bernadette reached for her water bottle as sweat flowed down her neck.

The two blondes tried to take off their saris. Nayla smiled and repeated the dress code. Ashley and Lucinda did an eye roll and gave their husbands a look that silently said how much this was going to cost them.

Bernadette walked with Chris through the gates that opened into a wide plaza. Shops and restaurants bracketed both sides. The smell of curry, tea, and incense hit her nostrils. She breathed in slowly. The chatter of people surged towards the massive statue of Lord Murunga. Monkeys jumped from pillars and put their hands out for food.

She stared up at the statue. The brochure in her hand claimed it was forty-two meters high. It gleamed in gold. Shielding her eyes, she looked over to Chris. "All this for a god of war."

Chris nudged her. "How big would a god of peace be?"

"Hilarious, my Catholic priest back home would be all over you on that one," Bernadette said. She took a few pictures with her phone and looked at the extensive set of stairs going up to the caves.

"I guess that's the major attraction up there, right?"

"Yep, pretty much. I'm up for it if you are," Chris said.

The stairs were twenty meters wide with large stone handrails on each side. They began their journey upwards.

The heat grabbed at Bernadette's lungs. She pushed herself forward, one step at a time, leaning into the steps. She'd lost count of the steps when she stopped again to bend over. A drop of sweat fell off her forehead.

"How are you doing?" she asked Chris.

"Well... if this... is hard for us... I can't imagine how those two older guys are doing," Chris said, panting.

He turned to see Nigel and Fred close on their heels. The guys had game. They were having a chat as they walked up the stairs. The two blondes were far behind, pulling themselves up the stairs and complaining with every step.

Bernadette looked behind them. "I think George and

Nigel are moving fast to keep away from the noise pollution of their wives."

They reached the top and stood there to catch their breath. George and Nigel were right behind them.

"Looks like you Canadians can't take this heat," Nigel said. "George and I were born and raised in South Carolina. This is like a good day in August where we're from."

Chris looked up and smiled. "Good for you. I have to say I'm more suited to the cold than the heat."

The two men walked by them, satisfied they'd showed the young ones a thing or two, and disappeared into the crowd.

Bernadette and Chris walked into the main chamber of the cave. A massive altar to the Hindu gods took up one side of the cave. Priests chanted; people clasped their hands in prayer while the smell of incense wafted in the air.

"I'm kind of done with this," Bernadette said. "The heat and the incense are getting to my gag reflex."

"I hear you," Chris said. "Let's go over to the back of the cave, then we'll head back down. I think I saw a place for a beer and some naan bread."

Bernadette smiled. "Now, you're talking my language, which is why I love you so much."

The back of the cave was quieter, a little cooler, and the sheer magnitude of the place had them enthralled. They were about to leave when they saw Nigel wandering around. He looked lost.

"What's up Nigel, did you lose George?" Bernadette asked.

Nigel looked up; he seemed a bit dazed. "Yes, we were together. George said he wanted to look at a cave in the back section." He took off his hat, running his hand through his hair. "Then I lost him."

"We'll help you find him," Chris said.

They heard a scream; it was Ashley's voice. "George has fallen—someone help."

Bernadette looked at Chris. "I think we found him."

9

Bernadette and Chris ran to the back of the cave. There was a small opening with an international no entry sign. George lay just inside it. Ashley was standing over him, stroking his head.

"Did you see him fall?" Bernadette asked. She put her hand to his neck, checking for vital a sign. He was breathing. A small trickle of blood came from his ear and his hearing aid lay on the ground beside him.

"No, I came in here to look for him. Nigel said he'd lost him," Ashley said. "Looks like he tripped. Is he okay?"

"He's breathing, but I think he may have suffered a concussion," Bernadette said. She looked up as Nayla came to her side.

"I called an ambulance. We will take him to the hospital," Nayla said.

"No. Not happening," Ashley screamed. "I'm not having my husband in some foreign hospital. And I'm not staying here by his side while the ship sails off without me. Do ya'll hear me?"

"Yes, madame, we hear you. But your husband may have

suffered something severe. Only a doctor will know," Nayla said. She stood up, folding her hands together with her eyes down, trying to be as passive as possible for the deranged wife.

"We have a doctor on our ship. If he says George needs more care, that's fine. That's my order. Now, get him to the bus," Ashley said. Her voice had dropped below a screech. The pilgrims in the cave returned to their prayers in the main cave.

Four maintenance men of the Batu Caves came into the small cave. Nayla spoke to them. There was an excited exchange back and forth, and Bernadette could see Nayla was making many apologies for being in the restricted area. Finally, Nayla calmed them down and got them to carry George down the steps.

Nayla came beside Bernadette. "We must pay a fine for going into a restricted area. I will take care of it."

"Yes. I'll speak to the captain and make sure he knows this was not your fault. And that the ship reimburses you for the fine," Bernadette said.

Nayla bowed her head and placed her palms together. "That would be most appreciated. This is my only job."

The men put George on a stretcher, taking him down the steps with Ashley by his side, while she berated them the entire way to be careful. The men sweated, guiding the stretcher down the steps. They seemed adept at this maneuver. Obviously, many others had succumbed to the heat of the cave.

Arriving at the bus, they laid George on the four seats in the back. Elizabeth Redstone bowed to them and gave them a large tip for their efforts. They bowed and walked away.

Azim, the driver, pulled the bus out of the parking lot.

They made their way back to the ship. Nigel sat in the front with his head down.

Bernadette sat behind him wondering if it was concern for his long-time friend or if he'd been overcome by the heat.

Elizabeth sat across from Bernadette. She placed her hand across the aisle and touched her shoulder. "I'm so sorry our group has caused all this excitement. Here, you and your husband were looking for a nice day out and we've ruined it."

"Not to worry, these things happen. I hope George is okay," Bernadette replied.

"George is a tough guy, don't let his age fool you," Elizabeth said. "He was an athlete in track and field back at college, active in hiking and mountain climbing until six months ago. He probably let the heat get to him, trying to show off to that young wife of his."

"You've known each other for a long time, haven't you?"

Elizabeth took a sip of water, looked behind her, and leaned over. "We started our electronics company forty years ago. My God, we were young and full of all kinds of ideas. My husband called George and Nigel in South Carolina and told them to get their butts out to San Francisco. They were his buddies from electronics engineering school. My Fred saw the opportunity the electronics industry had." She closed her eyes as if going back in time to see all of them in their youth.

"It seems you did well."

Elizabeth opened her eyes wide. "We made a killing. The company was in the top of Fortune 500 in five years. We invented electronic technology that no one else could dream up—not even the Chinese. Although they tried to copy it, they failed, so then they tried to steal it."

"What did you invent?" Bernadette asked.

"Microprocessors and circuit boards. We sold them to IBM, Apple and every new startup cell phone company. Our New Wave Electronics was at the forefront of new technology. We owned that market for over thirty years," Elizabeth said with a smile.

"You still have the company?"

Elizabeth looked down at her hands, massaging a brown spot. "Yes, we're major shareholders and active on the board. We stepped down from being active in the business, one by one, as we realized the company needed younger people along with their ideas." She looked out the window. "Hard to believe so much time has gone by that our young and fresh ideas would be out of date."

The bus drove to the harbor. As they pulled up to the ship, a group of officers waited with a stretcher, the captain standing amongst them.

They got out, letting the ship's crew enter to put George on a stretcher and bring him to the ship.

Bernadette saw the captain approach Ashley. He entered into an earnest discussion with her, pointing at George several times. It was obvious he wanted a doctor to examine George on land. Ashley shook her head and put up her hand. No way they would sway her.

The ship's doctor checked George's vitals and accompanied him onto the ship. Bernadette watched them go, then motioned to Chris. "I think I need a shower and a tall beer."

"Sounds good, let's hit the mini bar like it was an oasis in the desert," Chris said with a wink. "Then we can order room service and hang out on the deck."

They followed the others onto the gangway and into the ship. They scanned their passes at security and went through the security checks. Bernadette saw Cynthia standing off to one side. She walked towards her.

"You have a minute, Cynthia?" Bernadette asked.

"Sure, it's slow, we'll have a rush of passengers in a few more hours. Is the passenger you were with okay?"

"He had a fall. His wife wanted him brought back to the ship."

"Captain Prodromou will have a fit, that's not protocol in a big port," Cynthia said.

"It was the protocol of his screaming wife."

Cynthia nodded. "That's not unusual on this ship. The rich get their way and there's often little reasoning with them."

"I wanted to ask you about the enquiry from the Singapore Police yesterday before we set sail."

"What about it?"

"You said you accounted for the crew, that everyone was on board."

Cynthia held her gaze. "How did you hear that?"

"I was walking by as you spoke with the Singapore Police."

Cynthia rolled her eyes. "That's so like you. I think you put your nose into everything I did in cadet school. But that's correct, we do the same scan of crew we do of passengers, it makes sure we have a time and date stamp of all on board."

"Do you know how many of your crew left the ship in Singapore to see the sites?" Bernadette asked.

"There wouldn't be that many. Singapore is a quick turn-around. We stop longer in other ports and some crew get a day off. We have some crew changes in almost every port. Some have to go home, or their rotation is up," Cynthia said.

Bernadette looked around. The other security officers were checking some passengers in. "Would you mind indulging an old friend and checking if any female crew members got off the ship were in their early twenties and blonde?"

Cynthia put up her hand and shook her head. "Bernie, giving you that kind of info will get me fired. I like my job here. I almost have a condo paid off on Vancouver Island. I don't want to screw this up."

"I totally understand, Cynthia," Bernadette said.

"I hate it when you say that. You said that all the time in our basic training, then asked for shit anyway. Remember, I helped you qualify for constable."

Bernadette put her hand on Cynthia's shoulder. "Okay, all I need to know is if there was anyone who matched the description, I gave you. That's all."

"Is that the description of the dead girl in Singapore?"

"Yeah, it is."

Cynthia's shoulders dropped. "Ah, you got me, I'll check on it. The police officer in me never faded away. I'll check the port scans of the crew and pull some pictures."

"Thanks, girl, I'll see you later," Bernadette said. She made her way up the stairs to get some exercise and found Chris in the room coming out of the shower wearing a towel.

"Well, did you interrogate Cynthia in search of the missing blonde?" Chris asked.

"How did you know?"

Chris walked up to her and kissed her. "Because you just have to tie up the loose ends. It's just who you are. Did you find anything out?"

"No, not yet, but I'm hoping she'll give me something to work with."

"You still think there's a connection to this ship and the girl's death in Singapore, don't you?"

"Right now, I have only a feeling. Give me time and make the connection," Bernadette said as she pulled off his towel.

10

BERNADETTE SLEPT IN UNTIL EIGHT. She'd woken up at six, rolled over, and looked out to sea and decided she needed sleep more than anything else. Chris was already up. She found him on the large deck with a pot of coffee and orange juice. The coffee was in a silver carafe with china cups, and the orange juice had its own chilled carafe. She smiled at how elegant it was.

"I can call room service to bring up breakfast," Chris said when he saw her.

Bernadette came over to him, kissed him on the cheek, and poured herself some coffee. She spooned her usual two sugars and added cream. "Let's just hang out here for a while. I'd rather enjoy the sea view, and besides our dinner last night was exceptional. I don't think I'm ready to eat yet."

"That was a fantastic dinner," Chris agreed. "I loved your idea of dinner in our room last night. We might as well put this penthouse to use."

Bernadette looked over her shoulder at the six-seat mahogany dining table. The waiter had wheeled everything in on a silver platter and served them. She wasn't sure if she wanted to tell her detective partner back in Canada about this. She didn't take any pictures to put on Facebook as she'd never live it down with the uniforms in the force.

"I'm not sure if I enjoyed your company, the food or the dessert more," Bernadette said.

Chris reached over and stroked her arm. "I thought I was your best dessert."

Bernadette arched one eyebrow. "Honey, they served salted crème caramel."

"Oh, sorry, hard to compete with that."

The phone in the room rang. Bernadette got up and walked into the living room. She thought it might be someone from the concierge desk trying to put them on another tour. They'd decided they'd do as many solo things as they could.

"Hello, Bernadette Callahan speaking."

"Hey, Bernie, it's Cynthia. Look I can't talk long but there are two things you need to know."

Bernadette sat down in the armchair. "Sure, what's up?"

"George Compton passed away last night."

"Whoa, what happened?"

"He died in his sleep in his room. The ship's doctor said George woke up in the infirmary, his vitals were good. He claimed the heat got to him. The doctor sent him back to his room with Ashley and Lucinda."

"I'm sorry to hear of his passing. Must be tough on his wife," Bernadette said.

"Well, she's threatening to sue the ship for letting George go on such a strenuous excursion. Seems she bounced back pretty well."

"You need me to fill out a statement, don't you?"

"You're on the case as always, Bernie. Your statement would be a big help as you were there at the scene. All passengers sign a waiver for shore excursions, but you'd be an extra asset in the report."

"I'll come down to your office. That's too bad about George," Bernadette said.

"We do have some deaths on the ship. That's why we have a morgue on board," Cynthia said.

"I guess you'd have to. Can't be throwing them in the food locker."

"Oh, God, your humor hasn't changed."

"All those years on the force. So, what's the other thing?"

"I checked for the crew scans for re-entry in Singapore— they're missing."

"Has that ever happened before?" Bernadette asked.

"No, and I've been on this ship and others for seven years. The only one who can change data on our system is the chief of security, that's Mateo Taomia, he's a Maori from New Zealand, served in their armed forces. He's a top-notch guy. I asked him about the files, told him I was doing a routine scan. He's pretty pissed about it."

"Who else has access to the files?"

"Has to have high level access on the ship," Cynthia said. "That's a close circle of the captain and high up admins— look I have to go. I'm supposed to be doing rounds with another crew member. I'll call you to get together to do your incident report."

"Okay, sure, why not come up to my suite, we can have a coffee and talk more?" Bernadette asked.

"Sounds good, talk soon."

Bernadette walked back onto the deck and sat beside Chris.

"What's up? You look concerned."

"Yeah, George Compton died in his sleep last night. The

doctor is calling it heat stress," Bernadette said as she picked up her coffee cup.

Chris leaned forward in his chair. "I know the guy was old, but I remember them both saying how hot weather didn't bother them. They claimed they were from South Carolina."

Bernadette shrugged her shoulders. "I guess heat, old age, maybe he had an advanced heart condition. Who knows, life can hit you fast with things."

"Okay, sure, but what else is bugging you? You've seen more dead guys than most. What's up?"

"Cynthia told me that the crew scans of re-entry are missing for Singapore. That's kind of a big thing," Bernadette said, looking Chris directly in the eyes.

"That means you're going to dig deeper, doesn't it?"

"Totally. Something like this is too coincidental to let it pass," she said.

"Okay, no problem, you run it down and let me know when you need my help," Chris said.

Bernadette leaned over and kissed him on the lips. "I'm so glad you don't mind, as this is our honeymoon and all."

Chris laughed. "Hey, I'd rather you chase leads than see you unhappy because you thought you were missing out on an investigation. Where are you going to start?"

"Back in Singapore. I found the number for their police department and the name of the inspector on the case."

11

BERNADETTE POURED herself more coffee and went into the bedroom to make the call. The bedroom had a writing desk, phone, paper, and pens. She picked up the phone and dialed the number in Singapore. She knew her satellite call would be expensive, but her need to find out about the dead girl negated the cost.

It took a while for the sat phone to ring in Singapore. A female voice answered in perfect English, "Singapore Police Department, how may I assist you?"

"I wish to speak to Inspector Lee," Bernadette said.

"Is this concerning a case?"

"Yes, my name is Detective Bernadette Callahan. I'm with the serious crime unit of the Royal Canadian Mounted Police in Canada. Please tell the inspector I'm calling from the *Orion Voyager* that is at sea right now."

"Hold the line, please."

A minute later Inspector Lee came on the line. "Inspector Lee, here."

"Thank you for taking my call. I saw you on the *Orion* the day of our departure. Your request to search our ship

intrigued me. I hope I can shed some light on events that
have transpired."

"Well, yes, perhaps," Lee cautiously replied. "You say
you are a detective and you're on the *Orion*?"

"Yes, I hope you'll share with me some details of your
victim's last movements and conversations on her last night,
and perhaps, if you're willing to send me a picture?"
Bernadette said.

"Why would I do that?"

Bernadette hesitated; she was about to give confidential
information from Cynthia. But you don't get unless you give.
"Because I found out someone on this ship deleted the crew
arrival information in Singapore."

There was a pause. "This would be interesting."

"Yes, it would be. Only if someone killed your victim in
Singapore, then used her identity to gain entry to this ship. I
have a security officer doing a check on this."

"May I ask what your rank on the ship is?" Lee asked.

"Ah... I'm a passenger. I'm on vacation, my honeymoon
actually, but as a detective there are things I cannot let go."

Lee let out a low chuckle. "I fully understand. I have
done the same things on many vacations with my son. He
would rather do things without me."

"So, you'll fill me in on your case so far?"

"Here is what I can tell you. The young lady told the
man, Thomas Addington, she was working on a small ship
for three months with two hundred passengers that were
mostly millionaires. I think that's about all I can share at
present."

"Did she mention her job on the ship?"

"No, I asked Mr. Addington many times. He claimed she
said it was a very important job, and that was it."

"Who is Thomas Addington?"

"A very unfortunate Englishman who thought he was going to have... I believe the young call it a hookup for the evening. We had to report his name to the papers. I believe he will have some explaining to do when he returns home."

Bernadette scribbled some notes in her usual style that only she could understand. "I thank you very much for this, Inspector Lee."

"Will you let me know if you find the lady who might have taken the place of our victim? This might shed some light on our case. We have very little at present. I'll give you my email address."

Bernadette wrote the address down. "I'll forward anything I find on board. Thanks for sharing what you did, I know it's tough in the middle of an investigation."

"Yes, you are right, you are a good detective, you understand the process. If you need a job, Singapore could use you."

"Thanks, Inspector Lee. Too hot and the beer is too expensive."

She looked at her notes. Here lay a missing piece of the puzzle. If someone, a close match to the dead woman, was on this ship, she had an important job and she'd just started a three-month job. She circled the three months and wondered if any of this would pan out. Was it just bar talk? Or wishful boasting or, with the deletion of entry files on the security manifest, a way for someone on board to do something. But what?

A picture of the dead girl appeared in her inbox. It made her pause for a moment. Photos of murder victims always made her angry and want justice, the very reason she became a police officer. Pictures of victims clarified it.

She got dressed, threw a bit of makeup on to not scare

the other passengers, and went to the deck. "I'm going down to meet with the ship's doctor." She said to Chris.

Chris lowered his coffee cup. "You sick?"

"No, I have to fill in an incident report and there's something about George's fall I want to discuss with the doctor," Bernadette said.

She walked out of the suite and headed down the of stairs. Passengers wandered around in shorts and t-shirts, with smiles and holiday vibe. They had some sea days ahead, with time on the decks, several lectures from the on-board botanist, geologist and an archeologist who claimed to know of all the ancient religions of the ports they were visiting.

The infirmary was on a lower deck, just off the main security office and the lower entry port for passengers when boarding from the dock. The door was open; she stepped inside.

A female nurse with the name badge, Achara, looked up. She was Asian, in her late thirties, with thick black hair cut to encompass her round face. "Yes, may I help you?"

"I'd like to speak to the doctor," Bernadette said.

"If you have an injury or a medical concern, I'll need you to fill this form and please put down your room number for billing."

"I'm sorry, I'm here to speak with the doctor about the death of Mr. George Compton. My name is Bernadette Callahan."

"I see, I'll get the doctor for you," Nurse Achara said.

Bernadette stood to one side, looking around the small room. It had the usual posters about covering a sneeze with your elbow, greeting fellow passengers with a fist bump instead of a handshake, and covering everything in hand sanitizer.

The doctor appeared from the back room. He was a tall black man in his late fifties with thinning hair and black glasses set low on his nose. Bernadette thought he looked like a professor stepping out of a lecture. His name badge read Dr. Kamau. Below it stated Kenya.

"Please step into my office," Kamau said.

Bernadette followed the doctor into the examination room. The room was small with an examination table, a chair and writing desk. The doctor offered her the chair; he pulled up a small rolling stool to sit on the other side of the desk.

"How may I be of help?" The doctor asked. He took off his stethoscope and placed it on the desk.

"I wanted to ask you a question about how George looked when you examined him."

Dr. Kamau adjusted his glasses. "Why would you want to know that?"

Bernadette leaned back in her chair. She didn't want to seem demanding. "Sorry, Dr. Kamau, I'm a detective in the serious crimes division back in Canada. The ship's security asked me to give a statement. And It's in my nature to know how someone died where I was present."

The doctor nodded his head. "Yes, I understand. I worked as a coroner for a short time in Kenya."

"Let me explain further. When I discovered Mr. Compton, he was lying on the ground. I saw no contusions on his forehead, but I saw blood coming out of his ear. Did you see anything similar?"

"Yes, I saw dried blood on his left ear, I thought it might be from his fall. I put it in my report. But you must understand, my medical examination is rudimentary. I'm sure they will perform a full autopsy once they send the body back to America."

"Yes, doctor. I just wanted to confirm what I saw for the report to the ship's security," Bernadette said.

"I understand. But Mr. Compton was fine when he left my office. His vital signs were good, and he showed no distress. His wife found his hearing aid and gave it back to him. He walked out of here in good spirits," Dr. Kamau said.

"Thank you for your time, doctor," Bernadette said and walked out of the office. She made her way up the main deck and was about to take the stairs to meet with Chris.

Elizabeth Redstone came to her side. "I need to speak with you."

"Sure," Bernadette said, "what about?"

"George's death was not an accident," Elizabeth said.

12

ELIZABETH GUIDED Bernadette to a small café with few patrons. Most of the passengers were in the main dining room for breakfast. They ordered coffees. Elizabeth pulled her chair close to Bernadette's. She looked around and lowered her voice.

"When I left George last night, he was fine, but Ashley kept telling him he needed to take his medication," Elizabeth said.

"What type of medication?"

"She had him on some kind of heart medication from some quack doctor she took him to in San Diego," Elizabeth said. She waited a moment as their coffees arrived and the waiter left. She leaned forward again. "Ashley told George the medication would make him a stud in the bedroom, supposedly better than Viagra."

"Was he taking it regularly?"

"No, he told me the stuff made his heart race, and he got the sweats from it."

"Why did he take it at all?"

"To please that wife of his and make her stop nagging

him," Elizabeth said, then moved closer. "George was going to file for a divorce when they returned to America." She raised her head and looked around the café. "And I'm sure Nigel is going to do the same to Lucinda. Right now, he's saying nothing as he's devastated over George's death."

Bernadette moved back a little and looked at Elizabeth. "What you're telling me is circumstantial evidence. When a professional autopsy is performed, perhaps they'll find the medication Ashley was giving him caused his death, but other than that—"

"There won't be an autopsy. Ashley told me this morning; she wants George cremated when we dock in India. She claims George was in love with the Hindu religion and wanted someone called a Brahmin priest to perform his funeral. She wants to bring his ashes back to America."

"Was he about to join the Hindu religion?"

Elizabeth shook her head. "He was an elder in the Baptist Church. You couldn't get more strait-laced than George. Sure, he read about other religions, but a cremation? Hell no, I'd never see him wanting a cremation. His family has a crypt in his hometown in South Carolina. There's so many Compton's buried there; they have their own section."

"It's the wife's prerogative to decide her husband's final burial details. You'd have to get some kind of court injunction from one of his surviving relatives. Does he have any?"

"That's just it, he hasn't. Why do you think that blonde bombshell hung onto him for so long? He made her sign a prenuptial agreement that only gave her five million, but she'd burn through that in a heartbeat. With his death, she inherits a one hundred-million-dollar life insurance policy that buys her out of our company."

"Didn't the prenuptial keep her out of his company?"

"George blew it with his lawyer. He was supposed to will the insurance to the partners to buy out the surviving spouse. But Ashley convinced him to put her in there."

"I'm sorry for the loss of your good friend, but I'm not in a position to open an investigation into George's death," Bernadette said. "You might take your suspicions to the captain, but I'd say you're opening yourself up to a major libel lawsuit from Ashley with your suspicions if they prove unfounded."

Elizabeth fixed Bernadette with her gaze. "I thought you were a detective, not a lawyer."

"Sorry, I've been in the courts enough times in cases to know what gets traction and what doesn't. You'd have a hard time getting an autopsy on George unless you call your corporate insurance company and inform them. They're on the hook for your company's death benefit. They hate to pay insurance claims at the best of times. If you told them what you just told me, they'd have an investigator at the next port."

"That's a great idea, I'll speak to Fred about it."

"Sorry I couldn't do more for you," Bernadette said.

"That's fine, you've been a great help. But you know, you Canadians say sorry a lot, don't you?"

Bernadette smiled and shrugged, "Sorry."

Elizabeth laughed and went on her way. Bernadette continued on up the stairs to her suite and found Chris finishing a large breakfast of eggs, bacon, and fried potatoes.

She sat down beside him, put some bacon and potatoes on her plate, smothering everything in a sauce that looked like ketchup from a small silver container.

"I take it everything went well with your doctor's visit?"

Bernadette swallowed and took a drink of water. "The

doctor's visit was fine. But Elizabeth Redstone thinks Ashley killed her husband."

"Oh, then everything is normal in the world of millionaire cruising," Chris said. He pushed a white envelope towards her. "Security dropped this off."

Bernadette put her fork down and opened it. "This is the witness statement I need to fill out for Cynthia. I'll finish it after breakfast and take it back to her."

"You're loving this voyage of mystery, aren't you?"

Bernadette smiled. "Well, yeah, makes it more interesting than listening to some guy talk about fish of the Indian Ocean."

13

Bernadette put on makeup, changed into shorts with a casual top, and found her sandals. Checking herself in the mirror, she gave herself her usual talking to. "Okay now, you're on this trip to enjoy yourself. Spend more time with Chris and quit being a detective. You got that?" She smiled at herself in the mirror. She rarely listened to her own advice.

There was, after all, the mystery of who'd paid for their trip. She planned to check the ship's purser to find out. The dead girl in Singapore was another issue that wouldn't leave her consciousness. She sighed as she closed the door. She was a victim of her mind that needed to solve every mystery presented to her.

She bounded down the stairs to the security office, hoping she wouldn't run into Ashley or Lucinda. Her police training ingrained in her a "sorry for your loss" statement. The words never seemed enough. With the blondes, she feared it might seem too shallow.

Finding the security office, she let the office know she wanted to drop a statement off to Cynthia McCabe.

"Please wait a minute, Officer McCabe is here, she might want to go over it with you," the office said.

The officer knocked on the door, and Cynthia came out. She smiled and waved for Bernadette to come on in.

"How's your morning going, Cynthia?"

"Normally our days at sea are easy. But with the death of Mr. Compton we have reports to write up and both the chief of security and the captain were in conference calls with the head office in Fort Lauderdale. They've had to speak with the company doctors, the lawyers, and our insurance people. Everyone wants to know if we did everything possible to absolve ourselves from litigation."

"What's the verdict on that?"

"A bit of an ass-grinder, as we say in the business. We should have sent Compton to a hospital for a full examination. Our onboard doctor is excellent at handing out Aspirin or Dramamine and fixing the odd sprain."

"But his wife insisted. I was there when she refused the on land medical care," Bernadette said.

"I hope you put that in your statement."

"Yes, I did."

"Is it legible?" Cynthia asked with a grin.

"Yes, you little shit, I did it in block style, just for you," Bernadette said with a laugh.

Cynthia took the report and looked it over. "You've come a long way in your writing style. This will be great. I think this gets our ship off the hook. I'll scan and send it to our head office. I'm sure your detective signature at the bottom will carry a lot of weight. Thanks for including that."

"You're welcome. Now, I'm not sure if I want to share this with you..."

"Okay, spill, you got a wrinkle on the death, don't you?"

"Just a strange conversation I had with Elizabeth

Redstone," Bernadette said. She filled her in on the conversation and waited for her reaction.

"Oh my god, this ship is turning into one of those soap operas I used to watch after school. These passengers never cease to amaze me. This ship charges some of the highest fees in the industry for a cruise. We attract the ultra-rich and crazy."

"On another note, any ideas of someone who could have come on this ship in place of the murdered girl in Singapore?" Bernadette asked.

Cynthia took a deep breath. "Yeah, about that. I obtained our personnel roster, and I only three candidates. All of them came aboard in Singapore. I kind of forgot about them. One is a pastry chef, she's a Mexican girl; one is the Asian nurse that you probably met this morning, and the other is our director of hotel services. Her name is Holly Marsden, she's from Portland, Oregon." Cynthia pulled up her picture and turned her computer screen towards Bernadette.

"Well, she is blonde and close to the same age, and she might be a candidate from a distance," Bernadette said. She got a quick glance of her birth date before Cynthia turned the computer around.

Cynthia shrugged. "Might be hard for someone to impersonate her. She comes from the Silversea Cruise Line. She's well known."

"What hotel would she stay at in Singapore?" Bernadette asked.

"All the crew stay at the Pan Pacific Hotel. It's only a few kilometers from the dock. The ship gets a comp rate there, the crew then head home or come aboard."

Bernadette wrote Holly's name and the hotel. "Thanks, looks like we may have run into a dead end. I'm just going to run this by someone—without mentioning you."

"Appreciated. Now, you need to get with that good-looking husband of yours. Enjoy this beautiful ship. There's a bunch of cooking demos from the chefs, and the bartenders are mixing some mean cocktails. You need to get involved."

"Thanks, I will."

Bernadette got up to leave. She saw the security chief, Mateo Taomia, walk into the outer office. He gave them both a friendly wave and a special look to Cynthia. He was tall, with a muscular body, curly black hair, brown skin and Maori tattoos on his neck and arms. His face was wide with dark brown eyes. He was a poster boy for good looking natives of New Zealand.

Bernadette turned back to Cynthia. "You didn't tell me your boss was such a dreamy-looking guy. What's your story with him?"

Cynthia blushed, "Ah... well, kind of ongoing..."

Bernadette gave her two thumbs up and a smile. "Way to go, girl. You need to rock that!"

She headed out of security to the main deck where the purser's office was. This was the admin of the ship. She gave the young man at the desk her name and asked if she might see Ms. Holly Marsden.

Holly came out of her office with a confident stride. "How may I assist you today, Ms. Callahan?" She was all of five foot three with blue eyes, clear complexion and natural blonde hair—or the best dye job.

"I'm hoping you can help me, Holly. My husband and I received this cruise as a wedding present. I've lost the email address of the people who gave it to us. I wanted to send them an email with some pictures, and I really hope you can help me," Bernadette said with a big smile.

"Let me just check my files. I'll be just a minute," Holly said. She turned and walked back to her office.

Bernadette watched her walk away. Could she be the imposter? This job was one of the most important on the ship. Could someone assume her identity and replace her?

Holly came back without her smile. "I'm so sorry, Ms. Callahan, but the people who purchased this cruise for you wished to stay anonymous. Perhaps if you contact them by phone...?"

Bernadette smiled. "They're traveling. I'll just have to wait until I return home. Thanks for your trouble."

"My pleasure," Holly said. "Sorry I couldn't have been of more help. Anything else I can assist you with?"

"No, that's fine," Bernadette said. She smiled, turned, and headed back to her stateroom. She knew asking for the benefactor of her cruise was a long shot, but getting an up close with Holly Marsden had been her goal. Now, she'd have to find out more about her.

14

—————

BERNADETTE RETURNED to the room to find a note from Chris. He'd gone to the cooking class in the main dining room. She smiled; he was a great amateur chef who did most of the cooking at home. She was good at microwaving or ordering food online for delivery. Everyone had to have their strengths.

Opening her laptop, she checked Facebook for Holly Marsden. There was nothing there. She checked Twitter and Instagram and found the same. She sat back in her chair. What twenty-something doesn't have a social media page? Her Google search turned up nothing.

"Okay, this is strange," Bernadette muttered to herself. She went to her email and sent a quick note to Inspector Lee, telling him that the only one who fit the description of the girl in Singapore was Holly Marsden. She put in the hotel name in Singapore Holly stayed at but didn't have a date of arrival.

She then emailed her detective partner back in Canada. This was going to be weird. Bernadette had the date of birth for Holly Marsden. You can get just about anything with that in the government records system in both Canada and the United States.

Her problem was explaining her request to her partner. Detective Evanston was a sassy, opinionated mother of two with a mortgage and kids' sports equipment to pay for. She knew all about Bernadette's trip, had drooled over the brochure and website. Now, what would Evanston think about a request for someone's ID?

"Aw, crap, I'm just going to do it and live with the heat I get on this," Bernadette said to herself. She emailed the request, then spent a half hour looking over case files from her RCMP Detachment in Red Deer. She felt guilty as hell, but there was nothing she could do about it. After glancing over the files, she felt better. Closing the file, she was about to close her laptop when she saw an email from Inspector Lee.

Bernadette read the email. It took her breath away. The inspector claimed that they'd traced the dead girl back to the Pan Pacific Hotel. A cab driver had remembered picking her up and dropping her off at the Raffle's Hotel. He wondered if he could speak to her on the phone. He would call her, his email said.

Bernadette entered her number, and that she was in her room.

The phone rang. "Bernadette Callahan, speaking."

"Thank you for taking my call, Ms. Callahan," Inspector Lee said.

"You're welcome. I see the victim was at the same hotel as our hotel director on this ship," Bernadette said.

"Yes, and the hotel had no missing guests. They accounted for all of them."

"Any surveillance video in the hotel show the victim?"

"We have one photo of a girl that looked like the victim

getting into the cab," Inspector Lee said. "The hotel is very busy this time of year. But only one Holly Marsden registered at the hotel."

"This is the only blonde who possibly matches the age and height of your victim. This is all I have at present." Bernadette said.

"Now that we have a name, we can run a facial match with the name you gave us," Inspector Lee said.

"Please let me know what you find."

"Yes, I will be happy to," Inspector Lee said and hung up.

Bernadette changed; she felt the shorts weren't appropriate for the dining room where she wanted to meet up with Chris. She put on a pair of white capri pants and a yellow sleeveless blouse. She kicked off the sandals and put on a pair of casual pumps. After a quick primp of her hair and freshening her makeup, she headed downstairs.

Walking down the stairs she could hear the music playing in the main dining area. A band was doing some Caribbean music with a Reggae beat. Voices were loud and glasses were clinking. It was only eleven in the morning, but the ship's passengers were already enjoying themselves.

She found Chris in the dining room, standing beside Paul Weber, the head chef working with him to do a flambé of shrimp. Chris held the bottle of Pernod in his hand. He raised it high and let a stream of liquor hit the pan. Flames erupted into the air while Chris did a quick flip of his wrist with the pan to swirl the shrimp. The head chef, Paul Weber, nodded his approval and the crowd erupted in applause.

"I see we have an up-and-coming chef on board," Chef Weber said. He had a thick Swiss German accent. A stocky man with piercing eyes, he missed nothing in the culinary world, nor was he easily impressed.

Chris plated the shrimp, placing the pan to the side. He was wearing a chef's apron with a tall hat. Bernadette thought he looked fantastic in his outfit. She pulled out her cellphone to take a picture.

Some other passengers were doing the demonstrations, though most of them had stepped away when the flames shot up in the air and none had the flair or the technique of Chris. Chef Weber smiled in approval.

Two loud female voices rose over the crowd. "Let's hear it for the tasty-looking cook."

Bernadette turned around to see Lucinda and Ashley, with drinks in their hands. They looked like they were several cocktails ahead of everyone and pushing happy hour to the limits.

Bernadette wasn't sure what to do next. Her police officer training kicked in. That was to speak calmly to drunks and try to diffuse the situation. She walked over to the women. They smiled at her as she walked towards them.

"Hi, Ashley, hi Lucinda, I just wanted to say I'm sorry for your loss, Ashley," Bernadette said. She sat in an empty chair and put her hand on the table. She made sure she didn't put her hand on Ashley in case she found that too forward.

Ashley looked at her with a blank stare. "Look, Bernadette, me and Lucinda are having a wake. Isn't your last name Callahan—Irish, you know about it, don't you?"

"Yes, I do, I've never been to one, but I know it's held during the funeral," Bernadette said.

"Well," Lucinda said, her words slurring somewhat, "we're getting a head start. Why don't you join us?"

"It's too early for me." Bernadette said.

"What's the matter? We're not good enough for the likes of you?" Lucinda asked. She leaned towards Bernadette; her breath stunk of stale alcohol, the sign of long bingeing. "Let me tell you, once Ashley gets what's coming to her from those tight ass company pricks George was a partner in, she'll have so much money she could buy anything she wants." She turned to Ashley. "Isn't that right?"

"Damn straight, get my own yacht if I wanted. Not have to sail around with anyone on a shit can like this," Ashley said as she drained her drink. She looked around and waved her hand at the waiter.

"This service here is slow," Lucinda said. She raised her empty glass at the waiter.

Bernadette saw the waiter hesitate. He went to his barman; they had a quiet conversation, then he came over.

The waiter was a good-looking black man named Silas; his name tag stated he was from Jamaica. He walked over to table. "Ladies, how are we doing this fine morning?"

"We need more drinks," Lucinda demanded.

Silas squatted down, so he was at eye level. "Well ladies, we're closing this section down now. The cooking demonstration has ended. Why not take a break, have a nice nap in your rooms, then come and see me at happy hour? I'll make sure the barman makes you something special."

"Special, my ass. You just want us out of here," Lucinda said. "Listen, we're paying guests, the booze is included and you're a damn waiter. You got that?"

Silas winced. He wasn't getting anywhere. "Okay, ladies, you've had a bit too much to drink. My supervisor has asked me to stop serving you, but you can go to your rooms and open your mini bar."

"Who's going to make us drinks?" Ashley demanded. "My husband is dead. Are you coming up to my room to make me a drink?"

"Well, no, I couldn't do that. You could have room service bring you cocktails," Silas said.

"This is bullshit," Lucinda said in a loud voice. "I want a double dirty martini and I want it now. Are you going to bring it to me or not?"

"No, madame, I cannot do that," Silas said firmly.

Bernadette saw Lucinda's hand clench. She saw her arm draw back. In an instant she blocked the punch with her right arm, using her left hand to pull Lucinda's hand into a backwards wrist lock. She now controlled her.

The entire restaurant went quiet.

"Listen to me carefully, Lucinda. From this position, I can break your wrist, or I can let it go," Bernadette said in a quiet and firm voice. She turned to Ashley. "You've both had too much to drink, you need to go back to your rooms now."

Lucinda opened her mouth to speak, and Bernadette applied more pressure to her wrist. Lucinda's face registered the shock.

"I'm going to release your hand, Lucinda, and you're going to leave quietly. Am I understood?"

Lucinda nodded her head. Bernadette released her hand. She stood up, giving the ladies ample room to walk away.

"This isn't over. I'll get you for this," Lucinda said as she walked by both Silas and Bernadette.

Chris came over to Bernadette. "That went well."

Bernadette shook her head. "I walked right into that. I should have left those two for the crew to deal with."

Elizabeth appeared at her side. She placed her hand on her shoulder. "You did the right thing, Bernadette. Lucinda cannot treat someone like that."

"Thanks for your support, Elizabeth," Bernadette said.

She turned to Chris. "I think I'll take myself back to our room and stay out of harm's way."

"Have dinner with Fred and me tonight. Come to our penthouse, we'll order in," Elisabeth said.

"Well, I don't know..." Bernadette said, eyeing Chris for a way out.

"I insist. Come by at seven, I'll have Chef Weber prepare a surprise dish for you. Fred will order in some special wines."

"Okay, sure," Bernadette said. She smiled at Elizabeth and made her way back to her room. She knew that Elizabeth would want to bring up the death of George over dinner. No matter what dish Weber prepared, it would not go well with accusations of murder.

15

BERNADETTE GOT BACK to the room, took a beer out of the bar, checked her watch, noted it was eleven thirty in the morning and opened the bottle. "It's noon somewhere," she said to herself. "Cheers to me."

The phone rang. "Bernadette Callahan."

"Hey Bernie, Cynthia here. Lucinda Braithwaite called down and made a complaint that you'd attacked her in the dining room."

Bernadette laughed. "I love it. Was she coherent enough to file a complaint?"

Cynthia chuckled. "Look, I heard what happened from the bartender. I think what you did was outstanding. The entire bar staff thinks you're the reincarnation of Wonder Woman for stopping that punch. But it's my job to let you know another passenger filed a complaint."

"Is the ship going to let the complaint stand?"

"Company policy. I put my notes in, and the ones in from the head bartender, and we file it," Cynthia said.

"Won't be the first time I've had some shit follow me for something I've done."

"I think you were right to stop Lucinda from hitting Silas, but as one woman to another, I think you need to steer clear of her. She's a drunk with a nasty streak and I don't want to see her try to piss you off. I know what you're capable off. I've seen you in combat at cadet school. No one wanted to challenge you."

"Aw, I'm glad you have such fond memories of me, Cynthia."

"Those weren't memories, those were bruises," Cynthia said with a laugh.

"Okay, I promise to stay clear of the toxic twins from now on. Let the record show, I stopped them from abusing a ship's employee by using less than deadly force."

"You got it. I'll talk to you later," Cynthia said.

Bernadette hung up the phone and wondered how she was going to avoid Lucinda Compton on this ship with only two hundred passengers. She went on the deck, sipped her beer, and watched the waves roll by.

CAPTAIN PRODROMOU STOOD on the bridge of the *Orion* watching the horizon. Every day he felt grateful he'd become the captain of such a beautiful ship. She was 545 feet long and seventy-two feet at the beam, which laymen called the width, with the latest technology in propulsion. He could push this amazing ship to over twenty-five knots while the passengers hardly felt the speed.

His road to this ship had been in the Greek navy where the mainland Greeks had belittled his Cypriot Greek heritage. They hated the way he spoke, but he knew all of Greece was jealous that Cyprus was the banking center of the Middle East and enjoyed an above average standard of living.

He bided his time until he took a position as the second in command on a large container ship. From there he applied to every cruise line in the world. A Greek cruise line hired him as captain. He took it to move up, but he hated it.

A ship with a water slide was not a proper ship, and to top it off, it was one of the oldest in the fleet. The engines hardly gave him the propulsion he needed and constantly were breaking down. He tired of having to make announcements of delays and missed ports.

Good fortune came his way when he became captain of a Princess Cruise ship in the Caribbean. From there he jumped to a Windstar. They were just coming out with their new line of small yachts. He loved them.

No more water slides, climbing walls, and ice rinks. These were ships that had purpose. They plied the ocean to ports larger ships could not venture. The passengers were more into the journey, the experience, than some silly on-board feature. A skating rink on a ship? His mariner heart cringed at the idea.

The *Orion Voyager* was a true ship of adventure with no extra features on board other than the restaurants, bars, spa and gym. With the submarine, helicopter, and zodiacs, this was a ship you could take anywhere.

In a few months' time, they were sailing for the Antarctic; the very idea of it excited him. This ship was double hulled, and ready to take on the world.

He scanned the weather reports. A small cyclone was forming south of them. It would be directly in their path after they made their journey to Andaman Islands. They planned to be there for a day of excursions, then sail to Sri

Lanka. They'd have a bit of a rough sail in the Bay of Bengal if they crossed its path.

He looked over at Felica, his second in command. She'd been checking the weather data and already plotting a course around it.

He watched her move about the bridge in her usual competent fashion. He was immensely proud of her work. And attracted to her. He was trying hard to push her out of his dreams at night, but she entered anyway.

Felica Torres was ten years younger than him, but she shared his passion of the sea. She'd grown up in Lisbon, a bustling port town. Her first time on a ferry ride across the harbor to Barreiro had sealed her fate. She loved the water. Her family were lawyers. She went against her father's wishes to enroll in marine engineering and obtained her master's degree at the prestigious South Tyneside College in England.

Captain Prodromou felt conflicted by her. She was smart, superb at her job, and ready to take command of any size of ship on the sea. His need for her would damage both of their careers.

He had a wife and two sons in Cyprus. A romance with Felica would be inappropriate, it would ruin his marriage, destroy the faith his sons had in him, and be immoral. He knew he was doomed to act on it.

Felica walked over to Captain Prodromou. "I have the latest weather updates." She laid the chart on the console and touched his hand. His heart felt like it melted.

He looked over the charts. "It looks like the storm system will move towards us after we leave Andaman Islands. That's very early for this time of year."

"Yes, but storms can happen almost any time with the earth's increased temperature," Felicia said. "The low depression has been building south of Sri Lanka for the past three days. It will miss us if it veers south."

"Let's hope so, we'll plot our course north. I don't think I can take any more bad news to send to our head office this week," Captain Prodromou said.

"You mean with the death of the passenger?"

"Yes, and that altercation with the two in the bar this morning," Prodromou said. "You know how our company takes these things. They want only happy passengers and excellent reports."

Felicia put her hand next to his on the desk, her fingers caressed his. "Nicolas, you can't let this bother you. Everything will be fine."

Captain Prodromou smiled. "It would be even better if you came to my cabin tonight."

She put her head down to view the charts. "We'll see," she whispered.

16

BY SIX O'CLOCK BERNADETTE WAS RESTLESS. She'd done another tour of the ship, knowing the two blondes were probably sleeping their liquor off. She'd attended a lecture, after being coaxed by Chris, on the sea creatures of the Andaman Islands they were visiting next. The lecturer was a young Australian woman who seemed excited to discuss the many reefs and creatures of the islands. She'd mentioned with a great tone of despair that they could not see the whale sharks this time of year, but the shark diving was exceptional. She'd made the statement as if she was attending some kind of supper party.

Bernadette filed out of the lecture theater with a mental note of how she wanted nothing to do with a shark dive. She'd been amongst them once off the Florida Keys, and that was enough.

They had a brief nap, and now they needed to get ready. She looked over at Chris. He was throwing on some khaki pants and a casual shirt.

"I see you're doing the casual dress thing tonight?"

He turned to look at her. "One night in a tuxedo is one too many. I saw Fred in the corridor, he said it's a casual evening. You know, some beers, some laughs ... that kind of thing."

"Okay, works for me," she said, pulling a simple blue dress out of her closet followed by some low-slung pumps. "You know what Elizabeth is having the chef prepare?"

"No idea, but I'm starving. That sushi at lunch is just a memory to my stomach now," Chris said.

They walked out of their room and down the corridor. All the penthouse suites were on their deck. Chris rang the doorbell; Fred answered the door. He was wearing gray gaberdine wool trousers, a blue button-down shirt and a black blazer. Elizabeth came beside him. She had on an elegant but simple dress adorned with a large diamond pendant.

"Please come in, let me get you a drink," Fred said.

They followed Fred and Elizabeth into the suite with Bernadette giving Chris only the slightest nod to the elegant casual dress their hosts were wearing. Bernadette chose scotch and Chris a Tiger beer. Fred poured chardonnay for Elizabeth and himself.

Bernadette noticed a difference from their suite to the Redstone's. It was larger, and if the word opulent meant over the top in decoration, this was it. Most of the room was some kind of French, late nineteenth century, with tapestries on the walls and figurines of small cherubs holding up the table lamps. She was sure one cherub was looking at her disapprovingly.

They discussed pleasantries over canapés until the doorbell rang.

Elizabeth jumped up to get the door. Two waiters

pushed in a large silver trolley with Chef Weber walking in behind them. He was beaming.

"Good evening, ladies and gentlemen, I hope you will enjoy the special dinner I have prepared," Chef Weber said. He was wearing his dazzling white chef's uniform with his Italian style chef's hat raked to one side, giving him an elegant flair.

The waiters took warm plates from the trolley, placing them on the table, and poured wine.

"This is a specialty from my home in Zurich, Switzerland," Chef Weber said with pride. He spooned portions of the dish on each plate and placed it before them.

"I present to you, Zurich Geschnetzetes, a Swiss style veal in cream sauce with rosti potatoes. And, with this I have chosen a Cote de Bordeaux—Saint Macaie white wine. I was lucky to find the last bottle in our cellars."

"Bravo, Chef Weber," Elizabeth said, clapping her hands. "You've outdone yourself again with such simple but elegant fare."

"Bon appetite," Chef Weber exclaimed and left them with a bow as his waiters pushed the carts out of the room.

"I hope you don't mind our indulgence," Fred said. "This was the most elegant meal Elizabeth and I could afford on our first trip to Europe."

"Taste's wonderful," Bernadette said. She knew Chris would classify this dinner as something resembling beef goulash with hash browns, but she loved the memory they were sharing.

They finished dinner, then Elizabeth rang down for dessert. A classic flambés of cherries jubilee arrived with a stream of liquor to make the flames rise. Chef Weber exclaimed how so few people ever ordered this, but he loved making it as it brought him back to his years of cooking on larger ships.

They retired to the living room with cognacs. Elizabeth motioned for Bernadette and Chris to sit on the sofa while Fred and she sat in the two large armchairs. Bernadette could see a change in Elizabeth. There was something on her mind.

"What are your plans for our stop in Andaman Islands?" Elizabeth asked.

"Nothing much really. We thought we'd paddle around in the ship's kayaks, grab some snorkel gear, and do a bit of sight-seeing on the reefs. Then maybe go on shore."

"Were you thinking of going on the shark dive?" Fred asked.

"Not particularly. I dove with bull sharks once. That was enough," Bernadette said.

"Hmm, did you know that Nigel is going on it?" Elizabeth asked.

Bernadette sipped her cognac. "I hope he enjoys it."

Elizabeth put her glass down, looked at Fred, and then to them. "I'm not sure how to ask this, but Fred and I need your help."

"What for?" Chris asked.

"We're afraid for Nigel. This shark dive was a bucket list thing for George and him. They'd talked about nothing else for the past two months," Elizabeth said.

Fred nodded his head. "Just about made us crazy."

"But there's a dive master on each boat. We attended the lecture, and they said you're behind a rope and holding on. No one comes forward to be with the sharks unless they're with the dive master. I think there's one guide for every five divers. I doubt if they'd take him down if it wasn't safe."

Fred narrowed his eyes and crossed his arms. "It's not the sharks we're afraid of."

"It's Lucinda," Elizabeth said. "She's going down with him."

"You think she's going to feed him to the sharks? That'd be rather obvious. There are thirty divers on the excursion. That's a lot of witnesses," Bernadette said.

"We know if you're there, Lucinda and Ashley won't try anything. We think since Ashley got rid of George, Lucinda will try the same with Nigel," Elizabeth said.

Bernadette sipped her cognac and shook her head. "I can't imagine the dumbest person in the world trying to do that, and believe me, in my line of business I've seen a lot of silly crimes. If Nigel had an accident with the sharks, there'd be an investigation into George's death."

"We know it sounds like a strange request, but we wanted to be sure of his safety. We'll pay you very well for it. Just name your price," Fred said.

"I couldn't in all honesty take money from you. And besides, I'm not licensed to be a bodyguard," Bernadette said.

"Would you do it for our peace of mind, then?" Elizabeth said. "We've lost one dear friend on this cruise and we don't want to lose another."

Bernadette blew out a breath. "Okay, I'll do it if makes you feel better."

Elizabeth clapped her hands and hugged herself. "That's just grand. Thank you so much for doing this. This means the world to us. I'll book it with the concierge right now."

They finished their drinks and said their goodbyes. Bernadette and Chris walked back to their room, poured themselves a Pellegrino, and went onto the deck.

The waves rolled by, a few clouds hid the stars, and a gentle breeze blew a fine mist onto the deck.

Bernadette sipped her Pellegrino and looked up at Chris.

"Is there something bothering you?"

"I think I've just been fed to the sharks by someone using Swiss goulash," she said with a smile.

17

INSPECTOR LEE'S eyes were burning. He felt an empty pit in his stomach that he'd been trying to fill with tea. It was past eleven at night, he'd asked his neighbor to take care of his son, William. There'd be more hateful eyes in the morning when he woke him up to go to school.

But there was so much his young son did not understand. The killers, murderers and even those killed by accident, by manslaughter, needed to be brought to justice.

He felt it with every unexplained death, and this one, of the young, beautiful blonde woman in the canal, this was the worst one he'd ever experienced. To know that two men had taken her away spoke to a premeditated murder.

Who would want to do this, and why? He looked over the reports in front of him. The coroner had taken dental impressions of the dead woman's teeth and skin, hair, and DNA samples.

Lee had obtained a complete file on Holly Marsden from her birth date Detective Callahan gave him. He'd stared at the picture of Holly beside that of the dead girl. There were a few similarities, but Holly was not a match.

But nothing added up. The story of the dead girl, the missing entry files for crew members on the ship, and same hotel. Chance could explain none of this in his mind.

Lee pulled up a file from his phone. He used it often when he faced situations like this. It read, *Chance is none other than cause and effect; cause and effect is none other than chance. If this were not the case, it would render all three marks of existence false.*

This was a saying from Zen. He put the phone back on his desk and looked at the files again. It related the chances that the death of the girl lay in cause and effect. What effect did her death have to the ship that left port two days ago?

He emailed the detective on the ship to ask if anything unusual had transpired. He put his files on his desk and headed out the door. Sleep would not come easily tonight.

BERNADETTE COULDN'T SLEEP. She tossed and turned for a while in bed while Chris lay on his back snoring softly. Her mind kept mulling over recent events. The woman in Singapore was such a crazy outlier of the trip. The death of George; none of it seemed right. Now, she'd agreed to be a babysitter between an elderly man and his young wife who might want to do him harm.

She rolled out of bed, slipped on some clothes, and decided on a walk around the deck to clear her head. She grabbed her ship's card before stepping into the passageway.

The smell of cigar smoke wafted into her nostrils. She breathed it in like an old friend. The cigar lounge must still be open. Walking down the stairs, she heard the faint strains of jazz music. It drew her like a magnet to the heavy wood door.

She placed her hand on the door and pushed it open.
The aroma of tobacco and cognac enveloped her like a
welcome glove. The jazz melody "So What," by Miles Davis
was playing. It was her favorite jazz tune. Ernesto looked up
from his small desk and smiled. Only one other patron
occupied the room. He was an older gentleman with thinning brown hair and bushy eyebrows that folded over soft
blue eyes in his large and kind face. He sat in a leather chair
smoking a pipe and he looked up and smiled, then
motioned for her to join him.

She walked over to him. He wore sports coat, shirt, and
trousers all in black with a western bolo tie and black
cowboy boots. Bernadette had never seen the likes of him
on the ship.

"Good evening, come join me if you wish. The name's
Bill Loving, what's yours?"

Bernadette walked over to him. "Bernadette Callahan.
Nice to meet you, Bill. You come here often?"

"Most every night. Ernesto lets me smoke my pipe and I
think a bit, dream some, and solve life's problems," he said
with a smile.

Bernadette smiled. He had a kind smile and his voice
was so warm it felt like a hug. She almost wanted to shake
her head; he had the same voice as her grandfather, who'd
passed away many years ago.

Ernesto walked over to her and made a slight bow.
"What may I offer, madame?"

"I think a cognac and one of those fine Cuban cigars you
showed me a few days ago."

Ernesto walked to the humidor room and returned with
two cigars. "Which one would you prefer? I still have both."

"The Esplendido," Bernadette replied. She turned to
Bill. "I used to puff on these with my grandfather back in

northern Canada. Just the smell of them brings back memories."

Bill puffed on his pipe; the smoke rose in a lazy curl towards the ceiling and lay there. "Wonderful memories are good things. They keep us going sometimes."

Ernesto brought Bernadette a snifter of cognac, then expertly cut the end of her cigar and lit it for her. She pulled on the cigar, let the smoke roll around on her tongue, and blew it out. Her grandfather had taught her never to inhale.

They puffed in silence for some time before Bernadette finally said, "Where are you from, Bill?"

"El Paso, Texas, and you?"

"Canada, from a little city called Red Deer in the west."

"Pleasant country, that. What do you do there?"

"I'm a detective with the Royal Canadian Mounted Police."

Bill grinned. "Well, isn't that something. I'm a retired Texas Ranger."

"You come from a storied history of the law enforcement, Bill," Bernadette said as she blew a smoke ring into the air.

"Well now, so you do. I read up on your force. One historian claimed we had a lot in common. Tamed the west, kept the natives in check, and protected the ranchers."

Bernadette nodded. "Yeah, that's the history of the RCMP, and I'm part Cree Indian. My force is responsible for the suppression of my people. I can't say I'm proud of that era of our story."

Bill puffed on his pipe. "I know what you mean. I have some Cherokee in me, same here."

"Did you enjoy your service with the rangers?" Bernadette asked.

"I loved it. I was a special ranger in investigations. How about you?"

"Serious crimes division as a detective."

"So, Detective Callahan, what brings you wandering the halls of the ship at this time of night. Something on your mind?" Bill asked.

"Am I that obvious?"

"I guess it's from all my years in the rangers, you get to sense where people are at."

Bernadette pursed her lips and looked at Bill. His nature seemed to be one she could trust. "There are lots of unanswered questions on this trip. I don't know about you, but I rarely believe in random acts or coincidence."

Bill let out a low chuckle. "Ah, the dreaded line-up of things we see that no one else does. That's why you're a talented investigator. When everyone else takes something at face value, you look inside. What are you working on?"

"A dead girl in Singapore. There's a rumor she was supposed to be on this boat."

"Anything else?"

Bernadette swirled the cognac her glass and looked at Bill. "How do you know there's more?"

"The frown on your face," Bill said with a low chuckle that seemed to reverberate around the room.

"I saw some men follow my husband and me to the ship. They weren't pickpockets. They were watching to see if we get onboard."

"And you're confounded because you can't see the connection?"

"Is that my problem?"

"No, it's your gift. That's what makes you good at your job."

Bernadette blew another ring of smoke, watching it ascend into the air. "So, I'm cursed with this, then?"

"Yes, you are. Do you want to talk it over with me right now?"

Bernadette put her cigar down. "You know, I think I'll work on this a bit longer, but I've enjoyed this conversation, Bill."

"I have as well. Drop back any time, I'm here most nights. Ernesto keeps the place open a little later just for me." Bill said.

Bernadette left the cigar lounge and made her way onto the outer deck. The skies were clear; the stars shone down in a blanket of light. She wandered along the deck, looked over the railings, and thought about what Bill had said. Her intuition made her good at her job, she needed to accept it.

She would follow her instincts to find out what was happening on this ship. Returning to her room, she went into the bathroom to give her mouth a good rinse from the cigar smoke. Would Chris smell it on her the next morning? She'd have an early shower before he got up.

She undressed, got back into bed, and thought about how the conversation with Bill had made her feel better. There was just something in his manner that put her at ease. She hoped to drop into the cigar lounge again or perhaps she'd see him on the ship in the daytime and introduce him to Chris. But then again, perhaps not. There was just something in the tone and the manner of the conversation she'd like to keep between just the two of them. At least for now. She fell into a dreamless sleep.

18

BERNADETTE WOKE up early and showered. She washed her hair and hung up the clothes she'd worn in the cigar lounge beside the shower to get the smell out of them. Why she felt guilty about her visit to the cigar lounge and the meeting with Bill, she wasn't sure. Maybe she'd tell Chris in a day or two. He'd see the room charge for the cigar if he looked at their bill online.

She'd wash the smoke off and deal with the situation later. One of her dominant themes in her own life was to deal with everything in time. Her work as a detective always came first.

She ordered coffee from room service and went onto the deck. The sea was like glass. She could see the islands of Andaman coming up over the bow. A slight feeling of dread came over her of swimming with the sharks this morning. Most of it had to do with seeing the two women again. Few of their encounters were good. At least she knew where the sharks stood.

The ship dropped anchor just off the main island. Those

who wanted to go ashore could take one of the two tenders. The stern of the ship dropped to reveal a landing dock and marina. Those wanting to join the shark encounter made their way aft along with those going kayaking and stand up paddle boarding.

Chris decided he was going to do some stand up paddle boarding. As Bernadette stood in a group getting her diving gear, she watched him put a paddle board in the water, step on it, and begin taking expert strokes towards the reefs. She had to stop herself from sighing. She so wanted to be with him. He looked amazing out there, in his board shorts and t-shirt with those big arms propelling the board.

She heard Ashley and Lucinda behind her making whistling sounds. She didn't turn. This time she was going to put them both on ignore and watch over Nigel. Then, when this day was at its end, she'd have a few beers and relax.

The head dive instructor was a blonde, athletic Australian woman in her mid-twenties named Mia. She called everyone around her.

"Everyone, listen up." Mia said. "I want everyone here to show me their hands." She watched as everyone in the room put up their hands. "I count thirty-one pairs of hands. That means when we come back to the ship, everyone should have the same amount. Is that clear?"

A low and nervous chuckle emanated from the room.

"I'm very serious people," Mia continued. "There are a lot of sharks down there today. We've got the harmless nurse and guitar sharks, but there's also bulls and tiger sharks. They're big fellas that require your respect. If you've decided you'll be taking part in the feeding today, you must keep your eyes on the sharks at all times. Am I understood?"

A chorus of yes's came from the group, with a few smart-ass remarks.

"Okay, all you smarties, at this point we've never been able to retrieve a hand from a shark. So, if you turn to your mate for a selfie snap with your hand extended, you will become our YouTube example of what not to do. Questions?"

The group went deadly quiet. A few coughed and shuffled.

Mia smiled. "That line always gets everyone's attention. Now, here's a major item, we've provided you full wetsuits. We know it's hot, and you'd prefer short ones. The big reason is your lovely white skin flashes like bait to a shark. Keep yourself covered at all times. Is that clear as a bell?"

"And another thing, you'll notice there's an ambulance on shore. We've always have them at the ready for our shark dives—so far, we've never called them. Let's keep that record, shall we?"

The crowd looked over their wetsuits. Some men who'd made comments now pulled on the sleeves. Almost as one, they began checking each other for any skin showing.

Mia turned to the other dive masters. "Right then, let's shove off."

The group of divers made their way to the zodiacs. Each diver was wearing their full suit with their BCD, buoyancy compensator device, strapped on. The air tanks were in the zodiac.

The group was quiet now. They got into the zodiac, checked they had their masks and flippers, and gave their names to their dive captains. The zodiacs fired up their engines, and the convoy of divers sped off into the bright morning.

Bernadette sat beside Mia, with Nigel and Ashley. She'd pushed her way past Lucinda when she was pulling on her wet suit to fill the sixth seat in the boat. Lucinda looked pissed, muttered something in her direction, then jumped into the one behind them.

The sea was still calm, hardly a cloud in the sky and it was hot. The heat and humidity baked its way into the neoprene suit. Although they were thin, Bernadette felt like she was being microwaved. Every part of her was perspiring. She could feel the sweat dripping down her legs. The ocean looked inviting, and every spray of saltwater that flowed over the boat was welcome.

The boats took a hard right before the reefs and continued on. Bernadette saw Chris happily paddling his board over the reefs. He looked in his element with no group to contend with. She envied him. That pang of regret hit her, the one that always came when she'd agreed to do something because either she couldn't say no or was cornered to do it.

She looked at Nigel. His look of excitement was palpable. He could hardly keep still. Ashley looked bored. Several others on the boat spoke in low tones.

Mia looked at Bernadette. "First time with sharks?"

"No, I dove with them once before. But this should be a breeze," Bernadette said.

"Why is that?" Mia asked.

"Someone was trying to kill me and my friends then," Bernadette said with a smile.

Mia opened her mouth and then closed it. She wasn't sure if Bernadette was joking or not. The zodiacs slowed down. They were over the site.

"All right then," Mia yelled to all the boats. "Get your

gear on, let your dive master check your regulator, and no one goes in early. As you can see, the sharks have arrived, they've heard the motors. That's a dinner bell to them."

Bernadette looked at the ocean, it teemed with fins and dark shadows. Her stomach did a small flip.

19

DIVERS PULLED on masks and checked their regulators. The dive masters in each boat gave the thumbs up to Mia. They positioned themselves for a backwards flip into the water with their hands over their masks.

Bernadette flipped into the water, feeling relieved by the coolness of the ocean but still anxious about the sharks. She let out the pressure on her BDC and followed Mia down toward the feeding area.

A long rope attached to concrete pylons lay on the bottom. The divers positioned themselves along the rope, holding on with both hands. This kept them in check. A master diver watched them to ensure no one tried to reach out from the rope to 'play with a shark.'

The water was full of schools of snapper, angel fish and small groupers. The sharks glided in and out of view. The water was crystal clear in front of them, but two hundred meters out, the water became dark blue.

The dark blue patch got Bernadette's attention. Two large shapes lurked just inside the edge of the blue. Several of the dive masters had long poles with a crook at the end.

They pushed any shark away that came too close or looked too aggressive.

Mia took a large fish head out of the canister and waved it in the center of the line. Some smaller sharks ventured by, they shot in, took the bait and disappeared. She took out some smaller pieces and motioned for the other divers to take a turn.

Nigel swam forward. He offered a piece of bait to a silver tip reef shark. A docile nurse shark came by and picked up the bits off the sea floor. Nigel went back to the line, giving a thumbs up to Bernadette and Ashley. Bernadette could see that Lucinda was now beside him. She watched her. She seemed more interested in the sharks and hardly noticed Nigel.

A large shark came into view. He glided in from the deep blue edge with a grace that made him look like a small submarine. His wide eyes regarded the line of divers in black with their noisy air bubbles. But the bait drew him in. He'd smelled it over a kilometer away.

Bernadette recognized it as a bull shark, over two meters long, and some ninety kilos. His head moved side to side, scouting, sensing, and looking for the source of the delicious smell.

Mia waved a large fish head at him. It got his attention. He came by slowly, as if approaching the drive thru at a MacDonald's. He grabbed the fish head in his jaws. His enormous eyes went white as a protective cover slid over them to ensure he was never blinded when attacking prey.

He did a shake of his head and tried to make a turn. Another master diver guided the big shark away with a pole. The divers on the line felt the water pressure of the shark as he moved away.

Bernadette looked down at her air gauge, they'd been on

the bottom for all of twenty minutes, but she'd used up half her tank of air. The single tanks were good for one hour, but that was in calm waters while gazing at docile sea life. Watching a bull shark rip a fish head from someone's hand produced a breathing pattern in most divers similar to that of a marathon runner.

Another form made its way from the edge of deep blue. The entire line of divers looked in its direction. It came slowly into view. The bull shark looked at it and slipped away.

At first Bernadette thought it was a great white shark. As it got closer, she could see the distinct markings on its side. A full-grown tiger shark. Four meters long and some six hundred kilos of predator swam towards the line of divers with a few flicks of its tail that showed it owned this space.

The schools of fish parted for the new king of the seas; the other sharks slinked away to not become dinner. Mia pulled out an extra-large fish head, waving it at the shark. The gigantic head and steely black eyes looked in her direction.

The shark swam towards the line first, as if it wanted to show its dominance over these fragile creatures that dared venture into its domain with their breathing apparatuses. As it swam slowly by, the pressure wave felt like a small boat going by the divers. The air bubbles increased tenfold from the divers as they collectively gasped at the site of this fearless beast.

Mia held the fish head in her hand. A diver was ready with a pole. The tiger shark opened its mighty jaws and grabbed the bait. The other diver guided it away with the pole. The tiger did a slow circle and came back for more.

Mia reached down into the bait bucket, there was only one more fish head left. She offered it to the big tiger; he took it with ease, gulping it down, inhaling it as he swam around in another circle.

When Mia looked into the bucket, a few small pieces remained. Nothing big enough to extend to a massive tiger without putting her hands in danger. She signaled to the others that the feeding was over.

Bernadette looked down at her air regulator—ten minutes left. They were at ten meters, which meant they could ascend without decompressing, but the big shark was still circling.

The diver masters motioned for everyone to ascend as a group. They would watch over them with their poles at the ready if the big tiger got aggressive. One by one they let go of the rope and made for the surface.

Bernadette let go of the rope. She saw Nigel and Lucinda in front of her. Ashley floated into her view. There was a flash of white on her leg—a long rip exposed her flesh.

20

BERNADETTE DID two quick strokes with her flippers to get beside Ashley. She tapped her on the arm, pointed to her own leg, then pointed to Ashley's hoping she'd see the danger. Ashley waved her away. Bernadette tried to motion for her to get inside the circle of divers. Ashley pushed her away.

Bernadette looked around. The tiger shark had seen the flash of skin. It was hungry. Feeding time was not over—he smelled bait in the water. The shark rose to within two meters of Ashley. The other divers were rising, focused on the surface.

Mia was leading the group up, her attention was on helping a diver who seemed in distress, she had the pole in her hand. Bernadette needed that pole. She quickly swam to Mia and grabbed it. Mia turned to Bernadette—she pointed at the shark.

Mia's eyes went to saucers. She saw the danger—she motioned for the other divers to form a circle. Bernadette took the pole and made hard kicks to get back with Ashley. She was too late.

The tiger saw a chance with Bernadette out of the way. One flick of its tail put it in striking distance. Mighty jaws opened. Multiple rows of teeth extended. It clamped down on Ashley's thigh.

Bernadette propelled herself to the head of the shark. The water turned red with blood. She could hardly see. She pulled out the diver's knife in her vest. There was one chance. The shark's eye was covered. She hoped to inflict enough pain on it to let Ashley go.

She collided with the shark's head. Her hand felt rough skin. Moving her hand along the head her hand touched its lips, teeth were just below. She moved her hand up. The blood dissipated. She saw the eye and stabbed it. Her hand worked in a piston motion, stabbing again and again.

With a shake of its head, it let Ashley go, twisting and shooting off into the deep blue from whence it came.

Ashley was listless. She'd gone into shock. Bernadette grabbed her by the shoulders and took her to the surface. They broke the surface in a pool of blood. The divers who had made it into their boats looked down in horror.

Bernadette motioned for a boat to come to them. Suddenly Mia was by her side helping to get Ashley into the boat. They pulled her in, fell on top of her and assessed her wounds.

"The big bugger nicked the femoral artery," Mia yelled. "We have to stop the bleeding."

Bernadette applied pressure to the artery while Mia pulled out the medical kit. The bottom floor of the zodiac was awash in blood. Ashley was going white.

"Hang in there, Ashley," Bernadette said. "You're safe now. Just stay calm, we'll have you to a hospital in a minute. You'll be fine." She tried to keep her voice calm.

"No, take me back to the ship..." Ashley said with her voice fading.

"We need to get you patched up properly, don't worry," Mia said. "You just had a little love bite from the big fella, but no worries, we'll have you okay in a jiff."

"She's going on us," Bernadette said. She started chest compressions as the zodiac fired its engines and headed for shore towards the waiting ambulance crew.

The zodiac roared onto the beach to a team of Indian EMT's. They started an IV and kept up with the chest compressions. An attendant gave her oxygen.

The dive team stood on the shore and watched as they tried to stabilize her. They pulled out a defibrillator and gave her multiple shocks to start her heart. Nothing happened. They upped the voltage. Ashley's body was lifting off the stretcher with the increased current. There was no response.

The EMT's finally looked up and called it. The head of the ambulance came over with a sad face. "I'm sorry. The shock of the attack was too much for her. She is gone."

"Oh god, I can't bloody believe it," Mia said. "The bite was big, but not that deep. She must have had a heart condition."

"I think being in the jaws of the big tiger put her into cardiac arrest," one diver said. He looked around to the other four divers. No one said a word.

The EMT looked to Mia. "You want us to take care of the body?"

Mia shook her head. "No, she's the ship's responsibility. We'll take her back."

The EMT's placed Ashley's body in a body bag, zipped it up, and brought it to the zodiac. Mia washed the remnants of the blood out of the boat's floor. She knew it was bad enough for the passengers to be with a dead body; the added blood would put them over the edge.

Mia steered the zodiac, so it came into the side of the ship facing away from shore. The passengers usually lounged on the side facing the beach. She didn't want them staring down at a body bag returning from a sea adventure.

As they pulled up to the back of the marina, the captain and first officer were standing there.

Crewmen docked the boat. Four others pulled the body out of the boat. Captain Prodromou walked up to Mia, demanding to know what happened.

Mia put her head down; she was in tears. "A great bloody tiger grabbed her as we were heading to the surface. No one saw it until it was too late."

"Where the hell were your dive masters?" Captain Prodromou asked. "You've done this before. How did this happen?"

Bernadette walked up to them. "Her suit was ripped at the leg. I tried to tell her and get her on the inside. She pushed me away."

The captain moved closer to Mia. "You let a passenger go on a shark dive with a ripped suit?"

"No, we checked all the suits before the dive. Most of the suits were brand new. We bought some new ones in Singapore," Mia said.

First officer, Felica instructed the crew to take Ashley's body to the morgue. Then she turned to Mia. "You must inspect the suit and find out where it came from and when it went into service." She looked at Bernadette. "Will you give a full report to security on this?"

Bernadette nodded. This was a déjà vu all over again as Yogi Berra, the baseball player once said. This was getting crazy. She peeled off her wet suit and got under the marina shower. As she was about to put on her cover-up, she noticed a cut on her forearm.

"You best get that looked at," Mia said. "Tell the doctor you're covered by us. It's the least we can do for your actions today."

Bernadette nodded and patted Mia's arm. "Don't be too hard on yourself. I warned her, but she didn't listen. Sometimes people cause their own destiny."

Mia closed her eyes. "I know, it's the chance we take with hanging with those lovely beasts down there, but this has never happened before. I feel sick."

Bernadette gave Mia a hug. There was nothing more she could do. She had to leave her with her team to pull herself together.

Bernadette found her way down to the doctor's office. Dr. Kamau appeared from the back room and beckoned her to come in.

"You have brushed up against a shark?" Dr. Kamau asked.

"How do you know that?" Bernadette asked with surprise. She hadn't mentioned how she'd received the injury to the nurse.

"Your arm looks like it has been brushed by sandpaper. Only a big shark does this. Did you fight with the one that killed Mrs. Compton?"

"I helped get it away from her, more than fight. Did you see the body already?"

"Yes, the crew brought it into the morgue, and I had a look at it. The shark did not make much of a bite to my thinking."

"What do you mean, doctor?" Bernadette asked as he attended her wound.

"His bite nicked the femoral artery, that would mean a

lot of blood, but I looked at the damage. I could see it, the incision the shark's tooth made was not that big. You must have scared him away before he got a good grip."

"There was a lot of blood."

"The femoral artery is the largest in the leg, it supplies all the blood to the lower body. You only have to make a slight cut to get a lot of blood flowing."

"But I watched her in the boat, her color drained, and she went into cardiac arrest." Bernadette said.

Dr. Kamau continued dressing her wound. "She might have had an underlying heart condition. I understand the shark was big. This can cause severe stress on someone and put them into cardiac arrest. That is my best guess."

"You were once a coroner, were you not?" Bernadette asked.

"Yes, in Kenya, I had a practice in the town of Malindi on the coast. There is a marine reserve there. I saw many bites from sharks there," Dr. Kamau said. He took an envelope from his desk. "This pendant was around her neck. Would you give it to her friends? I believe you know them?"

"Yes, I do," Bernadette said. She took the envelope and walked into the corridor and opened it up. It was a heavy pendant with the letters NW on it. She turned over the letters and saw what looked like a microprocessor underneath.

She went back to her room. As she opened the door, Chris was waiting for her, and he took her in her arms and hugged her hard.

"I saw what happened out there. I made it back to the ship to wait for you to see if I could help," he said. "How are you holding up?"

"Well, I was at the scene of the shark attack. I made it

out alive, but Ashley is dead. I'll get over it, but she won't," Bernadette said.

"I think you need to rest for the remainder of the day," Chris said.

The phone rang, but they let it go it go to voice mail. It rang again.

Bernadette looked over at the phone. "That's probably Cynthia calling. She'll need me to make an incident report —you know that no one leaves this world without a report."

She walked over to the phone and picked it up. "Bernadette Callahan."

"Hey, Bernie, it's me," Cynthia said. "I need your help."

"Yeah, I know, the incident report regarding Ashley's death. I can be down in a few minutes to write it out."

"No, not about that," Cynthia blurted. "Our helicopter had to land on a deserted island some ten klicks from here. My security team is on shore in Port Blair, and I need some backup for a bit of a delicate extraction."

"How delicate?"

"The island is home to some aboriginals who don't like foreigners. It's protected by the Indian government and off limits. Any trespassers are killed by the locals," Cynthia said.

"Who's in the helicopter?"

"The Redstones. They went on a helicopter tour. The copter shouldn't have been near those islands," Cynthia said.

"We'll be right down," Bernadette said. She turned to Chris. "We got an adventure tour to go on. I'll let you know about it on the way downstairs."

BERNADETTE AND CHRIS met Cynthia and Mateo at the marina. They climbed into the zodiac, and Mateo hit the throttle, racing towards the island.

Cynthia turned and put her head close to Chris and Bernadette so they could hear.

"Here's the situation," Cynthia said. "The Indian Coast Guard is standing off the island. They are accusing our helicopter of doing an overflight and say it's our duty to retrieve the chopper and get it off the island. The pilot said he had an electrical system failure. We have a replacement part, but we need to get it to him so he can fix it and take off."

"What's the major concern then?" Bernadette asked.

"There's a group of natives heading towards the chopper," Cynthia said.

Mateo pushed the throttle forward on the zodiac. He sat in a covered wheelhouse at the helm of two twin seventy-horsepower engines. The sea was calm. He set the speed at fifty knots; they were cruising at 90 kilometers an hour. He wasn't about to lose more passengers or crew that day.

The island came into view and they saw the small helicopter sitting on the beach. There was a line of palm trees and scrub brush some three hundred meters away. Cynthia took a pair of binoculars and scanned the trees.

"I see three native males armed with bows and arrows," Cynthia said, handing the binoculars to Bernadette.

"Any idea of how aggressive these people are?" Bernadette asked.

"They murdered an American a few years back who came to this island to preach Christianity to them."

Bernadette put the glasses down. "Yeah, that would be a hard no." She turned to Mateo. "What's your plan?"

Mateo turned from the captain's chair. "I was thinking of going ashore with the part. Cynthia can run the zodiac on the beach, then back off. I'll run the part to the copter."

"I think you'll have a problem with that. The locals are moving towards the chopper," Chris said. "You don't have any weapons, do you?"

Mateo shook his head. "It's against maritime law for security on cruise ships to have weapons. I have a flare gun —that's it."

They turned to see the three natives walking towards the helicopter. They had their bows in front of them, with arrows at the ready. The men were tall, dark-skinned, with red bandanas and red armbands. They wore simple loin cloths. Their movements were slow, as if they were hunting this great mechanical beast that had landed on their island.

"I need to get between them and the chopper," Mateo said.

Chris stood up. "I'll go with you."

Bernadette stood up, putting her hands on their shoulders. "If you do, you'll both be full of arrows. You're big guys, you look threatening as hell. Cynthia and I will go."

"No way, I won't allow it," Mateo said.

"Yeah, you will," Cynthia said. "We go in, show them we mean no harm, and we're out of here. You go in, they'll put all their arrows in you—you know I'm right. For Christ-sake you're a Maori, you know what threats look like."

"Okay, but we see any trouble, Chris and I are coming in," Mateo said.

"I don't doubt it." Cynthia replied with a smile.

Bernadette turned to the Mateo. "Take us in to five meters off the beach into the shallows, we'll wade in, less of a threat, and Cynthia, take your shirt and bra off."

"My what now?"

"You heard me—their women probably don't cover their breasts. You want to be non-threatening; we go native," Bernadette said, throwing her cover up off. She walked to the bow of the zodiac and unhooked her bikini top, throwing it on the seat. "Okay girl, take it off."

Cynthia stood beside her, unbuttoned her shirt and took off her bra. "The shit you get me into Bernie—"

Bernadette looked at her and smiled. "Nice rack, by the way."

Cynthia smiled and looked at Bernadette. "You have a nice set yourself. Let's try to keep them inflated—no arrow holes."

They jumped into the waist deep water. Cynthia held the chopper part overhead. Making their way to shore, they could see the pilot in the chopper's front with the Redstones in the back. The pilot looked concerned. The Redstones looked terrified.

"How do we play this?" Cynthia asked.

"You remember all the times we were in practice combat at the academy? I told you that the Goju Ryu Karate I learned meant hard and soft. Show your hands to them, palms facing outward. It's the don't hurt me sign. If they come too close with those weapons, we show them what hurt is."

"You're asking me to remember karate techniques I learned from you over twenty years ago?" Cynthia asked as they neared the helicopter.

"Just like riding a bike—get inside the opponent and hit hard," Bernadette said, keeping her eyes on the natives.

Collin, the pilot, opened the door on the beach side. "Are you ever a sight for sore eyes, and I don't just mean having the part delivered," he said with a smile. He was a former bush pilot from Canada's far north. If he lived through this day, he'd have a rescue story that would get him free drinks for life.

"How long until you get airborne?" Cynthia asked.

"I just have to switch out this board. It got fried somehow," Collin said. "I'll have this bird up in five." He took the part, pulled out the old board, put in the new one, and began his system checks.

"There, that's easy," Cynthia said. "We catch a few rays of sun and we'll be out of here."

Bernadette stared at the natives. "Looks like our escorts are getting restless—"

The native men walked up to the other side of the helicopter. First, they tried to open the doors. Collin had locked them. They banged on the bubble of the helicopter with their arrow tips.

"They can't break it can they?" Bernadette asked.

"They'll scratch it, but it won't break," Cynthia said.

Two of the natives ran back towards the trees and returned with rocks.

"Okay, now we got a problem," Cynthia said.

"Let's move towards them, remember palms up," Bernadette said.

The men stopped what they were doing, watching the women come towards them. Only one of them had a bow in his hands, the others dropped their rocks.

"Hi guys, I'm Bernadette, this is my friend Cynthia, we want you to leave the helicopter alone and let it fly away," Bernadette said, smiling and making motions with her hands of a bird flapping its wings.

"I don't think they get it, Bernadette. What's the use in talking to them?"

"To calm them down and give Collin time to turn the rotors, when he does, we might have to subdue them," Bernadette said.

Cynthia looked at the men; they looked fit and strong. "How do we take on three men?"

"I'll take the two on the right, you take the one on the left. But wait until the rotors turn. Their eyes will be on the chopper and not you—you copy that?"

"Sure, I copy that, but your plan scares the shit out of me, Bernie."

The helicopter revved its engines. The top rotor made slow revolutions. Then the fan tail started. The men became agitated. They yelled and reached for the rocks.

"Wait for it," Bernadette said.

The helicopter rose, the sand from the beach threw up a cloud of dust.

"Now," Bernadette yelled.

She moved with lightning speed at the first man on her right—his arm was extending to a rock—and she grabbed his arm pushing it behind him and dropped an elbow on his head. He went down. The man beside him turned to her—she struck his leg with the heel of her foot on his shin; he howled in pain. She hit him in the throat and he dropped.

The sand storm turbulence from the helicopter was blinding. She looked for Cynthia. She was on the ground with a man who was holding a knife at her throat.

Bernadette disarmed the man by grabbing his wrist. She twisted it until he dropped the knife. An elbow to the head sent him to the ground. He tried to get up. Bernadette grabbed a rock and hit him on the side of the head. He went limp. She checked his vital signs, finding him still alive.

She pulled Cynthia up and they ran for the shore. The zodiac had beached, Chris was running towards them.

"Ladies, if you're done with your Amazon show, we can leave now," Chris said.

They ran to the zodiac, throwing themselves on board. Bernadette pulled on her cover and tossed Cynthia her shirt. Mateo threw the engines into reverse and pulled away as fast as he could. He hoped the natives didn't recover from the pounding the ladies had given them.

An arrow flew overhead, letting them know the natives had woken up and wanted to show their displeasure. Mateo slung the zodiac around. In seconds, the twin engines shot them out of there. A few arrows splashed behind them as they headed home.

Bernadette and Cynthia sat in the back seats with their arms around each other.

"I'm sorry I screwed up," Cynthia said. "I forgot about the keep moving part you always warned me about. You told me never to hesitate. I did."

"Any battle you live through is good. You survived, I had your back, Cynthia. Never sweat another day you get."

"Thanks girl, you're awesome!" Cynthia said.

"You're welcome. Will you be opening an investigation

into Ashley's death and this helicopter incident?" Bernadette asked, fixing a gaze on Cynthia.

"There are no coincidences in your world, are there?"

Bernadette looked up at the helicopter that roared over-head towards the ship. "Maybe in bullshit poker. In the actual world, no."

22
───────

BERNADETTE TOOK a long shower before she felt anything close to relaxed. She knew a return to normal would be some time away. She sat on the deck wrapped in a bathrobe staring at the harbor where the shark attack had been. Sipping on a second beer, she placed it on the table beside her.

There was no use in trying to turn off the vision of the large fish biting into Ashley. It would always be there, just beyond the periphery of her consciousness. To deal with it, she tried never to focus on it. The event had happened; it was real now she'd move on, to deal with the next event that came up.

The life of a police detective exposed her to the worst things that humans could do to one another. This event today had been bad timing between a human and a massive predator... or was it?

Chris came out and sat beside her, putting his hand on her shoulder. "Can I get you another beer?" he asked, staring down at her to see how she was doing.

She smiled up at him. "No thanks, if I go for a third, I'll be in the drunk tank by midnight."

"Hilarious. Anything you want to talk about?" he asked.

"Yeah, in a few days' time two of the people we met on the first night on this ship are dead. And it looks like the Redstones had an attempt on their lives with the helicopter malfunction. Lucky for them, the pilot was good at making an emergency landing."

Chris ran a hand over his face and looked at her. "Seems odd as hell to have three events like this. Has Cynthia said anything of what the ship is going to do?"

Bernadette shook her head. "No, not yet, but I intend on finding out."

"I take it you will not take it easy and rest up today?"

She got out of the chair. "No, not an option. I have some people on this ship I need to talk to. Besides, I read an email from Inspector Lee asking me if we had any unusual events on this ship. The latest events have been so unusual, I doubt he'll be able to comprehend it."

Chris took the envelope with the necklace off the side table. "While you were in the shower, I looked at the back of this necklace. It's interesting."

"Interesting in what way?"

"It looks like a normal necklace, but when I put my phone next to it, the back of it pulsated."

Bernadette took the necklace. "Show me."

"I tried some different apps on my phone with it. It doesn't seem to be a GPS, because there's no sync, but it could activate something. I just don't know what it is," Chris said.

Bernadette put the necklace back in the envelope and got up.

"Where are you going?"

Bernadette kissed Chris on the mouth. "I'm getting dressed and doing some rounds on the ship."

"You mean you're about to open your own personal investigation, don't you?"

"Totally. But the good thing is, I don't have to file any reports, I just have to find out who's responsible for these accidents. And maybe the Redstones know what this necklace is all about," Bernadette said. She went into the suite, threw off her bathrobe, and put on capris and blouse. She ran a comb through her hair, did a quick make up fix, and was heading out the door ten minutes later.

She walked into the hallway and stood there for a moment. The ship would sail for the next port in one hour. There were already some sounds from the ship's address system that they would weigh anchor at five. The ship's horn sounded once, letting the passengers know they would be getting under way.

The tenders were coming in from Port Blair. The local authorities considered the death of Ashley Compton an *Orion Voyager* problem. They wanted nothing to do with it.

Bernadette walked to the Redstone suite and rang their doorbell. It took some time before the door opened slowly. Fred stood at the open door. He seemed at a loss.

"May I come in?" Bernadette asked.

"Oh, yes, please come in. The events of the day have sent a shock into us. Please let me get you a drink," Fred said. He wore casual slacks with a golf shirt with a Pebble Beach logo.

"Thanks, Fred, I'm okay. I'm just checking to see how you're doing," Bernadette said.

Fred smiled and lowered his eyes, "We're okay now... thank God, you arrived when you did—"

"What Fred is trying to say," Elizabeth said, walking into

the room, "is he can't forget you, half naked, saving us from those savages. He has been waxing poetically all afternoon to me about those incredible moves you made to take out those horrible heathens."

Bernadette shook her head. "Those men were local natives, who unfortunately had never seen a helicopter before and wanted to protect themselves. I'm sorry I had to treat them that way, but we wanted to make sure you were safe."

"Well, damn girl, you rocked it. What were those moves you made on those guys?" Elizabeth asked.

"It's called Goju Ryu Karate. I've studied it since I was a teenager. It helped me deal with the bullies I encountered in my school days," Bernadette said.

Elizabeth directed Bernadette to join them in the living room. She held a large martini in her hand. Two giant olives looked like they were drowning in vodka.

Elizabeth took a long sip of her drink and placed it on the coffee table. "Whatever it was, you were impressive. My granddaughter is fascinated with Black Widow movies. She would have loved to have seen you in action." She rolled her eyes towards Fred. "With more clothes on, perhaps, so my husband doesn't have a cardiac episode."

Fred shifted in his chair and picked up his martini to examine it as if the olive had become fascinating. His eyes did one quick scan over Bernadette then dropped back to his glass.

"Well, thanks for the compliment, however, my martial arts prowess wasn't enough to save Ashley. I'm here to say I'm sorry for the loss of your friend's wife," Bernadette said.

Elizabeth lowered her voice, her speech slurred a bit from the alcohol. "Look, Bernadette, yes it's sad that crazy blonde met her end that way, but I cannot in all honesty put my hand on my heart and grieve her passing."

"Now, now, my dear, that's most unkind..." Fred said. He looked at Elizabeth. She waved her hand in his direction as if to dismiss him. "I mean, we cannot in all conscience be happy for the demise of Ashley," Fred continued.

Elizabeth turned her head quickly towards him. "I didn't say I was happy she's dead, I just admitted I wasn't sad with her gone. I'm sure when I email the insurance company, they'll be doing a dance of joy in San Francisco."

"You contacted the insurance company, then?" Bernadette asked.

"We did. George Compton is on our board of directors. We had to let them know that his wife Ashley would collect the one hundred-million-dollar payout," Fred said.

"Did they want to investigate it?"

"You bet they did," Elizabeth said, taking a drink and almost draining her martini. "They were planning on having an investigator and lawyer at the dock in Mumbai. When I told them she was going to have George's body cremated without an autopsy, they went ballistic. They planned on having an injunction in their hands from an Indian court."

"Did Ashley or Lucinda know of the insurance company's intentions?" Bernadette asked.

"No, not that I know of," Elizabeth said.

Fred went quiet, dropping his head into his hands with a low groan. "Oh God, I told Nigel."

"That was foolish," Elizabeth said, throwing a glare at him. "You know he's smitten with that airhead wife of his. He'd have told Lucinda. She would have informed Ashley in a heartbeat."

"Yes, I'm sorry, I forget how Nigel oscillates between

wanting to divorce Lucinda, and the moment she nails him in bed, he forgets and tells her everything... Sorry for my lewd description," Fred said.

Bernadette grinned. "I've heard worse. Now one thing I wanted to know is who did you tell about your helicopter tour today?"

"Pretty much everyone," Elizabeth said. "We were told we needed to book the tour well in advance as it books up quickly. We put out our itinerary for all the others to see months ago. That's why we knew about the shark feeding. Nigel and George talked about nothing else for months."

"I need to go now," Bernadette said. "I'm glad you're both okay."

Elizabeth put her martini down. "You suspect something, don't you?"

"My profession is a detective. I see dots and I want to connect them. There's been two accidental deaths in your party, and what looks like an attempt on your life. I want to speak with the security on board. There are so many things that make little sense to me here."

Elizabeth downed the rest of her martini and turned to Fred. "You see Fred? I told you so." She looked at Bernadette with her eyes narrowing. "I told Fred there's no way these are random accidents. And I'll bet that Lucinda and Nigel are behind it."

"Why would you say that?" Bernadette asked. "I thought George and Nigel were the best of friends. You told me that Nigel was looking to divorce Lucinda."

"All a ruse, he's been playing us all. When we get back to the states, I'm going to put a detective on that man. I'll bet Lucinda has been draining his bank account dry. With George and Ashley out of the way, Nigel and Lucinda look to profit from the extra shares that come to them from the buyout on George's passing. And, if he would have successfully killed us in the helicopter crash, he'd be in for a cool two hundred million," Elizabeth said. She pushed her martini glass towards Fred to make her another drink.

Bernadette stood up. "Thanks to you both for sharing some enlightening speculations. If what you claim is true, I'm sure the FBI will become involved."

"The FBI, why them?" Fred asked.

"I believe that since you're all American citizens and this ship is American with headquarters in Fort Lauderdale, the laws of the USA will probably apply to any felonies," Bernadette said.

Elizabeth glanced at Fred. "I thought we'd be dealing with the Indian government," Elizabeth said. "This ship flies a flag from the Bahamas. Don't the laws of their country apply to our ship?"

"I did a quick check on the FBI website. They can take over when there are American fatalities on an American-owned ship. There's another major factor—"

"What's that?" Elizabeth asked.

"This ship left the port of San Francisco to start its world tour. It will stop in Los Angeles in six weeks. The FBI gets to claim jurisdiction in this case," Bernadette said. She eyed Elizabeth's movements.

Elizabeth ran her hand through her hair, then clasped her necklace. "Well... that's good news, I guess. I'm sure the FBI will investigate these incidents."

"I'm sure they will," Bernadette agreed. "And one other thing..." She pulled the pendant out of her pocket. "The doctor gave me this pendant from Ashley's body. I'm sure you have someone to send it to."

Elizabeth took the pendant. "Not really, we knew none of her friends or relatives. I'll give it to Lucinda."

"I saw some kind of transistor on the back. What's it for?" Bernadette asked.

Elizabeth turned it over to look at it. "I'm not sure." She handed it to Fred. "What do you think it is?"

Fred took it, turning it over to look closely. "No idea. Perhaps George put some kind of GPS tracking device in it to track Ashley on the ship, or if she got lost... Hard to say unless I opened it up and looked inside."

"Okay, just wondering. I best be going now, I'm glad you're okay," Bernadette said as she walked to the door and left.

It relieved her to get out of the suite. There were enough accusations and double dealings to make her head spin. She almost wished for her life back in Canada, simple drug dealers, murders of passion, and low-level greed. This was high stakes and getting complicated.

The ship's horn sounded several times to signal they were leaving port. She made her way down towards the marina. She wanted to meet with Mia, and perhaps the pilot, before the end of the day. So far, she had more questions than anything else.

She headed down the stairs and met Cynthia coming up the stairs.

"Hey Cynthia, I was just coming to see you," Bernadette said with a smile she hoped hid her lie.

"I was on my way to see the Redstones," Cynthia said.

"You won't have much luck there, they're on their third or fourth martini. How about if you and I go have a talk with Mia? I can just be the fly on the wall, not involved..."

Cynthia laughed. "Sure, I'll tell Mateo that." She looked up towards the Redstones suite. "Yeah, let's go do that, you can fill me in on the conversation you had with them. I hate drunken interviews. I've done enough of them on this ship."

23

THEY STARTED with Collin the pilot first. The helicopter sat back into its own hanger with the rotors folded in. Bernadette looked at the thing. It was small; she disliked anything to do with helicopters. The very idea of them with their spinning rotor on top and the little spinning one in the back was, to her, a strange way to fly.

She'd been in bush planes with pontoons that had dropped over a mountain range and bounced to a landing on a thin strip of lake in Canada's far north. She'd rather take her chances in a little plane than a helicopter.

Collin was in a tiny cubbyhole of an office just inside the hanger typing on his laptop. He looked up as they came in.

"Well, what a surprise, my two lovely ladies who saved my ass from the natives. Although I have to say, you looked so much better on the beach earlier," Collin said with a wide grin.

"I'm glad we can add to your memories," Cynthia said dryly. "And I take it you didn't have a GoPro camera active on the chopper?"

Collin hung his head. "You surprised the hell out of me

with your beach landing. I forgot to turn the camera towards you. Sadly, a moment in time... lost forever." He looked up with a sigh.

"Do you believe him?" Bernadette asked, looking at Cynthia.

"We'd have been viral on YouTube by now if he had a picture, so yes, I believe him," Cynthia said.

"What can I do for you ladies, as you've already done more for me than any single man my age can ask for," Collin said, the smile returning to his face.

"I'm sure you'll be filling out a complete incident report to the captain, but I'm curious about how often you have electrical failures," Bernadette said.

"Hardly ever. These whirlybirds have double backups. I'm still trying to figure out what went wrong. One minute I'm flying, the next minute I've got no electrical. I had to put the chopper into autorotation to make the landing."

"Why were you doing a flyover of the Sentinel Islands?" Cynthia asked.

"I wasn't and they'll check my flight recorder to see that. I flew south from Port Blair. The Redstones wanted to see the coral reefs and some dolphin pods. When the malfunction happened, the islands were my only landing choice. No pontoons on our chopper."

"Was the itinerary yours or theirs?" Bernadette asked.

"It was a mix of both. I took them on the standard city tour, then Elizabeth asked for the coral reefs. I always do what my passengers request as long as it's safe."

"And there's a good tip involved," Cynthia added.

"Without question." Collin beamed.

"Was that a safe route?" Bernadette asked.

"As long as I'm within sight of land. My primary concern

is to keep a certain altitude in case I have to do my superman style landing. That's the no power thing."

"So, you were high enough when the malfunction occurred, then?" Cynthia asked.

Collin nodded his head. "Yeah, the saint of helicopters was on my side. I'd just gained altitude for our return to the ship when the electrical went. Had I been lower, we'd have been swimming."

"Lucky break, Collin," Cynthia said.

"How often does the thing get serviced?" Bernadette asked.

Collin raised an eyebrow. "This thing as you call it, which is my pride and joy, gets serviced every time we're in a major port. I had a tech come in and do a complete service in Singapore."

They thanked Collin and heading below decks to the marina. At first, they walked in silence, then Cynthia turned to Bernadette.

"I'm waiting for you to say it," Cynthia said.

"Say what?"

"That someone sabotaged the chopper by installing a faulty circuit board in Singapore. That everything leads back there," Cynthia said.

"Let's wait until after we've met with Mia."

They found Mia in the equipment room; she was stowing the dive tanks and washing down the wet suits. She looked up as they entered the room, her eyes moist from tears.

"Hey Mia," Cynthia said. "How are you holding up?"

Mia turned off the water and ran her hand through her hair. "Not well, actually. I'm getting fired over this. I don't blame them. I was the head of the dive. It was my job to get everyone back safe. I should have seen that big bugger shark."

"What had your attention?" Cynthia asked.

"A diver named Mandy Stogner. Her regulator was giving her problems—she wasn't getting enough air. I swam with her to the surface, sharing my oxygen as we ascended," Mia said.

"It's not your fault. You saved another diver's life. That distracted you," Bernadette said. "Your team of diver masters should have seen what you were doing and covered for you."

Mia brushed a tear from her eye and shook her head. "No, it doesn't matter, this will come back to me. I'll never be able to work in this industry again. I love diving, it's my entire life since I was a kid in Oz. I grew up with my mom and dad doing dives on the Great Barrier Reef. I'll be heading home soon."

Cynthia placed her hand on Mia's arm. "When the captain sees our notes from the enquiry, he'll understand. Everything will be fine."

Mia lowered her head. "No, it's over. Felica was just here. I'm to leave the ship when we dock in Colombo. The company's legal team has already been in contact with the captain and told him my actions were negligent in their eyes."

"Then we need to sort this out soon," Bernadette said. "How many of the crew have access to this equipment?"

"The marina and dive shop is open to both crew and passengers whenever it's in port and during sailing. If someone wants to come down to get fitted for dive gear, we meet them here," Mia said.

"You have four others on your dive team besides yourself, is that correct?" Bernadette asked.

"Yeah, most of them are good, only one of them—her

name is Astrid—I'm not too jazzed about. She's done a few daft things lately, but mostly just being lazy. I've been on her about keeping the gear stowed better and keeping it cleaner."

"What does she look like?" Cynthia asked.

"A real pretty girl, blonde, looks like she could be a model if she wanted," Mia said with a bit of a chuckle. "Maybe that's her problem, she thinks she can get by on her looks."

Bernadette put her hand up. "Mia, did you notice anything strange about her?"

"She's a bit of a loner. Somehow, she got her own cabin, which is rare on this ship. I know that she hung out with Collin a bit in the chopper hanger."

"You think they were sleeping together?" Bernadette said.

"Hard to say. Just about everyone on the crew suspects everyone else is hooking up and getting laid on a long voyage, but mostly never happens. We rarely have the time or the opportunity with our close quarters."

"But it's a possibility?" Bernadette said.

Mia shrugged. "Sure, could be. Collin would be a lucky guy. Hopefully she's as good a lay as she looks." She wrapped up the hose and looked at them with a grin.

"What's her last name?" Bernadette asked.

"Karlsson. She's from Sweden, thinks she's some kind of royalty from there," Mia said.

"Just one more thing," Bernadette said, looking around the marina, "did all the divers just select random boats and dive masters today or were they designated to boats and your team members?"

"Astrid made up the list the night before," Mia said, then

nodded at Bernadette. "You were the only late addition. Mrs. Redstone got you added in."

"What about wetsuits? How do you know who fits what or do you just fit them on the day of the dive?"

"Oh no, we require all the divers to come see us for a fitting. You were the only one we fitted the day of the dive," Mia said.

"I heard you mention to the captain that most of the suits were new," Bernadette said.

"We purchased ten new ones in Singapore a few days ago. Astrid picked them up on her way to the ship."

"What do you mean on her way to the ship?" Bernadette asked.

"She's a new hire, joined the ship in Singapore. She was diving in Malaysia before coming on board," Mia said.

Bernadette shot a glance at Cynthia. She looked stunned at the news.

"That's great, Mia, thanks for everything. I'll be doing a more in-depth inquiry in my office tomorrow," Cynthia said.

They walked in silence out of the marina and headed towards the upper decks. Cynthia stopped and turned to Bernadette.

"Look, I didn't know about Astrid. I received the new crew information from our ship's files. Someone must have changed them."

Bernadette leaned against the stair rail and crossed her arms. "I know it seems too simple. But I like this Astrid for a player in the shark attack. I don't know what you'll find in the wet suit of Ashley's, and as for the regulator of the Mandy lady, I'll bet someone tampered with it."

"You think Astrid somehow doctored Ashley's suit and made a regulator malfunction so Mia's attention would be elsewhere?" Cynthia asked.

"It seems like it to me. I'm going to send the name of Astrid Karlsson back to Inspector Lee in Singapore and see if it anyway lines up with the dead girl they have there. Also, you might check on the little Swedish Princess to see what she has to say for herself," Bernadette said.

Cynthia looked at her watch. "Damn it's already past 1800 hours. You need to slip into a nice dress and go hit a cocktail bar with your man."

Bernadette shook her head. "I've tangled with a shark and did a half-naked karate demo on a beach—I think I'm done. I'm going to get Chris to make me a biggie sized cocktail, order a hamburger, and go to bed early."

"Have one for me, I'm going to search for our Swedish cutie. See you later."

24

WHEN BERNADETTE GOT BACK to the room, she got a beer from the bar and found Chris on the deck. Big clouds formed over the ocean as they headed into the Bay of Bengal. A slight wind picked up. On their port side they could see the North Sentinel Islands.

"I hear the natives have no outside human contact," Bernadette said.

Chris ran his hand over her shoulder and gave her neck a massage. "They threw spears and shot arrows at an ocean freighter that ran aground on their island during the Tsunami of 2004. A helicopter had to come and rescue the crew."

"We were lucky that only three of them came to check out the downed helicopter, otherwise we'd be retrieving bodies—if they let us," Bernadette said. She took a swig of her beer and looked back toward the room.

Chris grinned. "You want to check some stuff on the internet and get in touch with Inspector Lee in Singapore, don't you?"

"You know me too well." Bernadette chuckled. "Do you mind?"

"Not at all. I'll order us dinner and some excellent wine. You get your detective fix in. I'm sure we'll find something to occupy ourselves with this evening. The events of this day wore me out," Chris said.

Bernadette went to her laptop. She opened the last email from Inspector Lee, filled him in on the events of the past several days, and let him know about the new suspect of Astrid Karlsson. She had to ask, did the female victim in Singapore have a Swedish accent? She'd never asked, and Lee had never offered that information.

She saw the email from her partner Evanston in Canada on her request for information on Holly Marsden. First, Evanston wanted to know why the hell she was chasing suspects and not enjoying her honeymoon cruise. Only then did she include the file Bernadette was after.

Bernadette opened the file; Holly Marsden was exactly the same girl she'd seen in the office. There was even a passport photo. No doubt about it, Marsden was not the girl that matched the victim in Singapore. Now it had to be the Swedish girl.

She took a swig of her beer. "What the hell is this all about and who's behind it?" she muttered to the laptop.

"Are you talking to me or doing your usual crime solving by discussing it with yourself?" Chris asked.

Bernadette looked up and smiled. "Hey, big guy, you know me, I try to hear what the thoughts sound like in my head to see if I'm making any sense."

The doorbell sounded and Chris went to answer it. "I ordered us some nibbles and a pitcher of margaritas."

"I'm hoping those nibbles are nacho chips and salsa," Bernadette replied.

"Nothing else goes with a good margarita," Chris said. He put the pitcher on the table and poured a glass for her and looked into her eyes. "So, how far along are you on your investigation?"

Bernadette took her glass and stared at him over the rim. "I'm not sure if we're going forwards or backwards. There's too many loose ends."

~

TWO HOURS LATER, the doorbell rang. Bernadette went to answer it, realizing she'd already drank too much. She wobbled slightly at the door.

Cynthia stood at the door with her head hanging down. She raised her head to look at Bernadette.

"Astrid Karlsson is no longer on this ship. I thought you should know that," she said.

Bernadette's hand went to the door frame to steady herself.

"Can you get on the phone to the police in Port Blair and stop her?" Bernadette asked.

Cynthia put her hand on Bernadette's shoulder. "For what? We have hearsay and involvement in an accident. I made a call to the Veer Savarkar Airport and told them we had a crew member named Astrid Karlsson who left some important documents on our ship. There was one flight leaving for Delhi tonight, no Astrid Karlsson on the flight."

"Maybe she's taking a flight tomorrow," Bernadette said.

Cynthia held up a Swedish passport. "Not without this she won't. I found this in her room and her driver's license and credit cards."

"Holy crap, this can only mean—"

"We found who replaced the dead girl from Singapore. And this looks like murder," Cynthia said. "We doubt if the captain will let us open any kind of investigation. We must make a report, it will get sent to Fort Lauderdale, and we'll know in a few days what they want to do about it. We have about as much authority on this ship as a retail mall cop."

"I'll email this to Inspector Lee to let him know. Maybe he can find if the dead woman is the real Astrid," Bernadette said.

"Sorry for the late news. I know you'll want to turn in soon."

Bernadette was about to close the door then stopped. "How did she get off the ship and no one knew she didn't return before sailing?"

Cynthia blew out a breath and rolled her eyes. "Another total screw up. She left one hour before sailing on the last tender going ashore. She told the tender crew she was bringing a zodiac back to the ship. She had someone run her ships pass through the re-entry system. We didn't know she wasn't on board until we searched the entire ship."

"Well, thanks," Bernadette said. She closed the door and looked at Chris.

He sat in the living room sipping on a red wine and listening to some music. "You have that look on your face."

"What look?"

"Like you're about to go all in on this case."

"Astrid Karlsson made a run for it, left her passport, everything..."

"Wow, that just made this turn from accident to murder. How is it playing with the ship?" Chris asked.

"Not well. They won't do anything about it. Probably too upsetting for the passengers. Cynthia said they'll make a report, it will go to their head office, and someone will get back to them. I'm going to send this information off to the inspector in Singapore. At least he won't have to wait while this cruise line drags its feet."

25

INSPECTOR LEE DID NOT GET Bernadette's email until late that evening. He was working another case. The information about the Swedish girl piqued his interest. He called Constable Chen into his office.

Chen sat there, fidgeting, like he wanted to be anywhere but in front of Lee. He glanced at his watch several times.

Lee looked up at him and waited for him to stop moving. "Did you determine the nationality of our victim from the canal from the interview with the Englishman?"

Chen bit his lip. "No, inspector, we listed her as Caucasian."

Lee looked down at his hands for a moment and back up at Chen. "Do you know how many nationalities of Asians are in this city?"

Chen brightened. "Well yes, inspector, there are several types of Chinese, and Malays as well as Thai and Cambodians."

Lee nodded his head slowly. "And the Caucasians come in many nationalities. Europe has many countries, just like we do here in Asia. Did any of the witnesses give you any clues?"

Chen thought hard for a minute. "Yes, someone said she sounded like Helena Mattsson in the American television show, Desperate Housewives."

"Is that actor Swedish by any chance?" Lee asked.

"Why, yes, she is," Chen answered.

Lee looked over his desk at Chen, his disappointment obvious. "You may go."

Chen walked out of his office while Lee opened his web browser. Opening the Facebook site, he entered the name of Astrid Karlsson. There were several, but in his scan only one matched the likeness of the dead girl.

He went to her page. She lived in a small town outside of Stockholm. Her profession listed her as a diving instructor with a myriad of photos from her dives. She also had her present job as dive master on *Orion Voyager*.

Lee shook his head slowly and spoke to the screen. "There you are, my lovely girl. Now someone has to inform your next of kin."

He found the police station in Sweden and called them. A polite female voice answered in Swedish, and Lee asked if she spoke English.

"Yes, what is this concerning?"

"This is Inspector Lee of the Singapore Police. We have a victim here that might be from your village. May I speak to one of your police on staff?"

"I am Constable Bridget Larsen. You can give me the details, please," Larsen said.

"We think the victim we have here might be Astrid Karlsson," Lee said. He waited a moment. The line went quiet. "Did you hear me—do you want me to repeat the name?"

"Did you say Astrid Karlsson?" Larsen asked.

"Yes, we think that is the possible name. We must confirm with the dental records. Do you know this person?"

"Ah... yes. She's my niece," Larsen said in a quiet voice.

"I'm sorry, but we are still not sure if we have a match. If you can give us the name of her dentist, we can send the impressions we have here and see if we have a match."

"Inspector Lee, please send them directly to me. I'll give you my email address. I will take care of it from here," Larsen said.

"Are you sure? If you are family, perhaps you'll want another officer to assist."

"No, please, I want to be sure. Her father and mother are worried about her. She usually posts something every day on Instagram from her travels. But they've heard nothing from her for days. I sensed something was wrong yesterday. I want to take the information to my brother if she is deceased."

Lee sighed. "Very well then. I will send all the files we have and the photos. I'm sorry for your loss if this is your niece."

"Yes, thank you for calling, Larsen." said.

Lee put down the phone. He looked at his watch; it was almost midnight. He needed to get home. His son would be sleeping. The neighbor from upstairs would take care of him, again.

Perhaps he'd solved the case as far as the identity of the girl in the canal. But what was happening on that ship? The dead girl in the canal was only part or the start of events. And he suspected things were about to get much worse.

He summoned his car and went downstairs. He felt the rain coming. There was an early cyclone brewing in the Bay of Bengal, it would hit Singapore with torrential rain in a few days. The *Orion Voyager* was heading straight into it.

26

BERNADETTE WOKE FROM A RESTLESS SLEEP. Everything about the last few days bothered her. From the day she'd heard about the dead girl in Singapore, to the deaths of George and Ashley, nothing fit. The suspect of Holly Marsden turned out to be wrong, it had to be Astrid, but how did they make the switch?

She looked at her watch; it was 11 pm. She wondered if the cigar bar was open downstairs. Pulling herself out of bed, she threw on some clothes and made her way one floor down to the lounge. The smell of cigar smoke wafted into her nostrils with a scent that smelled earthy and sensual.

The door pushed open. The familiar strains of jazz seemed to ooze from the wood-paneled walls and make itself comfortable in the soft leather chairs.

Bill Loving was there once again, puffing on his pipe. Ernesto sat at his desk. They both looked up and smiled.

"Care to join me?" Bill asked with a smile as he removed his pipe and blew a contented ring of blue scented smoke into the air.

"If that's okay with you," Bernadette said. She sat in a

large brown leather chair across from him, instantly feeling relaxed.

Ernesto appeared beside her. "What would be madam's pleasure this evening?"

"Well, I shouldn't..." Bernadette began with hesitation.

"You should," Bill said. "Ernesto, get Ms. Callahan one of those fine cigars and put it on my room."

"That's so kind of you, Mr. Loving, but I couldn't..."

"You must allow an old Texas Ranger the joy of being able to buy you a cigar." Bill leaned forward. "It's the least I can do. And the name's, Bill."

Ernesto brought over another Splendido cigar, clipped it, then lit it. Bernadette took a pull on it, blew a wide smoke ring, and almost moaned with pleasure. She looked at Bill and smiled.

Bill motioned for Ernesto. "And get the lady a nice cognac, not that cheap swill. I know you've got the good stuff behind your desk."

Ernesto smiled. "Yes, right away, Mr. Loving."

He returned and placed a snifter with a golden cognac laying in a liquid pool. "This is a Richard Hennessey, one of the finest cognacs in the world."

Bernadette raised the glass to her nose. It smelled of spice and leather with a hint of cigar. Raising the glass to her lips, she let a small amount fall onto her tongue. She rolled it around in her mouth and felt the smoothness of it. With an almost regret, she let it slide down her throat. She closed her eyes for a moment, then opened them. "That is one of the smoothest cognacs I've ever tasted."

Bill chuckled. "It should be at four thousand dollars a bottle. But then, I never worry much about what things cost anymore. I only think of the enjoyment of them."

"Thank you for letting me enjoy one of the finest in life," Bernadette said.

Bill drew on his pipe, blew a cloud of blue smoke, and looked at Bernadette. "Now, what's keeping you up at night?"

"I'm still that obvious?"

"You wear it like a proverbial crown of thorns. I could see it as you entered through the door."

Bernadette put her glass down and sat back in her chair. "The events of the past few days have me wondering if what I'm seeing is real."

"Ah, yes, we're back to the girl in Singapore and you being followed."

Bernadette nodded. "Then we add to that the deaths of George and Ashley Compton and the emergency landing of the Redstones."

"Someone has hired a killer to orchestrate a series of accidents, is that what you think?" Bill asked.

"That's exactly what I think. I just don't know how they killed George Compton. We have to wait for an autopsy in Mumbai and that could take time," Bernadette said.

"You think the killer could slip away in one of the next ports of call, don't you?"

"That's it exactly. How did you know?"

"I spent many years in detective work. Most killers never hung around after they'd done their job."

"You're right. The diver who helped create a diversion for the shark to attack Ashley Compton made a run for it."

"You think she was the only one involved?"

"No, there's too many other factors where Astrid wasn't present."

"Then you still have a killer on the ship," Bill said.

Bernadette sipped the Cognac, then puffed on her cigar. "Yes, that's exactly the conclusion I've come to."

Bill looked at her. He closed his eyes in thought then opened them. "You know, when I was a young Texas Ranger, just starting out, I had a strange case that bothered the hell out of me."

"What was it?"

"A man claimed he saw a woman abducted at gunpoint on a road in east Texas. We put out an APB for her, scoured the entire area. I must have had every ranger and volunteer in my territory working on the case. We couldn't find a trace of her. She'd vanished."

"Did you ever find her?"

"First I went back to the very beginning of the case. I retraced every step I'd made in my investigation and every conversation I'd had with all those I'd met over the past several days. Then I went back to the place the man claimed he'd seen her taken."

"And?" Bernadette asked, leaning forward in her chair.

"I stood on the man's porch, the one who'd said he'd seen the girl taken away at gunpoint. It was then I knew what happened."

"Okay, you've got me, what happened?"

"He had her. I looked at the bend in the road and knew you'd never see someone properly from that distance."

"Did he confess right away?"

"He took a bit of talking to, but he did eventually. He had the girl tied up in his root cellar. She was okay. He was waiting for us to stop looking for her before he did anything to her."

"That's a great story, Bill. Thanks for the cognac and the cigar. I think I'll turn in now," Bernadette said.

"Nice to chat with you, drop by again anytime. I'll be here," Bill said with a smile. He got up and bowed to her.

Bernadette returned to her room, slipped out of her clothes, and climbed back into bed. Chris was snoring softly beside her. She fell into a dreamless sleep.

27

Bernadette awoke to the rocking of the ship. She felt like she was going to get tossed from the bed. She slid to the floor and crawled towards her clothes, then pulled herself up to look out the window. The seas were high. White caps crested on top of four-meter-high seas. The wind howled; the ship groaned.

Chris woke up and stared at Bernadette on the floor. "What's up?"

"We've sailed into a storm," Bernadette said.

Chris got out of bed and fell to the floor. "I'd call this more than a storm."

The ship's intercom came on. "This is your captain speaking. We've encountered the edge of a cyclone. We expect winds of fifty to sixty knots and seas in the four-to-ten-meter range by late afternoon. We ask all passengers to stay inside the ship. Breakfast, lunch, and dinner will be available in the *Voyager* lounge. Please be careful as you move about the ship and avoid using the elevators."

"Is that the elevators I hear banging in their shafts out in the hallway?" Bernadette asked.

Chris lifted his head up and laughed. "Yes, I'd say that's it. I pity anyone who tried to use them. That would be one of the worst rides they'd ever taken."

The ship heeled over sharply. A loud bang sounded in the living room. Bernadette crawled along the floor and looked out.

"We just lost the coffee table and the left-over bottle of wine from last night. The chairs in the dining room look like there was a bar-room brawl in here overnight."

Chris pulled on his shorts and t-shirt. "I don't think we can even use the coffee machine in here. How about we venture downstairs?"

"Sure, sounds like a plan," Bernadette said. She found her shoes and together they crawled their way to the door as the ship made another violent lurch to the other side. Chris reached up, opened the door, and they crawled out of the room.

The Redstones were down the hall. They'd tried to stand but were now on their knees trying to hold on to the handrails on the wall for support.

"Stay low until you get to the stairs," Bernadette called out to Elizabeth.

Elizabeth nodded. Her face was a mask of fear. She motioned for Fred to follow her as they crawled along the floor towards them.

"Good morning," Elizabeth said as she reached them. "What kind of jackass captain would sail us into weather like this?"

Chris looked at Elizabeth from his crouching position. "I saw a notice on the ship's web that they were cruising north to miss this cyclone, obviously it traveled faster than they thought."

"You want to join us for a crawl to breakfast downstairs?"

Bernadette said. "I am hoping the dining room doesn't rock this much."

"Don't worry, the lower decks sway much less than this. The lower down we get the better we'll be," Fred said. "I've always told Elizabeth we should never book the upper decks and the penthouse suites because of this." He looked over at Elizabeth with an accusing eye.

Elizabeth looked at Fred with a scowl. "Don't give me that crap, Fred, you're the one who loves the penthouse suites for all the room and the enormous deck. You know damn well they rock like crazy in a storm."

"The ship feels like it wants to tip over," Bernadette said. "I know it won't but it's one hell of a strange feeling." She turned and crawled toward the stairs.

Fred and Elizabeth crawled after her with Chris following behind.

"These ships rarely tip in high seas," Fred said. "The center of gravity is in the ship's hull. It also has a series of stabilizers that act like wings under water to keep it from tipping. The problem is the ship is still heading west towards India, in a few minutes the captain will turn the ship into the wind and head south to Sri Lanka."

They reached the stairs. One by one, they grabbed the stair rails and made their way slowly down the stairs as the ship's motion swayed violently back and forth. The sound of the elevators clanging in their shafts made an ominous boom, followed by a clang.

The rocking motion felt less with each lower deck. When they reached the lowest deck with the restaurant, the swaying was mild compared to the upper deck. They took their hands off the rails and walked almost normally. Bernadette noticed that people still walked like they'd had far too much to drink or had an accident in their pants.

The restaurant was half full. Some people were eating, some were picking at food and wondering if what they ate would stay down. Others watched their partners eat with either envy or dismay.

The maître d came by and found them a table by the window. He smiled at them, bid them a good morning, then rushed to help a passenger about to fall over a table. He was a young man from Quebec in the Eastern Townships. Usually he was affable and joking, but this morning he was trying to hide the fear he felt at the size of the waves outside.

A waiter with dark hair and brooding dark eyes, came by with menus. "We're slow this morning," he said with a wide smile. "The kitchen lost power for a short time this morning. They had to cook with headlamps, but now they're fine."

"I wonder what happened to their backup generators," Fred said.

Elizabeth looked up from her menu to Fred and then Bernadette and Chris. "You'll notice Fred has an answer or a question to everything. It's the engineer in him, it's almost a curse. But I live with it."

"I'm always trying to figure people out, it's refreshing to see someone who questions the physical world," Bernadette said.

"I'm sure you'd stop finding it refreshing after forty years of it," Elizabeth said with a roll of her eyes.

Bernadette turned to look out the window. The sky was lead gray; the waves rolled with huge white caps on top. There seemed to be a valley in each wave as they rolled towards the ship. She turned back towards Elizabeth; her face had dropped to a scowl.

"Oh, my lord, it's Lucinda," Elizabeth said. Her body

stiffened as Lucinda marched towards them, although it was more of a swaying march that looked ridiculous.

"I've been looking all over the ship for you," Lucinda said, staring down at Bernadette.

Bernadette looked up at her and smiled. "It's a small ship, I don't know what took you so long."

Lucinda steadied herself as the ship rolled once again. She grabbed onto a chair from the neighboring table. "I want to know how you saved these two from some natives and you couldn't save my dear friend, Ashley?"

Bernadette lowered her eyes, then raised them to focus on Lucinda. "Simple, these two cooperated with the rescue."

"What the hell is that supposed to mean?" Lucinda said.

Bernadette waved her hand. "I'll be making a full report today to the ship and I'm sure there'll be an enquiry in either Mumbai or Dubai. You can read the transcript then. Until then, I will not discuss it with you."

"You're a total bitch, you know that?" Lucinda said.

Another table of diners raised their heads to watch the conversation. The maître d looked up from across the room.

Elizabeth raised herself slightly from the table. "Lucinda, we don't need your trash talk here, I suggest you leave."

The maître d appeared at Lucinda's side. "Madame Braithwaite let me find you a table. I'm sorry I kept you waiting. I have a lovely spot for you by the window and I'll order a mimosa for you. Please let me take you to your table."

Lucinda let the man babble on about how happy he was to see her and what a lovely looking lady she was as he walked her to another table.

"Nice save. He mentioned alcohol to her, and she's like a dog chasing a squirrel," Elizabeth said.

"You think she blames you for Ashley's' death?" Fred asked.

Bernadette pursed her lips. "It appears so. Comes with the job of detective."

"I'm so sorry for this, Bernadette," Elizabeth said. "We asked you to go on that dive. If you wouldn't have been there, Ashley would have suffered the same fate."

"No, it's not your fault, I said I would. What happened is a chain of events..."

"You think someone planned it, don't you?" Elizabeth asked.

Bernadette was about to answer when Fred grabbed the edge of the table. "I think the ship's about to turn into the wind. We'd best brace ourselves."

28

CAPTAIN PRODROMOU STOOD on the bridge. His hands gripped the chart table. A helmsman sat in the chair with the controls. The sea had an ominous look to it. The rollers were getting bigger; the wind getting stronger.

A ship further south was reporting seas of over seven meters. The ones battering the ship were three to five. He had to make the course correction soon to head into the wind. But, too soon and he risked taking them directly into the path of the storm.

The storm had hit them at midnight. At first it seemed only an annoyance. He slowed the ship's speed to eighteen knots, set all the stabilizers and told the ship's crew to rig the ship for a small squall. That little squall turned into a fiendish demon by four in the morning.

When Captain Prodromou came on the bridge at 6 a.m., he knew what they were facing. He slowed the speed to fifteen knots, then plotted the course they needed to make their turn into the wind.

He couldn't count the amount of times he'd been in storms like this, but those were bigger ships. This ship with its shorter length took the seas differently. There was, in the seaman's terms, more surge under the shorter hull, which resulted in a different sway and heave. The actual difference was how this translated to the passengers.

Cruise ships were an idyllic experience for all on board —until they sailed into a storm.

Captain Prodromou walked to the bridge's window. The ship was heeling heavily to the port side with the wind. He couldn't wait any longer. They needed to turn directly into the wind—to port. A risky maneuver they had to execute with care.

"Make your turn now," Captain Prodromou, commanded.

"Aye, sir," the crewman at the helm replied. His name was Lars Jessen, a tall blonde Dane in his late twenties from south of Copenhagen. This was his first experience of a cyclone. His stomach was churning, his mouth dry, and his palms sweating as he eased the controls to turn the ship into the wind.

The wing stabilizers on the starboard side would be almost flat out to keep the ship from rolling over, and the liquid bilge stabilizer in the ship's base would compensate to throw weight to the starboard side.

Lars Jessen knew the mechanics of the ship were working in harmony to keep them upright. But as he feathered the controls with his right hand gripped around the ship's rudder, all he could see were the giant waves looking like they wanted to tear the ship apart.

"Excellent, steady as she goes," the captain said as the ship slowly turned. The wind was easing up a bit as they turned.

Lars watched his direction. In just a few more degrees,

they'd be due south and hitting the waves head on. Then he saw it. It looked like a tower coming towards them.

"Rogue wave. Rogue wave," the captain shouted. "Hard to port. Face it straight on."

Lars had one chance to get the ship's bow to meet the wave. He moved the controls over to port and hit the ship's speed control to increase the engine speed. They needed to meet this towering monster head on with some speed.

The captain grabbed the intercom. "Attention. Passengers and crew. Brace for impact. Rogue wave. I say again, rogue wave. Brace for impact."

FRED'S EYES WENT WIDE. "Oh dear. I fear we're done for, Lizzie." He grabbed Elizabeth's hand, his face drained of color.

Bernadette looked out the window, she couldn't see anything. There was only one place to go. It was down. "Get under the table everyone. If the glass shatters it will break on top of us."

They dropped under the table as one. The ship's hull was trembling with the pounding of the waves. A sound like a freight train slammed into the side of the ship with a reverberating boom.

The ship rocked back as if it had taken a punch in a prize fight. Everything stopped. The lights went out.

"Are we going to sink?" Elizabeth asked.

"We'll be fine," Bernadette said, more for her own reassurance than for Elizabeth's. She raised her head up to look around. There was a gray half-light to the dining room. Chairs were overturned, dishes and cutlery had flown onto the floor, some guests lay sprawled as if an explosion had hit them.

She turned to Chris. "Let's check for injuries."

They checked the passengers on the floor. Some were literally shell shocked. The wave had thrown them to the floor with such a force they'd had the wind knocked out of them.

The waiters were not so lucky. They'd been trying to shield passengers and get them to the floor. Two of them had large cuts to their heads and hands from being thrown into the tables and chairs. Bernadette grabbed cloth napkins and tablecloths to stanch the blood and apply pressure to the wounds.

Chris picked up chairs to clear a path so the other crew members could come in to help with the wounded.

Lucinda appeared out of the rubble. Her blouse was ripped and covered in some kind of sauce. Her hair and makeup looked like she'd been in a fight and lost.

Bernadette looked up at her. "Are you hurt? Sit down. We'll get someone to look at you."

"Hell no. I was waiting for my cocktail when all hell broke loose. I'm going to the bar to get a drink."

"I'm sure the bar is closed right now," Bernadette said. "The impact of the wave probably threw half the bottles across the lounge. How about if you just sit for a bit? You look like you might have a concussion from the impact. I'll have the crew look at you."

Lucinda narrowed her eyes and steadied herself by a chair. "The hell you will. I'm going to my room for a drink. This cruise is bullshit."

Bernadette shook her head as Lucinda half walked, then dropped to her knees and crawled away. There were too many injured to get into a war of words with her. She'd ask a crew member to check on her later.

Crew members and security came into the dining room with medical kits and stretchers. Bernadette called them over to look at the two waiters, then she checked on more passengers.

Bernadette could feel a difference in the ship's movement. It rolled front to back instead of side to side. She wondered how much damage they'd sustained. She moved around the room helping passengers. The captain would have to make an announcement soon to let them know the state of the ship. She hoped it wasn't as bad as it looked.

29

"THE ENGINES ARE NOT RESPONDING," Lars said. He pushed the control—there was nothing. He looked up at the captain. He tried to mask the fear he felt looking out at the waves. They could pound a ship like this to pieces. Without power they were defenseless.

Captain Prodromou grabbed the phone and called the engine room. He got no answer. "I think the impact damaged our communication and electrical systems. I'll go see for myself. Keep her turned into the wind."

"Aye, Captain," Lars said with as much calm as he could muster. Keeping the ship turned into the wind needed not only his rudder control but the turning of the propellers. Soon the wave action would turn the ship. Electrical power ran the stabilizers and everything else on the ship, there were backups, but if the wave had damaged those—they were dead in the water.

Captain Prodromou descended to the engine room. He had to walk through the devastation of the ship. It had ripped her beautiful artwork from her walls; sculptures lay in pieces on the floor. Furniture lay in a pile against the wall.

Passengers walked like zombies with crew members helping them get to their rooms.

He couldn't console passengers, he needed to get to the head engineer to find out their situation. If this ship was without power, they'd need to call the nearest ship for a rescue tow. That was the only option. He couldn't abandon this ship in these seas, no one would make it out alive.

Descending further down the decks, he passed by crew members running around with fire extinguishers and checking systems. No fires had been detected, but they trained all crew to be on fire watch, one of the deadliest of situations at sea.

As he reached the engine room, the place was a glow of red warning lights. No sounds emanated from the machinery. There should have been the comforting sound of two high-tech turbines put into service just last year in Finland. The quiet produced an icy fear in the captain.

Captain Prodromou found the chief engineer, Valerijs Kronis, standing in front of a massive electrical panel with the chief electrician. Kronis was heavyset, with a dark complexion and an often-dour mood that came with his upbringing in Latvia, but he was first rate at his job.

Kronis looked up at Prodromou as he walked up. "The electrical got fried with the impact. Sparky here will have it reset in two hours."

The sparky he referred to was a short, round Mexican named Santos who had gained the nickname of sparky the moment he came on the ship. Santos looked up at the captain, rolled his eyes at the mess, and began pulling out circuit boards.

"You're telling me we're dead in the water until then?" Prodromou asked.

Kronis raised and lowered his bushy black eyebrows.

"Unless you can shift out some oars, that's it. With no electrical, I can't fire the turbines. These new turbines no longer run on the cheap bunker fuel. They're now sipping refined diesel, and they take an electrical charge. The old bunker fuel monsters I could light a rag, throw it in, and I'd have enough power to slam this shiny bucket through any enormous wave. But now...," he looked around the gleaming high-tech engine room, "...I need electrical."

Captain Prodromou shook his head. He could think of a stream of Cypriot Greek swear words that would be relevant in this situation, but none of it would do him any good. He made his way back to the bridge and gave the crew the news.

First Officer Felicia Torres came over to him. "We have no ship communications. I think we both go below to speak to our passengers. We can send some bridge crew to speak to the crew and security."

Prodromou and Felicia went below and spoke to everyone they could. They told the crew to pass the message on to others. The ship would wallow in the storm with no power and no engines for two hours. They would do the best they could.

An older gentleman came up to the captain. "Do any of the other ships know of our situation?"

Prodromou helped to steady the gentleman. "No, our communications are down. We have a global positioning system where other ships can see us."

"Ha, so no Morse code then?" the man asked.

"No, I'm sorry, we gave that up years ago for newer technology," the captain replied.

"Seems like you could have used a good backup system."

Captain Prodromou could only nod his head and walk to the next passenger. He saw Bernadette and Chris and gave them the news. They both just nodded and said they'd do the best they could.

Bernadette turned to the captain, and moved him to one side, out of Chris's hearing, "Have you run into Mr. Bill Loving today?"

"Ah... Mr. Bill Loving?"

"Yes, have you seen him? I just wanted to know if you've seen him, if he's okay."

The captain shook his head. "I don't believe I've met Mr. Loving yet on this trip. Funny, I usually know everyone on the ship by now. I'll enquire for you."

"Thanks, but I'm sure I'll find him eventually," Bernadette said. She turned to see if Chris had heard the conversation. He hadn't. She went back to helping passengers.

The captain approached Felica. "Take care of the passengers, I need to set a lookout." He took off at a run just as the ship lurched, and he slammed into the passageway, pushed himself forward, and went up the stairs.

30

CAPTAIN PRODROMOU FOUND the officer of the watch, Clara Hughes. She was a bright young woman from Liverpool, England with a quick wit and sharp mind. She stood at the bridge window, while Lars kept trying to keep the ship turned into the wind.

"Officer Hughes set out a watch on every point of this ship. I want crew with binoculars, radios, and flare guns."

"Aye, aye, Captain," Hughes said. She knew immediately what the captain meant. She should have thought of it herself. With their communications down, they couldn't alert other ships of their condition. In this weather, ships needed to hear from each other and monitor their radar.

Hughes went to her radio, called her crew, and gave them instructors. All crew were to have flares, wear life vests, and lash themselves to the deck. She didn't want any man overboard accidents. She hoped that her crew could see something in this weather—to let off a flare to warn another ship—if they saw it in time.

∾

THE OOCL SINGAPORE CONTAINER ship plowed through the rough seas of Bengal Bay with ease. At four hundred meters long and sixty meters wide, few waves were a match for this ship. Known as one of six G Class ships, few could match this monster for size or carrying capacity.

Only three crew members were on the massive bridge. The ship ran on autopilot most of the time. They were there to do a visual watch or listen for any alarms that sounded. They'd left Chennai, India early in the morning, and were now heading to Kolkata to pick up more freight.

Two of the crewmen, named Azmi and Asumi, were from Jakarta, Indonesia, the other was from Manilla in the Philippines. There was little interaction between them. They didn't speak each other's language; they used hand signals or pointed at instruments if needed and used some rudimentary English words.

The captain was in his quarters getting some extra sleep as the loading in Chennai had taken longer than usual. He planned to come to the bridge by 1000 hours.

The crew member named Joshua was a Pilipino, his eyes tired of looking at the gray sea and sky. He was losing his focus. He looked at the radar. Saw a blip on the screen. Then it seemed to disappear. He moved his face closer to the screen—there it was again.

He picked up his binoculars. He could see nothing on the horizon. The waves rose and fell in such large canyons that only ships such as the Singapore would be visual today.

Joshua looked over to the two Indonesians. He'd need to show them the blip on the screen, motion with hand signals to use their binoculars, and see if they understood them.

He approached them to get them to watch for the ship he'd seen. He got halfway across the huge bridge when one of them yelled something.

"Look—look—look. Container. Container!" the shorter of the Indonesians named Azmi yelled, pointing out the window.

Joshua looked down the length of the ship to see three containers coming loose. He grabbed his radio and called to the deck crew. They'd have precious minutes to secure them before the containers fell into the sea.

The deck crew radioed back they were on their way. The ship rolled to starboard, a container moved again. The containers were so far away they made no sound. But they were massive. At twelve meters long and three meters high and wide, these could hold several cars and tons of freight.

Losing them at sea was not only bad for business, it was bad for the shipping lanes. Countless small ships had sunk by running into containers floating just below the surface. The ones that were loose were empty, a minor loss for the company, but Joshua hated the thought of these containers causing a hazard.

He watched through his binoculars as the crew activated the winches that pulled the containers back into line. There seemed to be a problem with the last one. A crew member would have to strap himself into a safety harness and walk on top of the containers to attach a cable. Joshua watched, hoping the man on the container didn't injure himself.

His focus was off the radar. The slight blip was getting larger on the screen.

31

BERNADETTE AND CHRIS set themselves up in the inner lounge between the whiskey bar and the Sushi bar. The whiskey bar looked like it had exploded. Bottles lay everywhere, none remained on the shelves. A bartender was sweeping up large pieces of glass.

"This place smells like a distillery," Chris said.

Bernadette breathed in. "Yes, but a very high-class distillery."

"It's too bad the fish from the sushi bar doesn't have the same effect," Chris said with a grin. "If they don't get the power to the refrigeration units back on soon, this high-class ship will smell worse than a tuna trawler after a long day at sea."

Bernadette surveyed the lounge. Passengers lay on the sofas, sprawled on chairs, and several lay on the floor. The heat was becoming oppressive as the day wore on. The air conditioning no longer functioned, the lights were out, and even the fancy art deco fans that did nothing more than artistically paddle air downward were idle.

The Redstones lay a short distance away—Elizabeth with her haute couture linen dress hiked up as far as her personal decorum would allow and Fred with his expensive purple golf shirt unbuttoned and his yellow Bermuda shorts rolled up.

Fred tried to put his head in Elizabeth's lap, but she'd pushed him away. Human contact was too hard to handle in this heat. The passengers sat, swayed with the ship, and tried not to let motion sickness get to them.

Bernadette's one visit to the overflowing toilet was enough. She dared not go there now. Passengers were coming back with stories of toilets that didn't flush, and the smell of vomit that permeated the place. She sipped on a bottle of water and let the moisture sweat itself out of her body.

She glanced at her watch; the gigantic wave had struck over two hours ago. How much longer could the ship survive like this? A man in white coveralls rushed by heading for the stairs to the upper deck. There was a name on his back —Santos Electrical Engineering.

"I hope he's got some kind of hail Mary coming, because we need it about now," Bernadette said.

Santos pushed his short legs up the stairs towards the bridge. He hoped everything they'd done in the past hours would work. The system had to be rebooted from the bridge. The dumbest thing Santos had ever experienced. On other ships, he'd make his repairs, hit the main breaker, and they'd be back online.

Orion Voyager was a marvel of both propulsion and the new mode of computers. If this continued in other ships, Santos knew he'd be out of a job in five years and rewiring old buildings back in Guadalajara, Mexico at a quarter of the pay.

He reached the bridge and found the first officer, Felica Torres. "I'm ready to reset," Santos said. "You have the password?"

Torres looked at Santos. "Password—why do we need a password?"

"Because that's how this ship functions. It's like a big computer, when all its circuits fail, it needs to reboot itself," Santos said.

Torres shook her head. "I miss the days we used to sail these things and left the computer nerds on the shore." She picked up her radio, "Captain—Santos is here, we need the password to reset the system. You want to give it to me or do you want to come up here?"

"Oh my God," Captain Prodromou said. "It's in my cabin. I'll be back in five minutes."

Torres and Santos stood on the bridge, looking at each other. The wind was getting higher; the seas were rising. Jessen at the helm had figured out a unique way of keeping the ship pointed into the waves. There was enough auxiliary power from the generator to keep the rudder functioning and the stabilizers working.

Jessen was basically 'flying by wire,' an old term for maneuvering an airplane. He positioned the rudder with one hand, then compensated with the large wing stabilizers on the sides of the hull. The system wasn't great, it was awkward to use, but he'd kept them pointed into the waves, although they were moving backwards at a steady pace. Jessen did a quick computation in his mind that the ship would run aground in Bangladesh in forty-eight hours.

~

CREWMAN JOSHUA WATCHED the container being winched back onto the ship and secured. A sense of relief came over him. There was nothing worse than having to report the loss of a container on a shift. He hadn't been there at loading or securing; his only job was as a lookout and general crew hand, but still, he was happy he could report secured cargo to the captain.

The other two crewmen smiled and gave him a thumbs up for a job well done. They went back to their stations as Joshua walked over to the radar screen. He could hear a faint beeping amongst the rush of the wind outside.

He looked in horror at the screen. They were almost on top of another ship. "Alarm. Alarm," He yelled. "Collision."

He ran to the captain's chair in the center of the room. Jumping into it, he hit the switch from auto to manual. He moved the control to starboard hitting the collision alarms and ship's horn almost at the same time.

The other crewmen picked up their binoculars and scanned the horizon looking for the other ship. They saw nothing.

CAPTAIN PRODROMOU MADE it to the bridge. He looked exhausted. The ship lurched, throwing him against a bulkhead. He pulled himself to the console at the captain's chair and plugged in the password into the ship's computer. Santos did a quick punch of the new program and the lights came on.

"Can you restart now?" Prodromou asked.

"Yes, it will be automatic," Santos said.

"I have propulsion," Jessen said.

"Make our speed fifteen knots and set our original

course," Captain Prodromou said. He turned to Torres. "We should be out of this cyclone in six hours, then we can clean this ship up and get her into Colombo for some repairs."

"Does anyone hear anything?" Torres said.

They stopped and listened. They could hear a faint horn. It sounded like it was being carried by the wind.

"Check the radar," Prodromou said.

Torres ran to the screen. "It hasn't rebooted yet."

Prodromou's eyes went wide. He turned to Jessen. "Hard to port—now!"

Torres ran to the console. She sounded the ships' horns.

CREWMAN JOSHUA COULD HEAR something now, but he couldn't see it. The other two on watch were useless to him. They spoke so little English he only hoped they could point out the danger before he hit it.

He pushed the rudder control to starboard, then reversed engines hoping they might slow before his ship hit the other vessel. There was nothing to do now but hope and pray.

From his view on the bridge, he could barely see the horizon over the fully packed containers. Anything they hit would make a dent in the mighty OOCL Singapore. But they would pulverize the other vessel.

Joshua sent a prayer to God. Adding one to all the gods of the sea for safe measure.

CAPTAIN PRODROMOU and Torres saw the bow of OOCL Singapore crest the wave like a high-rise building coming at them.

"Hard to port, full speed," Prodromou yelled.

Jessen moved the control hard to the right and pushed the throttle full. His mouth was dry. He could only squeak out an "Aye—-aye captain," that was barely audible.

They watched in horror as the mass of metal approached. It seemed doomed to hit them. A moment seemed like a lifetime. They froze with fear.

The big container ship plunged down the waves—sliding by them to the right. The *Orion Voyager* seemed to do a pirouette. With an almost nimble move, the little ship leaped off to the left.

For a moment, the bulk of the freighter blocked the view. It roared by them as its mighty hull threw waves in their direction. What seemed to last forever was over in six minutes. The massive container ship missed them.

Torres and Santos looked at each other, then back at the captain and Jessen. They almost couldn't believe what they'd just experienced.

Bernadette and Chris stood up to watch the sight of a wall of steel pass by the window of the lounge. Some passengers screamed, some let out expletives in a steady stream in their favorite language.

The horns from both ships drowned out all voices, the noise was almost more than a human ear could handle. Bernadette looked around to see passengers fall to the deck in fear. Crew ran to them, checking vital signs.

The intercom sounded with a bell. "Attention all passengers, this is the captain speaking. We had a near miss from another ship. Everything is under control. The engines are running at full speed. The butlers will attend to your cabins and replenishing your personal mini bars. I suggest you return to your cabins and get some rest. We are sorry for the inconvenience. The ship will offer all passengers a selection of our premium wines and liquor for the rest of our journey to Colombo."

Elizabeth appeared at Bernadette's side. "I think I could drink them out of their Johnny Walker Blue label." She looked over to the bar. "I might start now."

"You seem to have recovered well," Bernadette said.

Elizabeth turned to her. "What's that saying about what doesn't kill you makes you stronger? Well, in two days, I've survived near death on a wild island with natives and a near miss with a giant hunk of metal."

Bernadette smiled. "Yes, I'd say you've had some adventures."

"How about you? You fought a shark, saved me, and now we've seen death pass before us blowing its horn," Elizabeth said. "Why not join me for a drink? It's going to take our butlers over an hour to put the penthouses together."

Bernadette cocked her head to one side. "Sure, but it's early for scotch, maybe I can find a beer." She turned to Chris. "How about you, sweetie?"

"I'm going to the gym to see if I can get a shower, I'll join you later. Good luck in finding a beer in this mess."

"On this ship, I doubt if you'll have a problem getting a beer," Elizabeth said.

They righted some bar stools and asked the bartender if he wouldn't mind serving them. He found some unbroken glasses, poured Elizabeth a large glass of Johnny Walker Blue Label and an Amstel beer for Bernadette.

They clinked glasses. "Here's to staying alive and afloat," Elizabeth said.

Bernadette sipped her beer. "What are your plans now?"

Elizabeth eyed her over her glass. "Do you mean for dinner tonight?"

Bernadette chuckled. "No, I mean this ship will have to

stay in Colombo for a few days to make some repairs. I heard the engineer say that in passing."

"I hadn't thought about it, but we'll probably stay with the cruise until Mumbai. If we tried to get George and Ashley's bodies shipped back to the states in Sri Lanka, we'd be there for weeks. I hear the place is okay, but I prefer Mumbai, better hotels and restaurants."

Bernadette sipped her beer, "Oh, I see—"

"Sounds a bit cavalier to you?"

"Yeah, pretty much in the entire scheme of cavalier statements and dead bodies," Bernadette replied.

Elizabeth moved closer to Bernadette. "Look, we were all business partners. We fought like cats and dogs over everything. But we grew one hell of a company together. This was our farewell cruise. We had an offer for all of our shares. Each of us was to make one hundred million dollars from the sale. I told Fred I would stomach those blonde bimbos that Nigel and George married for a few more weeks, then I never had to see them again."

"Thanks for clearing that up," Bernadette said. She finished her beer. "I'm heading up to our room and see if I can get a shower, I'm feeling kind of sticky."

She moved away from the bar, walked with swaying feet as the ship plunged forward into the waves. Walking up the stairs, she hung onto the handrail and pulled herself upward. She saw Mia walking down the stairs, coming towards her with her head hung low, like someone had handed her an executioner's sentence.

Bernadette caught up to her. "Hey Mia, you alright?"

Mia turned to Bernadette; she made an attempt at a tight smile. "I handed my report on the shark attack to the security office yesterday evening."

"Any news that absolves you and your crew?" Bernadette asked.

"Kaitlin on our crew remembered that Astrid tried to give a regulator and buoyancy vest to Ashley, but it didn't fit her. Kaitlin handed her a bigger vest and regulator and gave the other one to Mandy. It upset Astrid with the switch. She wanted to change the regulators. Kaitlin said there wasn't enough time."

"So, Mandy got the faulty regulator," Bernadette said.

"Yeah, that's how it went down."

"Where was Astrid on the line during the shark feeding?"

"I saw her swim beside Ashley. I thought she was checking on her wetsuit. She went down to the seabed—I thought maybe she dropped something. Now that I heard she made a run for it, I'm sure she caused the attack," Mia said.

"And you reported this to security, I'm sure you're in the clear now."

Mia shook her head. "No, not at all. Mateo said head office will review the accident. I get to stay on until Mumbai, but that's about it."

Bernadette put her hand on her shoulder. "That's a bit of a reprieve, I guess. You'd said that Astrid was bringing new wetsuits in from Singapore to the ship. Do you remember the name of the dive shop?"

"Sure, it's the Gill Divers on Hong Kong Street. It's the only one the ship uses. We asked Astrid to do it as it was on the way from her hotel to the ship," Mia said.

"Thanks, look, I'll do everything I can to see if I can save your job, Mia. I know you and your dive team had nothing to do with Ashley's death," Bernadette said.

Mia wiped a tear from her eye. "You're what we call a

cobber back in Aussie, that's a real good friend. If I get out of this and keep my diving license, I'll take you to the Great Barrier Reef for some good shark watching."

Bernadette smiled. "I've never been called a cobber before, but how about if I pass on the sharks and meet you for a beer somewhere?"

"No worries, Bernadette, I'd love to have some bevvies with you," Mia said. She turned and walked down the stairway.

Bernadette continued on to her suite. She hoped the internet was back up; she had an email to send to Inspector Lee.

32

MARCUS HAD FINISHED CLEANING the suite by the time Bernadette got there. She took a shower, managing to not do herself an injury with the rocking of the ship. The internet was up and running with the ship's satellite working. She emailed Lee with everything Mia had told her, plus threw a note in that perhaps the Singapore Police could check if any cameras had seen Astrid at the dive shop.

Chris walked in. "Sending emails to tell our friends we're okay or back on the case?"

She looked up and smiled. "Mostly about the case. I met Mia downstairs. She told me the faulty regulator was meant for Ashley. I just fired off an email to Lee. Maybe he can do something with it."

"What's the ship's security doing?"

"Nothing they can do. They filed a report to their head office, which gives Mia a slight breather until Mumbai. That's about it."

"But not for you, is it?" Chris asked. He opened the mini-bar, found a few bags of cashews and dumped them on the table.

"No, it's not," Bernadette said grabbing a cashew. "I guess this is the breakfast we missed until the ship's restaurants sort themselves out."

"We could call it high class camping," Chris said with a laugh. "Do we have a plan for Sri Lanka? I hear there's a few days layover that might extend our cruise. Can you handle it with your chief of detectives back home?"

"I will have to," Bernadette said.

"And why is that?" Chris asked with a knowing smile.

"I always follow the bodies," Bernadette said. "I just learned that Elizabeth and Fred are staying on the ship. I'd like to see where all of this is leading. If there's nothing by Mumbai, we catch a plane home."

"You think there's still a killer on board, even with the woman you think was posing as Astrid has left the ship?" Chris asked.

Bernadette chewed a cashew and swallowed it. "My jury is still out. There are too many other elements, like how did this Astrid get off the ship without her absence being noticed?"

After several hours, the wind died down. The raging sea became swells under a benevolent moon with innocent little clouds. To Bernadette this was mother nature's way of saying, 'sorry for the fuss, I'll make it all better now.'

They'd decided on the Italian restaurant for dinner once they'd phoned down to find it was in operation.

Bernadette put on her simple but elegant black dress, and threw on a silver shawl with some silver pumps. Chris wore dress pants and a long sleeve shirt that didn't make his muscles bulge like Sylvester Stallone. He stuffed his size twelve feet into black loafers that shone from Markus's attention.

They admired themselves in the bedroom mirror.

"We look good for two people who've been through a cyclone," Bernadette said.

Chris picked up her Navajo necklace and attached it around her neck with a kiss on her cheek. "Yes, we take a licking and come back ticking as they used to say in the Timex commercial."

They walked out of the room and down the stairs. The ship was slowly coming back to normal in a bandaged and patched up kind of way. Most of the paintings were back on the walls. The damaged sculptures had been removed. The ones that survived were back in their special alcoves. Some looked a bit scarred.

"I guess they never accounted for a rogue wave to hit this ship like it did," Chris said.

"Yeah, the place looks like taverns I've seen back in Canada after a Saturday night punch up," Bernadette said. She looked at a picture on the staircase that had suffered no damage.

"A passenger told me this is a Chagall," Bernadette said. "Looks like two people about to get married by a gigantic bird."

"Your grandmother would love it. She'd probably have some kind of story to tell you of what the bird is trying to tell the married couple," Chris said.

"Yeah, and if I told her this painting costs more than a small home back in Canada, she'd laugh hysterically," Bernadette said.

They arrived at the Italian restaurant. There were few diners. A headwaiter in black trousers and white shirt with a long white apron escorted them to their table by a window. The moon shone down off the rolling waves, providing an idyllic view with a frame of some low fluffy cloud's overhead.

A waitress appeared with water and menus. She was round-faced with bright blue eyes and blonde hair. Her name badge said Klara from Sweden. She told them of the specials which were put together with ingredients that survived the rogue wave.

Chris ordered some wine and looked over the menu. "You see anything that looks good?"

Bernadette leaned forward. "Yes. Klara."

"Ah, okay. I'm not sure where you're going with that."

"I need to know if she knew Astrid."

Chris shook his head and smiled.

"You don't mind?"

"No, I can't wait to hear what she has to say. This has become a whodunnit cruise. When we return to our simple lives in Canada, of you arresting regular convicts and me roaming the forests watching for poachers, we'll be bored to tears."

"Hilarious," Bernadette said.

Klara came back to the table with a bottle of Italian Ripassa Zenato Valpolicella. She cut the foil wrapping on the bottle, pulling the cork with expert ease.

"Klara, I hope you don't mind, but I have a question to ask you," Bernadette said.

"Sure, how may I help you?" she asked as she poured a small taste of wine into Chris' glass, deftly turning her wrist to avoid spilling a drop.

"Did you know Astrid on the diving crew?"

Klara's blue eyes became wide, then she recovered. "Yes, I knew her well. She was from a village on the coast just outside of Stockholm."

"Did she seem different when she got on the ship in Singapore?"

Klara poured wine for Bernadette. Her hand shook

slightly. She put the bottle on the table. "I hadn't seen her for several years, but she looked and acted very different. I asked her how she liked the ship—she didn't answer me. I thought that was strange."

"Did you ask her in Swedish?"

"Yes, I did," Klara said.

"Thank you, Klara. That's all I needed to know."

Klara looked to see if any of the waiters were nearby. "I know there's people saying some things about Astrid, since she jumped ship, but I cannot believe that was the Astrid I knew. She is a wonderful girl, sometimes a bit aloof, but nice all the same."

Bernadette put her hand on Klara's arm. "I hope the security on the ship can find the truth."

Klara looked at Bernadette, a small tear was forming in her eye. "I heard that you're a detective. Maybe you can find out what really happened."

"I'll try my best," Bernadette said.

"Thank you," Klara said.

She took their order and left them.

Chris sipped his wine and put it down. Bernadette stared out the window at the waves rolling in the moonlight.

"Well, are you going to say it?" Chris asked

Bernadette turned to Chris. "That my hunch is right? Yeah, I guess I am. That's something that the police in Singapore need to know. I'll send another email to Lee about the conversation we've had with Klara. I'm sure I'll get an answer back from Lee in a day or two." She sipped her wine and looked at the waves again. She hoped it would be sooner. There had to be an answer to the incidents on this ship.

33

INSPECTOR LEE HAD READ over the emails from Bernadette. The remaining link came the moment his phone rang.

"Inspector Lee, how may I help you?"

"This is Officer Bridget Larsen in Sweden. The dental impressions you sent me are an exact match for my niece, Astrid Karlsson."

"I'm sorry for your loss," Lee said. The words sounded hollow, but they had trained him to say it for years.

"Was she sexually assaulted?"

"No, I have the medical examiner's report. There was no penetration, no bruising of any kind," Lee said.

"How did she die?"

Lee paused. "That is uncertain. There was a trace amount of barbiturates in her bloodstream and no sign of drowning. The ME thinks she was dead before they put her in the water."

"Do you know who did this?"

"A woman matching Astrid's description was seen being taken away by two men, but there's been some develop-

ments on the ship she was on," Lee said. He filled her in on
Bernadette Callahan's report.

"I sense they used her," Bridget said.

Lee gripped the receiver tightly. "I have that same
feeling."

"We have to get these people, these evil people that
killed my niece. She was all that was beautiful and innocent
in this world. I taught her how to dive. Did you know that? I
taught her. She was in Singapore because of what I taught
her. You have to get these people." Her last words ended on
a sob.

"I understand. I will put out an APB on the woman who
fled the ship and assumed Astrid's identity. She had her
passport. That will make her culpable in the crime of her
death. I'm putting out a bulletin to all the airlines that flew
out of Port Blair last night. Perhaps someone saw her."

"Thank you, inspector, I know you'll do your best."
Larsen hung up.

Inspector Lee got busy on his laptop. He pulled up the
airlines from Port Blair on Andaman Island, checking all the
destinations the woman could have flown too. Detective
Callahan reported that the security on the ship found the
passport of the victim, Astrid Karlsson, in the room of the
woman who left the ship. The possession of the passport
warranted an accessory to murder charge.

The flights from Port Blair mostly went directly to India.
He pulled up Chennai and Kolkata, then did a quick search
of connecting flights. Both had many connections to Paris,
Amsterdam, London and Toronto. He needed to act fast.

But he needed to find the identity of this woman. He
started in Port Blair, where she'd fled from the ship. Pulling
up the name of the police station close to the International
Airport, he dialed it.

A woman answered the phone in Hindi, then said, "Andaman Police, South District."

Lee gave his name, his rank, and his police department headquarters in Singapore—happy they spoke English, his Hindi being non-existent.

"Yes, how may we help you?"

"I need to trace a young woman who left a ship off your coast yesterday. She may have taken a flight out of Port Blair. She is wanted on accessory to murder," Lee said.

"One moment, please."

A few minutes later a voice came on, "Inspector Chandra here, how may I assist you?"

Lee breathed deeply and went through his complete request again. He knew this would happen. He made himself ready for it. He'd dealt with the Indian Police before. The amount of times he'd had to re-explain himself could tax the very limits of his Buddhist teaching.

"Aha, aha, I see. What you want us to do is not possible. The airlines will not allow this, you see," Chandra replied.

"Inspector, this woman had the victim's passport in her possession. I'm sure you know how hard it is to solve a murder. This is our only chance to find out who this person is," Lee said. He tried not to plead, to sound weak. He had to appeal to Chandra's own sense of futility all police felt in solving murders.

"I will see what I can do. I know many of the people at the airport. I will meet with them directly. Can I call you at this number?"

"Yes, please, I will be here waiting," Lee said.

Lee waited at his desk for several hours, he did paper-work, drank more tea, making sure his cell phone was with him when he went to the toilet. He hoped the Inspector from Port Blair would come through.

Inspector Chandra phoned him three hours later. "I have good news," he said. "One of the airline operations is a good friend of mine. I told him what you needed and why. He has a daughter the same age."

"Yes, this is good, did you get a name and destination?" Lee asked. He knew the Indian Inspector could keep him on the phone for a long time, but he needed to get the information.

"Yes, yes, there was only one young woman matching your description, which is very lucky. She took the flight from Port Blair on Spice Airlines to Chennai. From there she is connecting to Amsterdam—she is traveling first class the entire way," Inspector Chandra said with much enthusiasm in his voice, impressed by the expensive taste of the fugitive.

"Did your friend give you her name?"

There was a long pause. Lee waited.

"Yes, he did. Her name is Catriona Visser, she is traveling on a Dutch passport," Inspector Chandra said.

"Thank you, that is most kind of you," Inspector Lee said, ending the call. He opened up his web browser's Interpol website and punched in her name. The name matched one of those stolen from the massive Marriott web breach several years ago.

The real Catriona Visser was a dark-haired, tall woman in her forties who lived in Harlingen, Holland. A simple passport to get by an unsophisticated airport like Port Blair would cost one thousand USD. One that could get her out of Chennai would cost five thousand.

Lee sat back and looked at his screen. He would check with the police in Chennai to see if Catriona had taken the next flight to Amsterdam. He doubted it.

First, he checked the flight status of the Spice Air flight

on their website to see when it landed in Chennai. They had delayed it. The flight left only this morning from Port Blair due to the cyclone in the Bay of Bengal.

The connection to Amsterdam wouldn't be for another three hours. Lee got busy on the phone. He needed an international arrest warrant. There was no use in calling the police in Chennai without it. If he wanted to catch this woman and solve his case in Singapore, he needed the next hour to work in his favor. He hoped the right judge would be available for the warrant.

34

"WOULD you care for more orange juice, Ms. Visser?" the flight attendant asked. She stood beside the passenger in seat 1A with a small pitcher of orange juice and napkins.

"No, take my tray away," Ms. Visser said without looking up or acknowledging her. "I still can't believe you don't serve alcohol on this airline. Not even a mimosa. I'd never booked into first class had I known."

The attendant took her tray away, gave her a nod, and went back to hiding in the galley. The surly passenger in seat 1A was her only first-class passenger. She'd been enough work for ten.

The passenger in seat 1A looked out the window as the plane descended into Chennai and realized everything she'd done wrong. The major screw up—fitting Ashley Compton with the wrong scuba gear. If she'd grabbed an extra-large vest to handle the woman's big breasts—what the hell had she been thinking?

Her cutting of the wetsuit had been a last-ditch effort. The shark bite had been a piece of luck, but then the questions from the dive team made her realize they were on to her.

Catriona Visser would exist until Chennai airport. Then she'd resume her actual identity as Charlotte Bowden of Sea Island, Georgia. She'd exit the airport, cash in her ticket at the airlines counter to Amsterdam. From there she would grab a taxi to the train station, take the train to Goa, hide out for a few weeks, then fly home.

Catriona would become thin air to the police whom she knew would be on to her by now. Someone had to figure out what she'd done. When she'd taken the job, it seemed simple. Her acting jobs were scarce, her diving instruction jobs were boring. She hoped the people who'd her hired wouldn't be too upset. Ashley Compton died an accidental death. Didn't that mean she'd done her job?

The flight arrived in Chennai; the plane taxied into the terminal. Charlotte hurried into the terminal. She presented her ticket to the airline and asked for a refund—in cash. The airline desk clerk's eyes went wide when she saw how much cash she had to hand over. Charlotte had paid for a first-class ticket in cash so she wouldn't be cramped in the back of the plane and get a few cocktails. Now she regretted it. The airline desk agent ran to several other cashiers. The first-class ticket had cost her just under five thousand USD. The ticket agent gave her over three hundred thousand in Indian Rupees.

Charlotte took the huge wad of Indian Rupees, folding them into her small backpack. The airport looked new and spacious, but she wanted out as fast as possible. Many police wandered around staring at passengers and talking to each other.

She felt eyes on her. She needed to move. The train to Goa wasn't until 1520 hours. The train station was only a twenty-minute taxi ride away—she wanted to get there—now.

She needed to get as far away from the air terminal as possible. A tingling feeling ran down her spine, as if something was pressing in on her. It was fear. The fear of being caught.

In her mind, she hadn't killed Ashley. But now, in this foreign country, she felt like she needed to get as far away from anything to do with the police as possible. She'd never been on the run before. A strong morning sun beat down on the pavement. Her skin crawled with icy fear.

The Vasco da Gama Express train to Goa would take twenty hours. She'd have time to think on the trip of how she'd approach her client for forgiveness.

Walking out of the airport terminal, she headed towards the taxi line.

A voice called behind her. "Hey Charlotte, we'll give you a ride."

Charlotte froze—she wanted to run. Terror held her in place. Turning slowly, she saw her handlers from Singapore. They called themselves Simon and Eric.

"Uh, hey, guys. I meant to call once I got to my hotel... and you know, give you my update from the ship," Charlotte said.

"What were you going to tell us?" Eric asked. He looked Chinese with a tall, muscular build that looked at home in a mixed martial arts arena. He no longer wore a suit like in Singapore. Now he dressed in black pants with a white shirt and black shoes. His dark sunglasses mirrored Charlotte's reflection back to her. She could see the reflection of her fear.

"Well... Ashley is dead. I did that right, didn't I?"

"Yeah, we heard you nailed it," Simon said with a slight

sneer his voice. He was a smaller version of Eric, more compact and looked edgy. "And then you ran. You've exposed everyone. Did you think of that?" He wore the same dark glasses, similar black pants with a white shirt and a dark sports coat. His hands clenched and unclenched in readiness for action.

"Sorry—had to run. Mia, who runs the dive crew, asked me a bunch of questions about why I left my position on the feeding line. When that big blonde bimbo wouldn't take the regulator I handed her, I had to think of something. I did a quick slice of her wetsuit to get the shark's attention. I thought it was a stroke of genius. You wouldn't want me subjected to an investigation on the ship, would you? This way, no one will know who I am. I used a fake passport out of Port Blair to cover my tracks."

Simon and Victor shared a look through their sunglasses.

"That's excellent, I think our client will be happy. Come with us. We'll get you paid, and you can be on your way," Victor said.

Charlotte's body trembled. The tone of Victor's voice was cold. Leaving with them would mean her death. She wasn't a killer like them, she'd only acted it. Now, here was the real thing. These men intended to kill her.

She took a deep breath. Putting on her best actor smile she'd used to get parts in commercials, she said, "You know, I don't want to trouble you guys. How about if you give me your cell number and I'll call you? You can do a bank transfer." She smiled again, holding her hands so they couldn't see them shake.

Victor opened his jacket, showing a gun inside a shoulder holster. "Charlotte, we said you're coming with us."

Charlotte backed away slowly. "Look, you don't want to

do anything here. Police are everywhere. I'm going to get into a taxi and be on my way. Tell the client to keep the money. I had a fun time on the ship and an enjoyable time in Singapore. Let's call it even, okay?"

Victor's hand gripped the gun. He moved towards her as she walked back towards a taxi. A driver saw her coming. He motioned for her to get into his taxi, thinking the tall Asian man was seeing her off.

Charlotte kept backing up. She felt the door—reaching behind she pulled the door open and threw her backpack in. She lowered herself into the back seat when Victor drew his gun. He placed it on her forehead.

"No," Charlotte said. The gun's silencer made a whooshing sound. The metal shell casing fell to the pavement.

The cab driver started the car thinking this man would close the door for the lady. He looked around to see the Asian man gone. The lady lay on the back seat—her head covered in blood.

Victor and Simon hurried to a black Mercedes sedan. They sped off, hearing the yelling of cab driver.

35

INSPECTOR LEE CURSED the slow judicial system. It moved with the speed of a slug when he needed to get an international arrest warrant. After several hours of emails and phone calls that included the writing of a long letter of request, Lee had a Red Warrant—also called an International Warrant.

He looked at the clock. Four hours had gone by since he'd spoken to the police in Port Blair. If the woman known as Visser caught the plane to Amsterdam, he'd call the police in Holland to get her apprehended there. He picked up the phone to dial the police station in Chennai. He found the one close to the airport.

It took much longer this time. The receptionist kept putting him through to one officer after another who listened to his story, asked him politely to hold the line, then wandered off to never return. Lee called back several times to speak to another officer.

Finally, Sergeant Rupinder came on the phone. "Yes, how may I assist you?"

Inspector Lee repeated his request for the fifth time. He

gave the description of the girl, the name on the passport she was traveling on, and her destination.

"I am hoping," Lee said, "her plane to Amsterdam has been delayed, and you might arrest her before she leaves India."

"This lady has been much delayed," Sergeant Rupinder said.

"Was there a problem with the plane, then?" Lee asked in hopes they'd be able to make her arrest.

"No, I have just returned from the airport. We have a victim that matches the description you gave us. They shot her, execution style, you see. A great bloody hole in her forehead at close range at the cab stand. They upset the poor taxi driver over the mess he has to clean up," Rupinder said.

"Did the driver see who did it?"

"Two Chinese men dressed in black. Was this woman involved in drugs?" Rupinder asked.

"I'm sorry, I do not know. She came off a cruise ship. We think she aided in two homicides, both here in Singapore and on the ship. Did she have any other ID on her?"

"Yes, she had the Dutch passport that we found is fake, and an American one under the name of Charlotte Bowman."

"Would you send me a copy of the American passport, we'd like to continue with the investigation, and we will share our findings to help you close yours, Sergeant Rupinder."

"Very kind of you, I will send you a copy right away."

Lee put down his phone and wiped his brow with his handkerchief, he'd been at his desk for too long. But he needed to inform Bernadette Callahan about the incident in Chennai.

He put together an email of his conversation from both

the police in Port Blair and in Chennai, so she'd know what had transpired. He finished and left for the day. Somewhere in this investigation they'd find the truth—he hoped.

～

BERNADETTE LOOKED at her laptop the moment she got back into the room. They'd left the restaurant late, lingering over a tiramisu and a glass of cognac with a coffee as they watched the waves out the window. But Chris could see Bernadette wanted to get back to the room.

The moment she'd entered the room, she knew she had to see what transpired in the hunt for the fake Astrid. She looked at her email, read it, then closed it. She walked over to Chris and sat down beside him on the sofa.

"You look disturbed." Chris said.

"The woman who was masquerading as Astrid Karlsson got shot at close range at the Chennai airport this morning," Bernadette said.

"Did someone witness it?"

"Yeah, the cab driver saw two Chinese guys. Inspector Lee thinks it could be the same ones who picked up the girl in Singapore. They're sending him a copy of the CCTV so he can compare."

"What do you make of all this, Bernie?"

"Gangland execution. It can only mean the fake Astrid was on board to kill someone. I have her actual name. She was Charlotte Bowman from Sea Island, Georgia."

"You're going to stay up and work this?"

Bernadette lowered her head and put her hands on his chest. "Yes, you know I can't let this go."

"Hey, beautiful, I married you not only for how amazing you look but also your incredible determination. I'm going to bed. You go chase down that criminal. But don't stay up too late," Chris said as he kissed her on the forehead.

"I won't, I promise. I'll be good," Bernadette said.

"Great, and maybe tonight you won't be talking in your sleep."

Bernadette looked at him. "Since when have I been talking in my sleep?"

Chris grinned. "Only the last few nights. I'm getting jealous..."

"About what?"

"About Bill. I hope I don't have to have a talk with this guy," Chris said with a wink.

Bernadette waited until Chris was in the bedroom before she opened her laptop and got down to business. The murder of Charlotte Bowman added a new level. Now, she knew there had been no accidents. These were murders. How was she going to solve it?

She searched for Charlotte Bowman. Her webpage showed her as an actor. Most of her credits were for commercials and some terrible reality shows. There was no doubt about her beauty, and—she was a dead ringer for Astrid Karlsson.

Charlotte Bowman had been a certified diver and diving instructor with several jobs in the U.S. Virgin Islands and around Georgia on St. Simons Island.

The girl looked so innocent, beautiful, and happy. Now, someone was going to have to tell her parents of her death and involvement in a murder, well, two murders, actually. Bernadette sighed and looked at the time on the computer. It was close to midnight. What time was it on the East Coast of the states?

She knew of one person who could put this investigation into focus. It was Carla Winston, an FBI agent in Washington DC, who got things done. She was a mid-forties African American who doted on her son who was in college and put up with her husband. They'd been on two cases together and so far; Bernadette never crossed her badly enough that she wouldn't take her phone call.

She picked up the phone in the living room, checked that the satellite phone was operating, and dialed a number. A world time zones website informed her it was past three in the afternoon the next day. She hoped Carla picked up.

"Agent Winston."

"Hey, Carla, it's me, Bernadette. I've kind of got a complicated case I need your help with."

"Um huh, and you reach out to your old lifelong friend, is that it?" Winston replied dryly.

"Ah, yeah, I'm on a cruise ship at the moment."

"Where did you say you're at now?" Carla asked.

"I'm on a cruise ship in the Bay of Bengal heading for Sri Lanka," Bernadette said.

"Did you throw someone overboard?"

"No."

"Did you shoot someone?"

"No."

"Then, why the hell are you calling me from a cruise ship? Why aren't you enjoying yourself? I hear those ships have food everywhere. I don't think I'd stop eating until I got off the ship. What are you doing there?"

"Well... it's kind of our honeymoon. You know Chris and I got married last May."

"Oh, yeah, I couldn't make the wedding. Sorry about that," Carla said.

"I know, you said it was the same time as your son's graduation ceremony," Bernadette said.

"Yeah, and the fact your wedding was so far back in the

sticks I think I had to paddle a canoe to get there," Carla said with a laugh. "Now, really, why are you calling me?"

Bernadette took a breath. "I've got a murder in Singapore attached to this ship and two deaths from suspicious accidents. I think the accidents were murder. There's just been another murder in India, the victim was Charlotte Bowman. She was on this ship as well and responsible for one of the accidents. This thing is complicated—hopefully you can help me solve it."

"My oh my, girl, you're having some fun on your honeymoon. I spent my honeymoon with Carl in Nantucket, stuffing myself silly with lobster rolls and chowder."

"Thanks for the vision, Carla. Now, can you help me with this? I have a strong feeling we have a suspect on this ship. We dock in Dubai in a week. If I can find out who's behind this, I could turn them over to the authorities when we dock."

"And you want me to do some investigating, where I don't open a case file, report to no one but you, and see how I can keep my ass from being handed to me by my boss if I'm found out. Does that about cover it?" Carla asked.

"Yes, that would be it." Bernadette said.

Winston laughed. "Why did I even ask? Okay, email me what you're looking—you got my address?"

"Yeah, I do. And look, I really appreciate this, but the quicker you can get anything back to me the better. I really need someone to check out Charlotte Bowman and who she was connected with."

"Oh, yeah, the usual Canadian approach. You're all friendly and nice and then get all pushy." Carla chuckled. "Don't worry, I've got agents all over the country that owe me favors. They'll keep it quiet and me out of it. Now, go back to that big stud husband of yours. I have a long and boring staff meeting that I just can't wait to get to."

"Thanks, Carla, you're the best," Bernadette said. She put down her phone and began typing out her email. She'd put everything in there about Charlotte Bowman. Then she stopped. Her fingers hovered over the keys. She remembered the conversation with Bill Loving. His story was about going back to the beginning. She threw in some notes about the Redstones, Comptons, the Braithwaites and the company, New Wave Technologies. Then, for good measure, she threw in the notes about the dead girl in Singapore and at first thinking Holly Marsden might be the replacement, then finding she wasn't a match for the dead girl.

She closed her laptop and headed for the bedroom, hoping she wouldn't talk in her sleep again. Soon, she'd have to come clean with Chris about her late-night visits to the cigar room and the charming gentleman from East Texas. But not just yet.

Tomorrow they were docking in Sri Lanka. There was a discussion she needed to have with the Redstones and the Braithwaites. She knew they wouldn't be happy with it. But they needed to hear. Yawning, she got into bed.

36

BERNADETTE WOKE to the sound of the ship's intercom. The captain wished them a pleasant good morning, gave them the ship's position in the Bay of Bengal, and their arrival time at the port of Colombo in Sri Lanka. He stated there would be an extra stop in port. They'd ordered some parts for the ship's repair from Miami, but the parts wouldn't be there until the next day. The captain apologized profusely, for the stay in Sri Lanka was now three days instead of the planned two days. She got out of bed and brushed her teeth, washed her face, then went back to bed.

Chris was still in bed. He lay there, opening his eyes. "Why do they have to make every announcement into the cabins?"

"Looks like our honeymoon is getting extended," Bernadette said as she climbed into bed to lie beside him. She ran her hand down his chest to his abdomen and kept going.

"Action's like that will get you laid, madam," Chris said.

"I was hoping you'd say that," Bernadette replied.

Chris rolled out of bed. "I'll brush my teeth, don't start without me."

Bernadette watched him go into the bathroom, then rolled over to look out the window. The sea was calm, the clouds a puffy white. Just another easy cruising day and almost like the previous day hadn't happened—only the ship had the bruises to prove it. It reminded her of domestic disturbances when she was in uniform. She'd arrive to find the home torn apart, the couple with blood and bruises, but they'd made up. All is well, they'd say, don't mind us or the mess. We're fine.

For now, she wanted to block last night's conversation with Carla Winston out of her mind and just be with Chris. This was their honeymoon. She wanted to focus on that.

Chris came walking out of the bathroom naked. She had no problem with her focus.

They made love, showered, and ordered room service. The deck was now accessible. They watched the waves and birds dance around the ship until the Island of Sri Lanka came into view.

"How long until we arrive in Colombo?" Bernadette asked.

"I think there's about three hours. Do you have some plans?"

Bernadette grinned and put down her coffee cup. "I thought I'd get Cynthia up to speed on their missing crewmember, then have a chat with our friends with the targets on their backs."

Chris looked at her and shook his head. "You know, it amazes me how you can wake me up in the morning, have sex—"

"Great sex," Bernadette interjected.

"Yes, great sex, then want to wander the ship and work on a case."

Bernadette got up and gave him a lingering kiss on the lips. "Honey, didn't I tell you, making love to you energizes me."

He laughed, running his hand over her arm. "Once again, you got three to my one. So, you must be bursting with energy."

Bernadette changed into a t-shirt and shorts then made her way to the lower decks. Her first meeting was with Mateo and Cynthia. They sat in Mateo's office while she filled them in.

"I don't think we've experienced anything like this," Mateo said. "I must report this to the captain and to head office." His hand went through his wavy black hair. The news unsettled him.

Cynthia looked at Mateo. "This will change everything about the shark attack. We need to report this to head office. This gets the security staff and the dive team some breathing space. But if someone else on board was working with the deceased Charlotte Bowman, we have other passengers in danger."

Mateo raised his hand. "Look, I'll take it to the captain, but I doubt if he'll have us make some kind of announcement. You have any idea how this will play with the cruise line?"

"What about the risk to the rest of the passengers while you drag your feet on this?" Bernadette asked.

"This is all speculation. This lady, Charlotte Bowman, could have had a personal vendetta against the Comptons. Remember, we're only security personal, and Bernadette, you're still a passenger and guest on this ship. If we do an active investigation on this and start interviewing every passenger and making statements, we'll cross so many lines of legalese, the lawyers in Miami will have us in knots. Not to mention passengers would launch lawsuits. I'm sorry, we have to keep this quiet."

"What if you just informed the Redstones and the Braithwaites about the recent events?" Bernadette asked. "This concerns them more than anyone else, don't you think?"

Mateo leaned back in his chair. "I'd have to get authorization from the captain for that. Remember, we're a cruise ship. Our mission is to provide a wonderful experience and trip of a lifetime while everyone takes selfies and checks off their bucket list. Our primary job in security is keeping their valuables safe and making sure they get safely back on the ship."

"You're right, Mateo," Bernadette said, "There's no use in pushing this issue. I'm sure the captain will consult with your head office and decide of what's best. Now, I'll get back to my vacation."

Bernadette got up and walked out of the security office. Cynthia followed her out. They stopped in the passageway.

Cynthia turned to Bernadette. "You're going to do what you want, aren't you?"

Bernadette shrugged. "Yeah, pretty much."

"I remember the same look from you in RCMP cadet school. The drill instructor gave you a lesson in doing take downs. You smiled at him until he went away—and resumed your techniques. You kicked his ass with your karate moves if memory serves me right," Cynthia said.

Bernadette laughed. "Yeah, old Sergeant Krivich. I remember him."

"Yeah, the cadets called him the beast—until you kept taking him to the mat."

"It wasn't fair, I'd just completed my black belt before I entered the force," Bernadette said. "I should have told him that."

"So, what are you planning to do, Bernadette?"

"I'll keep out of harm's way, enjoy my cruise, and let you know if I need you," Bernadette said with a wink.

Cynthia blew out a breath. "I figured as much. Please don't get into any trouble on the ship."

"You have my promise. I'm going to the main lounge for the talk on Sri Lanka's ancient history. That should be about my speed for the day."

She walked away, knowing Cynthia didn't expect her to keep her promise, but she'd done a C.Y.A. move. The classic Cover Your Ass in the world of security. She could always report that she's made a request that Bernadette not get involved. That would be good enough to keep Cynthia out of trouble.

The ship was buzzing with life. Passengers were hitting the small casino as they'd had no chance during the storm, and it would be closed once they docked in Columbo. Bernadette walked by the casino, saw a game of five card poker in progress. She was tempted to join in, but she knew the stakes were low on the ships. This prevented passengers from getting fleeced by those who preyed on the unsuspecting rubes loaded with money and no game sense. Poker games had paid for her schoolbooks and karate lessons in high school, then helped pay for her university tuition.

She stopped for a moment to watch someone try to pretend to bluff on a poor hand. It made her skin crawl at the tells the player displayed. Resuming her journey, she turned into the bistro café to see Elizabeth Redstone sitting alone with a daily printout of the *New York Times*.

"Hi, mind if I join you?" Bernadette asked.

"Please do, this *New York Times* edition is so skimpy it's like reading a menu at MacDonald's, little substance and not filling," Elizabeth said with a smile.

Bernadette sat down and ordered a cappuccino from the waiter. The waiter walked away and came back with water. She waited until he'd gone back to make her the coffee.

"Elizabeth, I'll get right to the point—"

"Go right ahead, I've noticed you usually do."

"They murdered the woman who bolted from this ship in Port Blair in Chennai yesterday. The police reported they shot her in the head at close range," Bernadette said.

"Oh, dear. That's terrifying. What do you think this means?" Elizabeth asked. Her hand was visibly shaking as she brought it to her face.

"It means she'd served her purpose. They terminated her. Only gangs do this. I need to know something, Elizabeth, and you need to tell me the truth," Bernadette said as she leaned close to her.

"What is it?"

"Is your company involved in anything even slightly illegal?" Bernadette asked.

"Well... I don't think so. We make circuit boards for customers all over the world," Elizabeth said. "I told you we have an offer to purchase our company by a reputable firm —sorry I can't divulge the information because it's with the accountants and lawyers and we can't say anything as directors. But I can't imagine why anyone would try to harm us."

"If you look at the events of the past few days, you can see that someone is after you. You realize that," Bernadette said.

Elizabeth put both her hands on the table. "My dear, the murder of the woman changes everything. I can see we are in danger."

The waiter brought Bernadette's coffee to the table and left.

"I think the four of you should make plans to fly home to the states," Bernadette said.

"No, my Fred will never leave George's body on this ship. I already mentioned it to him. Don't you remember? We discussed getting a flight from Columbo and realized how long we'd have to stay to do it. And besides, what's stopping these people from coming after us once we're off the ship?"

Bernadette stirred her coffee and looked at Elizabeth. "You have a point. You could call your company and have them arrange security for you."

"That seems like a lot of extra planning, when we could just stay on the ship, where we know we're safe," Elizabeth said, looking down at her hands.

"If you want to remain on the ship, you must be extra careful. The ship's security knows about the murdered girl. They claim they can't speculate there's a threat on your life," Bernadette said.

"I don't know what we'd do without you, Bernadette. If it hadn't been for you, Fred and I would be dead by now," Elizabeth said with tears in her eyes. "Would you reconsider being our bodyguard and watching out for us? We will pay you very well. Fred and I would pay you five thousand per day, just to have you by our side."

Bernadette shook her head. "I don't do personal security; I'm not licensed for it and not about to start. I suggest you remain on the ship and in your cabins while in port."

Elizabeth sighed, "well then, I guess we'll just be on our

own with Nigel and Lucinda." She pulled out a Kleenex and dabbed her eyes, "Maybe you'll say a little prayer for us."

Bernadette held her breath. How did she get pulled into these things? Looking at Elizabeth, she could see how fragile she looked. "Okay, I'll tell Chris we're coming along, but after this, I'm asking you to stay on the ship, okay?"

"Great, I'll let the tour guide know you're coming along. It is overnight, but don't worry, I'll have the concierge give you all the details," Elizabeth said with a flashing smile.

They got up from the table, and Elizabeth looked at Bernadette. "I feel so much safer now that you'll be coming along. Thank you so much."

They parted company, and as Bernadette walked back into the main atrium on her way up the stairway, she saw Cynthia.

"How's it going?" Bernadette asked her.

Cynthia looked around and guided Bernadette over to a small sitting area near a window. "It's not good. Mateo had like a ten-minute meeting with the captain—he went ballistic. He stated categorically that we should not involve you. He's doing a complete report to head office. I think the shit's about to hit the fan once the owners of this cruise find out what's transpired."

"At least you got their attention," Bernadette said with a weak smile. "Look, I've promised I'll go with Elizabeth on some tour they're doing. When we return to the ship, I'll sit on them until we leave for Mumbai. Is that okay?"

Cynthia put her hand on Bernadette's. "Just be careful, okay? I don't understand what's going on. In my three years of security duties on ships, I've seen nothing this crazy. It's like this voyage is cursed."

"Good subtitle for a mystery book," Bernadette said. "Now, I'm going to go hang out with my husband and tell him he needs to pack a small bag for tomorrow's tour. I'm sure he won't mind, but he's not great on surprises."

When Bernadette got back to the room, she found Chris had left a note he was going to a lecture on the history of Sri Lanka. She went to her laptop, opened it up and saw two emails, one from Inspector Lee and one from Carla Winston. She opened them up. Both of them caught her attention.

37

CHRIS ENTERED the room while Bernadette stared at her computer. He walked in, kicked off his shoes, poured himself a glass of water, and sat beside her.

"Did something major happen?" he asked.

Bernadette looked up. "Yeah, why do you ask?"

"You've been staring at the computer since I walked in. The only time I see you like this is when things fall together or fall apart in a case."

She sat back in her chair and looked at the screen. "I've been reading emails from Inspector Lee and Agent Carla Winston."

"You want to fill me in?"

Bernadette got up and poured herself a glass of water, she took a drink and sat down again. "First, from Lee. They arrested the two men suspected of murdering Charlotte Bowman in India. The Indian police sent the CCTV photos of the two men to Singapore and they showed up at the Singapore airport this morning."

"That's great. Have the men confessed to the killing of Astrid?"

"No, they lawyered up. Lee mentioned they got some high-priced lawyers."

"Which means they're members of a gang."

"Usually does," Bernadette said.

"So, you're no further ahead?"

"Yeah, pretty much, if the police in Singapore can't place these two with Astrid, then they have nothing. From what I read of Lee's report from the shooting in India, the taxi driver didn't see it happen. He only saw Bowman dead after the two walked away."

"No gun recovered?"

Bernadette just looked at Chris and raised her eyes to answer in the negative.

"There's a chance these guys will walk with a talented lawyer," Chris said.

Bernadette sighed. "Yes, the way of the legal system, good defense lawyers get wealthy criminals off. The worst part is, they couldn't connect these guys to Astrid. The CCTV video from the dive shop she visited showed her leaving with some woman."

"Will they send you the video footage?"

"I asked for it. I hope to have it soon. Maybe I can ID the woman to someone on this ship. Then I might have something to go on." She sipped her water and opened the other email.

"The email from agent Wilson has some major revelations."

"What's agent Winston say?"

"So far, she's filled me in on Charlotte Bowman. She did some acting. Had some bit parts in some reality television in Atlanta plus some commercials, then worked as a diving instructor on Sea Island in Georgia. She worked in hotels, did some bartending at a place called the Cloister. I looked it up online, a mere five to seven hundred a night during the summer."

"Right up our alley," Chris said.

"Yeah, right? The other interesting thing is our table-mates, the Comptons, Braithwaites and Redstones. Not as rich as they make out."

"What, really?"

"Yeah, Winston ran a credit report on them. I didn't ask her to, but then if you want to know the reason for someone chasing you, look at the money," Bernadette said, looking up from the laptop. "They have a less than stellar credit score with several of their properties in receivership."

"So, why would they be on this exorbitantly expensive cruise?" Chris asked.

Bernadette raised an eyebrow. "That's a good question. Elizabeth said their buyout would net them one hundred million each. With the Comptons gone, they get another fifty million each in shares. I assume it would fund their lavish lifestyle once again."

Chris laughed. "There's got to be a fairy godmother in this story or a genie in a bottle. Why am I feeling this is too good to be true?" He got up, stretched, and looked out the balcony window.

Bernadette got out of her chair and walked to his side. "I'm sorry honey, am I kind of boring you with all this?"

Chris slid his arm around her. "No, it's just kind of funny. Here we are, two working stiffs dropped into the world of the rich, and we find some are not so rich. But it looks like they'll do anything to stay wealthy."

"I wonder about that myself."

"You think the others aren't as innocent as they seem?" Chris asked.

"Lucinda could be doing a righteous act of playing the

bitch, but then again, she's doing it so well I'd nominate her for an Oscar. But that could be her way of hiding the fact she's behind the deaths of the Comptons," Bernadette said.

"I thought Lucinda and Ashley were lifelong friends?"

"I've seen a lot less money than a hundred million result in the murder of a friend," Bernadette said.

"Then Nigel would have to be in on the scheme as well?" Chris said.

"No idea. The only thing that makes them all suspects is they are broke, according to Winston's email. Money is the second biggest motivator for murder," Bernadette said.

"What's the first?"

"Being born into a family that wants you dead. Don't you remember your first lesson in homicide investigation? Look to the husband, the wife, or the nearest relative."

"You're right. Familiarity breeds contempt. I was lucky, I did most of my postings in the force on desolate islands. Most people got along because they hardly saw each other."

"There, I rest my case. Now, I need to fill you in on our little adventure we're doing tomorrow with our millionaire friends."

Chris winked at her. "You mean the broke ass millionaires?"

"Oh please, don't say that. The next time I see Lucinda and Nigel, it'll be the first thing to pop into my head. But I promised Elizabeth we'd go on some overnight tour to a big rock shrine."

"The lecturer covered it this morning. It's called Sigiriya, the Lion Rock. The temple is over one thousand years old, one of the most revered places in the country," Chris said as he rubbed Bernadette's shoulders. "The thing is, there's a two-hundred-meter climb to the top on one thousand steps.

If George died from less than half that amount in Kuala Lumpur, I doubt old Nigel has a chance."

"Elizabeth asked if we'd come along to keep them safe," Bernadette said.

"Sure, that's easy. I stand at the base of the rock and tell them all, don't go up, you'll probably die," Chris said, raising his hands in the air to show his instructions. "Oh, and one more thing. We have to listen for the cry of the devil bird."

"What's that?"

"A bird from the owl family that makes a noise like a lady screaming. The legend has it, when you hear it, someone dies," Chris said with a wink.

Bernadette closed her eyes. "Yes, wonderful advice. Let's pack a bag and get ready for tomorrow's journey. There's a one-hundred-and-fifty-kilometer ride to the site, we stay overnight in a resort hotel near the rock, then make our climb up early the next morning."

"And in that time, we watch over them for marauding monkeys and elephants?"

"I guess so. Someone got to the other two somehow. I don't know how yet. George died of what looked like a stroke or heart attack and Ashley's death wasn't caused by the shark, it was a heart attack. I have some ideas, but I'll work on them tomorrow when I see everyone on the dock," Bernadette said.

THE SHIP CAME in with the help of two tugboats at two in the morning. Normally with its high-tech propulsion systems it wouldn't need an assist, but the damage made it necessary.

Captain Prodromou stood on the bridge to ensure the ship docked with no further incident. This voyage was to be the start of a world tour. The deaths of the passengers on board and the murder of the woman in India were not looking good for his record. His crew had let the wrong woman come on board to replace Astrid—then let her leave the ship and fake her return. All of this would come back to him. It didn't matter what sinister forces were trying to eradicate a few passengers from some other land. This fell to him. He was the master of the ship. His chances of resuming the cruise after Dubai were slim. They'd probably have his replacement ready to take over command.

His life was reaching a crossroads. Last night Felica had told him their relationship was over. He'd seen it coming. Both of them knew they wouldn't be able to keep their affair a secret. They had a choice, an illicit love affair or their careers on the sea.

Felica chose the sea. She wanted to be a captain of her own ship one day. Prodromou thought she'd made a wise choice. He'd call his wife soon after they docked, ask her to meet him in Dubai when the company sacked him. He needed to reconnect with her and his children.

He sighed deeply as he left the bridge. Some of his life choices would be made for him in the next few days. He loved this ship; he'd miss it more than Felica. And he knew Felica felt the same way. She'd told him that last night as she left his bed.

38

BERNADETTE STEPPED out on her deck to see the harbor and city view of Colombo before her. The smell of spices and sea salt mingled with humidity assailed her nostrils the moment she breathed in. She loved it.

They docked at Queen Elizabeth Pier. The ship's guide map claimed a colorful fifteen-minute walk into the city, or you could take a short taxi as long as you negotiated the fare. But for the passengers of the *Orion Voyager*, free air-conditioned shuttles would be available.

Bernadette surveyed the dock with the vendors, the workers driving forklifts to provide food to the ships; the police standing guard and the ship's crew already busy making repairs.

She longed to grab a backpack and disappear off the ship with Chris into the city. But she had agreed to be with Elizabeth and the group for the next two days. There would be one more day in Colombo for ship repairs. They could roam the city on their own then.

They were both packed. Everything they needed was in one small carry-on bag and their two backpacks. Bernadette wore some knee-length shorts in those great fibers that wick so well no one knows you are sweating like a pig roasting on a spit. She hated the feeling of having her clothes drenched in sweat.

Chris was in his usual shorts with a tight t-shirt that made his muscles look like they wanted to get out. He came onto the deck and put his arms around her.

"You ready for our big adventure?" he asked.

Bernadette grabbed his hand. "No, not really, but I'm curious to see what happens this time."

"What do you mean?"

"Well, check our stats. Two outings with these people and two deaths. This is our third time on an excursion. I hope we're not batting a thousand, as they say, but I'll be looking for a clue or to see if they are in any danger," Bernadette said.

"And what should I be looking for on this trip?" Chris asked.

"Damned if I know. Maybe see if anyone suspicious is lurking around us as we venture into the sites," Bernadette said. "I saw nothing in the temple in Kuala Lumpur, but it was crowded. All the people at the shark feeding were passengers. This time, there is only us, our fake millionaire friends, and our guide. Anyone else is a suspect."

Grabbing their gear, they headed downstairs and joined the line of passengers exiting the ship. Bernadette saw Cynthia on the dock and went over to her.

"Hey, Cynthia, you going to spend a few days roaming the town while most of the passengers visit the island?" Bernadette asked.

"Not a chance. We have meetings with the entire security team. Mateo is going to take everyone through protocol training. He's pretty pissed on how the events of the past few days have gone down. Then we've got to work on reports."

"Sorry to hear that, doesn't sound like fun. I'm going to be a chaperone for Elizabeth Redstone and friends. I'm hoping to bring them back in one piece—so far their track record isn't good," Bernadette said.

Cynthia took Bernadette aside, turning her back to the others. "Are you sure it's wise? Lucinda has made two complaints to the captain about you. Did you know she filed a formal charge that you contributed to Ashley Compton's death?"

Bernadette shrugged. "That wouldn't surprise me. She's a bit off her head. I can't see from the events how she'd come up with that. But anyway, I'll be hanging with Elizabeth. I promised her I'd look after her."

"You're a big girl, you can look after yourself, but be careful with that crowd," Cynthia warned. "Do you have a way to keep in touch with the ship?"

Bernadette pulled out a cell phone. "I got this in Singapore. It has an international sim card. I'll give you my number and call you if we have anything happen. Here's hoping I come back with a cheap souvenir for you and we can share stories over a beer."

She walked away and found Chris chatting with the Redstones.

"I'm so glad you're coming with us, Bernadette," Elizabeth said. "I kept telling Fred I thought you might not come."

Fred stepped in. "I told her you'd be here. No woman who handled those natives on the island would back away from a brief tour to an ancient rock."

"I'm a woman of my word," Bernadette said, motioning

to Chris behind her. "And with my man rock or rock that walks like a man, I'm sure we'll be fine."

"Look, I'm just along because I heard there's some cool mountain biking around the rock near the resort. I need some exercise and a few days off the ship couldn't hurt," Chris said, adding, "And I don't look like a rock."

Lucinda walked up, placing her hand on Chris's bicep. "From where I'm standing, you'd be a mighty fine rock to climb."

Bernadette glared at Lucinda. She was dressed in her usual reveal-all style—a low-cut tank top and shorts that would look good on a cheerleader. A baseball cap with glitter that proclaimed '*Babe*' and a set of white tennis shoes finished her outlandish outfit.

"I see you're dressed once again for touring," Bernadette said dryly.

Lucinda let go of Chris's arm. "Oh, this is just something I threw together at the last minute. Nigel said it was going to be hot today—I thought I'd dress for it."

Nigel came up beside her. "My dear, we'll be in the air-conditioned bus for several hours, you'll be dying from the cold. I'll run back to the room and get you a sweater."

"You're a doll, Nigel, but I brought a wrap in my bag," Lucinda said. She turned back to everyone. "Now, let's get this bore-fest started. I'd rather be spending two days getting spa treatments and having some fat sucked out of me, but I promised Nigel I'd come along. Let's go, shall we?"

Lucinda and Nigel walked arm in arm towards the van, with Elizabeth and Fred behind them talking in low tones.

"I don't think I've ever heard a more compelling speech from someone to go on a tour, have you?" Bernadette asked Chris.

Chris grinned. "No, I haven't, but I have a feeling there's a lot more to come from her in the next few days."

They entered the Mercedes minibus with eight rows of seats, two on each side. The bus was tall enough they could stand up in it. The driver took their luggage and put it into the back; they carried their backpacks inside.

Fred and Elizabeth took seats at the front near the driver. Bernadette and Chris sat behind them, Nigel and Lucinda sat across from them, with Nigel in the aisle seat across from Bernadette.

The driver introduced himself as Anand. He was small with a boyish face, dark hair, and dark eyes. He looked all of twenty but was probably older. His voice was deep with an accent that had him almost clip the end of a sentence when he spoke.

"I need to make sure we are all here for my records," Anand said. He produced his clipboard and began announcing the names. He checked off the Redstones, the Braithwaites, and Bernadette Callahan and Chris Christakos, which was hard for him to pronounce. Then he came to the Comptons.

"Are Ashley and George Compton still doing the tour or are they late?" Anand asked.

"No, they're dead," Lucinda announced in a loud voice. "Isn't that right, Bernadette?"

Anand looked from Lucinda to Bernadette. "I see... So not coming on the tour."

Elizabeth looked up at Anand. "So, sorry, we forgot to inform you of that."

Anand put his clipboard away. He got into the driver's seat, put the bus into gear, and started down the pier. Other buses were ahead of them. They crawled along the pier until they made their way to the main road, then began their journey.

Bernadette scrolled on the phone as the bus drove through the street. She'd received an email from Carla Winston, saying, "Call me, I have more information regarding Sea Island."

39

THE BUS LEFT the city behind with its new high-rises and gleaming shops. Anand explained the newfound riches of Sri Lanka. The war with the Tamil Tigers had ended, there was peace. In peace, the world came calling and liked what they saw on the large island sitting strategically off the south coast of India.

So did the tourists, thought Bernadette as she watched bus after bus loaded with tourists either pass them or go by in the other lane. By the time they arrived at the first site of the day, the throngs of tourists looked like someone had announced a two for one sale at Walmart. Massive coaches lined the entrance.

Anand opened the door and announced they were stopping at Dumballa Buddhist Temple for a trip to the toilets and if they wished to see the Temple of the Buddha.

"If you will please follow me, I will get you tickets and escort you to a guide. The stop here will be one hour only," Anand said with both his palms pressed together in front of him.

"I am not getting out," Lucinda moaned from her seat. "I

don't need to pee, and I don't need to see no Buddha. I'm a God-fearing Christian, so there." She pulled her shawl around her and slumped down in her seat.

"God help us all," Elizabeth said as she headed out the door of the bus.

Bernadette came out of the bus behind Chris. "You go on ahead. I'm going to see if I can make a phone call to Winston. She asked me to call her regarding some information."

Chris followed the others to the entrance while Bernadette dialed the number. She had only two bars of reception. She hoped she had enough.

The phone rang several times. She got Carla Winston's voice mail. All she could do was leave a message. She looked at the time on the phone. It was noon in Sri Lanka. Pulling up a time converter on the web, she realized it was just past two in the morning in Boston. She'd have to wait until this evening when they reached the hotel to try again.

Thumbing through her messages, she saw one from Inspector Lee. He'd sent the CCTV video of Astrid with a woman outside the dive shop in Singapore in hopes someone on the ship could identify the person with her.

The screen on the cheap phone wasn't very good. Bernadette had to walk towards the entrance with the ticket booth to get into the shade to see the screen more clearly. The video showed Astrid walking out of the store, then a woman approached her. She was wearing a hat, keeping her head down, apparently aware she had to avoid the cameras. Waving at Astrid, she got her attention. Astrid followed her to a taxi and got in. The taxi drove off, the license plate wasn't in view.

Bernadette scrolled it back to run it again. This was a meeting by someone Astrid knew and trusted. There was something familiar about the woman. She'd seen that frame, that walk. She was good at identifying traits of people. It was her business to notice. But who was she?

Chris came over with a ticket for her. "You contact Winston?"

"No, I'll call her tonight. It's two a.m. there. But there's something else. Lee sent me the CCTV video from the dive shop in Singapore where Astrid was last seen."

"Anything of interest?"

"Yeah, but I need to review the video a bunch more times to place this person. I've sure I've seen her on the ship."

"You see her face?"

"No, I saw her walk."

Chris shook his head. "You never cease to amaze me. Let's catch up with the group. Remember, you're supposed to be looking out for Elizabeth. You can't do it from outside this fence."

They wandered around the site. Nigel and Fred stuck together, looking over the site and speaking in quiet tones. They seemed to commiserate over their friend George. Elizabeth stuck close to Bernadette and Chris and hung on every word of the guide. They learned everything about the Buddha and the temple before heading back to the bus.

Bernadette wanted to stop to view the video on the phone, then realized the battery was getting too low. The charger was in the bus inside her backpack.

Anand opened the door of the bus; he'd kept it running to keep the AC on with Lucinda inside. They walked into the bus to find Lucinda gone.

Nigel was furious. "Where did she go? I told her to stay here."

"I will go find her," Anand said. "Please wait here, no one leave. I will see if she has gone to the toilet or the vendors."

He turned to leave just as Lucinda showed up with a bag full of souvenirs.

"You scared me half to death," Nigel said. "You never told me were going to leave the bus."

"Well, I got bored, now didn't I," Lucinda said with a pout. "But look at all the trinkets I got for next to nothing. You just got to bargain with the natives, and you get what you want."

"These people are not natives, they are local people, Lucinda. And, they're trying to earn a living.' Nigel said. 'Now, get on the damn bus."

The rest of them got back on the bus. Anand started the bus and moved out of the parking lot and back on the road.

Nigel turned to Bernadette. "You know, I really haven't thanked you for what you tried to do for Ashley. I was there, I saw how you put yourself in harm's way for her. Fred told me how you saved Elizabeth and him on the island. You're a very brave woman, I thank you for that."

"Thanks, Nigel," Bernadette said.

Lucinda leaned across Nigel. "He's just hoping you'll attempt to save him somehow and show him your titties like you did for Fred and the natives. I'm sure you gave these old boys erections for the next week." She resumed her position against the window.

"I... I apologize for my wife. She can be crass," Nigel said.

"Yes, she can," Bernadette agreed. She plugged her phone into the charger and tried to watch the video again. The bus started moving. She lost the signal on the video. She'd have to wait until they got a better signal to see Astrid's killer.

40

THEY ARRIVED at Lion Rock at two in the afternoon. Tourist buses were already leaving the site. Anand told them they would tour the rock early in the morning. This afternoon, there was a tour of an elephant sanctuary or some mountain biking for the adventurous types.

Anand drove them to a small boutique hotel within sight of the rock. It surrounded a long and inviting lap pool with lounge chairs and open-air dining. The rooms were cabins in teak wood with grass roofs. The rooms were elegant with a clawfoot tub, glass shower and king size bed. A large patio deck with chairs and tables led onto the grounds. Bernadette could have walked into the room, closed the door, and gone into hibernation for the rest of the day. But the group was calling.

"Are you sure you don't want to go off mountain biking?" Bernadette asked Chris. "I'm certain I can handle this small group and some baby elephants."

Chris took a bottle of water out of the mini bar. "I know you're up for it, but I said I'd have your back, and that's what I'll do. Besides, Anand said the elephant thing would be only an hour. We'll be back at around three thirty, which gives me plenty of time to do a spin around the resort before dinner."

"No idea how I landed such a great guy like you," Bernadette said as she kissed him on the lips.

"Total luck on your part, and you picked a bunch of losers before me..."

"I will use you for some karate training later for that comment."

"Sure, as long as you take me to the mat—I could enjoy some of your grappling maneuvers," Chris said with a smirk.

They grabbed a backpack, her phone, and some water and headed out the door. Bernadette looked back at the lovely room with longing, shut the door, then followed Chris to the bus.

The group were already on board. Elizabeth was chatting with Anand about the elephants and how they'd arrived there, Lucinda was looking bored. Nigel stared off into space. He seemed more distant after his harsh words to Lucinda.

Bernadette hoped the two of them wouldn't have any more arguments on the trip. But having seen Lucinda's crass behavior, it might not be possible.

The bus drove on a dusty road for ten minutes, pulling into an archway with an elephant motif and wording in both Indian and English. Little elephants scampered about the paddocks following the bus.

Anand led them out of the bus, got them small snacks to feed the elephants, then led them inside the paddock. Baby elephants surrounded them.

"Oh look, they're adorable, and this one keeps touching my boobs," Lucinda said.

Bernadette and Chris had their own group of three come towards them. "They are amazing and adorable," Bernadette said as she waved their little trunks away from her chest. "And they have a fascination with breasts."

"Must be juvenile male elephants," Chris said with a wink.

"I'll bet you they don't grow out of it, just like men," Bernadette said.

"I'm saying nothing," Chris said.

The sanctuary keeper came over. "Hello, my name is Jabi, I'm in charge of these beauties. I hope they are behaving." Jabi was a slim young woman with dark hair and thick eyebrows over dark eyes. She wore a brown uniform of shirt and shorts with a baby elephant logo on it.

"They are so cute," Lucinda said. "I'd love to have one back home. Could I have one of these?" She looked at Nigel with wide eyes and a pouty mouth.

"I'm afraid not, my love, they grow far too big in time, don't they...?" Nigel looked at Jabi for help.

"Oh, yes, this baby is now one hundred and twenty kilos, and already a meter tall. In five years, he will be over four meters and weigh six thousand kilos," Jabi said.

"That's an awful lot of poop to pick up, Lucinda," Elizabeth cautioned.

"But they are just so beautiful," Lucinda said. "What happened to their mothers?"

"Poachers kill the mothers and the big bulls to use their parts for medicines to send to China," Jabi said with a catch in her voice. She'd must have given this same speech many times, but it was clear it bothered her.

Lucinda massaged the little baby's head and fondled its trunk. A tear formed at her eye. "I find it hard to believe that people would kill these wonderful animals."

Anand came forward. "Please, we must see the main elephant house and then be on our way." He motioned for them to follow him.

Bernadette stood by Chris and held him back. "Did you hear that?"

"Hear what?"

"Lucinda. Her voice totally changed. It became elegant. Her crass twangy diction left her," Bernadette said.

"Maybe she fell in love with the little elephant. Things like that can change people."

"Hmm, I've got a feeling she's hiding something," Bernadette said.

They wandered with the group, first to the big elephant house where the older three to five-year-olds were, then to an exhibit of what was being done to elephants by poachers killing them and sending hides and ears to the far east to use for strange medicines.

Bernadette was walking ahead of the rest of the group as they lingered over souvenirs and one last look at the paddock when her phone vibrated in her pocket.

She checked the number. It was Winston. "Hey, I'm glad we could finally figure out the time zones. This one day ahead is crazy."

"Where are you now?" Winston asked.

"I'm in Sri Lanka at an elephant sanctuary," Bernadette replied.

"Is the hotel you're staying at nice?"

"Too nice, I should be there in a half hour with a cocktail."

"Do you have time to talk?"

"We're rounding everyone up to get back on the bus. We can talk awhile, what's up?"

"I started searching all the names you gave me to look at, the one I did last was Holly Marsden."

"Anything interesting?"

"Yeah, she did a short stint at the Cloister's Resort on Sea Island."

"Same time as Charlotte Bowman?"

"Same dates. I called the hotel to confirm their employment records," Winston said.

Bernadette looked behind her. The rest of them were walking towards the bus. "I received video footage of Astrid being lured away by someone in Singapore. I wondered where I'd seen that figure and walk—Holly Marsden fits the bill. She joined the ship in Singapore. So did Astrid. They would have stayed at the same hotel. Marsden could have hidden Bowman in her room until it was time for her to assume Astrid's identity on the ship."

"Astrid would know Marsden was from the ship, her picture would be on the ship's roster, she'd take a ride with her, no questions asked." Winston said.

"Yes, and Marsden had access to all the files on the ship and passes. She had to be the one to delete the security records to get Bowman on the ship late at night."

"When are you due back at your ship?"

"Tomorrow, late afternoon."

"Are you going to call the ship, or do you want me to do it, as the official FBI. That might put them in motion."

"Sure, contact Cynthia McCabe, maybe tell her to monitor Marsden. I'm going to see what plays out here. I'm still not convinced there's only one killer on board the ship. I've got four people here who are likely targets. I'd like to see who shows up to try to take them out."

"That's an interesting game you're playing. I hope you can do it without getting yourselves killed," Winston said.

Bernadette saw the others approaching the bus. "Thanks for calling and catching up with work. I'm sure you have everything taken care of. Bye for now." She turned and clicked off her phone.

Elizabeth looked at her. "The nerve of your police force to call you while you're on vacation. Some people have no class."

Bernadette shrugged. "Sometimes they just have to get my take on things. Our criminal element never takes a holiday... well, they do when we put them in jail. But sometimes it's just not long enough."

She boarded the bus with Chris; they sat in the back.

"That wasn't work, was it?" Chris asked.

"No, I have an update on some of our players. I'll tell you about it back at the lodge."

Anand put the bus in gear and headed back to the lodge.

41

BERNADETTE FILLED Chris in on the conversation with Winston and told him to go for a mountain bike ride. There was nothing to do about it until they got back to the ship. She decided to take a swim in the pool that lay inviting like a big patch of liquid blue in the green forest that surrounded it.

She'd brought along a speedo swimsuit for that very purpose after viewing the lodge's pool online before leaving the ship. Swimming was something she loved but had so little opportunity back home. Their home in Red Deer, Canada, was on a fast-flowing river and the big Sylvan Lake was an hour away. Work and life got in the way.

Putting on her one-piece suit with the racer back and her swim goggles, she headed out the door for the pool. The light was fading. Stars were appearing in the southern sky with a chorus of birds welcoming the dark and the release from the baking sun.

The pool area was empty. People were congregating at the bar near the restaurant. Loud voices punctuated by a cocktail blender wafted toward her as she put on her goggles and slipped into the pool.

The water was the temperature of a warm bath. She pushed off the side of the pool and did a breaststroke for a few lengths. Then she did the front crawl, her favorite. If you did it right, you could go for hours.

The timing had to be right, with the head dropping to the side at the exact angle to draw in air, then breathe out under water while the arms came underneath with hands cupped like small oars to propel one forward with the feet kicking like scissors. And the head was a major item. The head must be level, too high it dragged, too low, you sank.

These were the words she remembered from a swim coach at university where she studied law enforcement in Canada. Her coach was Maryna Kubler, a tall lady in her fifties with a mop of curly blonde hair, bad skin, and a thick German accent that admonished everyone with a compliment, "Yah, not bad, could be better—back in the pool."

Bernadette happened upon the university team late one night when she was having the ultimate misgivings about her chosen field of law enforcement training. Most cops were a pain in the ass, too stodgy, too by the book. Did she really want to be one of those?

She ended up at the pool, watching women her age doing drills for hours. It was fascinating. Her swimming experience had been lakes in Northern Canada. You didn't jump into a northern lake until late June, otherwise you'd die from hyperthermia. By August, everyone was in, the nights were warm; the water was cool, but it didn't chill you immediately. Such a blessing.

Maryna had wandered over to her with the question, "You swim?"

"Yes, I can swim," Bernadette had said.

"You put on suit—show me."

Bernadette had tried to blow her off. "I don't have a suit."

"Ya, we have many." She'd yelled to a girl in the pool. "Linda, get this girl a suit. Now."

Linda had shot out of the pool like a dolphin, took Bernadette to the change room, found her a swimsuit and goggles. She was cornered.

She came out of the change room into the pool area. The others were treading water, waiting for the newbie to hit the lanes. This was obviously a rite of passage many of them had faced.

Bernadette dove into the water and began the smooth strokes of the Australian crawl her friends had taught her. It was a head up, side to side with all breathing above water. The Aussie lifeguards developed it to swim out to save swimmers in distress. Keeping their heads above the water gave them visual contact with their target.

She did two laps of the pool, stopped and pulled herself out of the water to see the legs of Maryna standing over her.

"Ya, you are a powerful swimmer. Good muscles, but your technique is shit. You want to learn. I teach you. Come back tomorrow. Training starts at sixteen hundred hours."

Bernadette was hooked. She'd trained with the team for the next year. Went to the finals against other universities and won a bronze in the butterfly and a gold in the team relay.

Swimming saved her from the doubts of her chosen career, a breakup with a dickhead boyfriend, and kept her focused.

Now, she relaxed into long smooth strokes with easy kicks. Her Timex lap watch told her she'd already done sixty-eight laps. The pool was Olympic size at fifty meters, which meant she'd done a mile. She felt good.

She swam back to the pool edge and pulled herself out. A towel appeared in front of her, but she couldn't see who was behind it.

42

LUCINDA STOOD behind the towel with a martini glass in her hand. "I thought you'd be in that pool forever."

"Thanks for the towel, Lucinda," Bernadette said. She looked around. There was no one else at the pool. The place was now close to pitch black.

"You probably wonder why I'm here, huh?" Lucinda asked.

"Yeah maybe. I can't deny you've been a bit off me for... the entire cruise." Bernadette said.

"Come and sit. I brought you a martini," Lucinda said.

Bernadette toweled herself off, wrapped the towel around her waist and followed Lucinda to a table with two chairs and a martini glass.

"Sorry, it might be warm. I've been here for a while, just watching you go back and forth and back and forth—you plumb tired me out," Lucinda said. "You're one hell of a swimmer. Were you in the Olympics or something?"

"No, just the university swim team," Bernadette said. She sipped the martini, it tasted mostly of Vodka. She had to take a breath after her first sip.

"That might be strong. I told the bartender to make it a triple. I doubted if they had service out here."

Bernadette waited until her breath came back. "Thank you. This is great." She met Lucinda's gaze. "So, what's on your mind?"

Lucinda looked up at the stars and took another sip of her drink. Bernadette waited for her. Her skill as an investigator was waiting for the other person to speak.

"I need to talk to you about something," Lucinda said. Her voice was quiet. It had lost the brassy edge.

"Sure, what about?"

"I received a warning from Ashley's lawyer that someone may be out to kill me," Lucinda said. Her eyes showed it all to Bernadette. There was genuine fear.

Bernadette put the martini down. "Why are you coming to me about this? I understand from ship's security you think I had something to do with Ashley's death, and we haven't exactly been best of friends on this cruise."

"Sorry, my bad, just my act. It gets away on me sometimes," Lucinda said. "I figured if I threw enough aspersions at you and everyone around me, someone might take me seriously."

Bernadette nodded her head. "Okay, strange tactic. Why do you think someone is out to kill you?"

"Well, the why is obvious. Ashley left me as the sole heir in her will. She had no real friends or decent relatives who kept in touch with her. I was her only friend, and I must admit, what we had in common was our pursuit of men and marriage for money," Lucinda said.

Bernadette said nothing. The night birds were the only noise.

"Okay, I see that look in your eyes. You might think poorly of me, but listen, I was a graduate of Columbia

University with a degree in psychology. I was on a good career path until I fell in love with a man who jerked me around. That bastard took my heart and my money. I swore that would never happen again."

"So, you teamed up with Ashley, and developed that backwoods country drawl, is that it?" Bernadette asked. The light was leaving the sky, a bright moon appeared to light up the pool area.

"You are good, I'll give you that," Lucinda said. She looked up at the moon, then back at Bernadette. "I left the world of psychology in Atlanta and moved to Sea Island to get into real estate. I did okay. Then I met another man who treated me like a queen and got me investing in all kinds of beachfront properties. You can guess what happened." Her voice had changed to a sophisticated southern lady.

"Did he leave you with anything?"

Lucinda made a low chuckling noise. "Yes, he certainly did. A stack of bills and several foreclosures. The bastard took all my cash and ran. It took me two years to get my finances in order. That's when I met Ashley."

"Was that on Sea Island?"

"Yes, it was, she ran a mani-pedi place that did relaxation massage. Her place was a sanctuary during my troubles. I unloaded on her. She told me how she handled men. She'd been married five times—walking away with most of the money every time."

"And she showed you her techniques?" Bernadette asked.

"Oh yeah, she was good. I became a manicurist and masseuse right along with her. She told me to hide my intellect and change the way I spoke to catch a man. She had an in with the Cloister Hotel to send us well-heeled men. My God, we did well."

"Is that when you met George and Nigel?" Bernadette asked as she shifted only slightly in her chair. The dots connected, Holly Marsden and Charlotte were both from Sea island.

"Yeah, they were on some kind of company retreat or whatever. We had the concierge there tell all the older gentlemen that we were the best place to go on the island with wonderful service. We gave them smiles and cleavage. The old boys always loved it, gave us great tips, and we had dates by the dozens. I had three marriage proposals inside of six months. But I ran a financial report on every man who asked me to marry him—no way was I getting taken again," Lucinda said.

Bernadette shook her head in awe "How did it work for you?"

"I went through two marriages in eighteen months. Did damn well in each one. Netted myself about five hundred thousand in each. But I thought Nigel would be my biggest score ever."

"There was a problem?" Bernadette asked. She already knew Nigel and the rest of them were in financial difficulties.

Lucinda dropped her head into her hands. "Why didn't I see it? The flashy watches, the expensive cars. Most of the men I chose were just these modest rich guys, I went for the big score. Nigel told me how loaded they all were. I even stalked him back to San Francisco, made love to him in a classy hotel where one of his old friends saw us."

"That you orchestrated, I assume?"

"I learned from Ashley, the pro. I had Nigel right where I wanted him. He hadn't had good sex in a while, or probably ever with what I had to teach him. But his wife divorced him when she found out, and I got him," Lucinda said with the arch of her eyebrow Bernadette could see in the moonlight.

Bernadette took another small sip of her drink, placing it on the table. The people at the bar were leaving now, heading off for dinner. She was waiting for Lucinda to tell her about the threat. The background on Sea Island was more than she hoped for.

"You haven't told me why you think your life is in danger," Bernadette said.

Lucinda looked at her empty martini glass with despair, then up at Bernadette. "Ashley's lawyer told me it's all about the insurance that New Wave Technologies carried. The company insured George, that in case of his death, the insurance would pay Ashley his full shares. She left me as her sole heir. I'm set to inherit one hundred million. There's no one, including Nigel, who wants that to happen. Don't you see, they'll be hiring someone to kill me. Then the shares go back to Nigel and the Redstones."

"I'm sure many wealthy people have a target on their back when they come into a windfall. But you'd need more than Ashley's lawyer's speculation," Bernadette said.

"Then you'll do nothing to protect me?" Lucinda said, rising out of her chair.

Bernadette sat back in her chair. "There's not much I can do other than to tell you to stay close to me. I'm willing to watch out for you. But you need to be careful. Once you're back on the ship, I suggest you confine yourself to your room."

"But it could be Nigel who's trying to kill me," Lucinda protested.

Bernadette stood up. "He could have done it anytime in the past few days, during the shark feeding or the cyclone.

He's had lots of opportunity, and here you are, still standing."

Bernadette waited for a reply. Lucinda stood there. Something caught her eye.

"Oh, no..." Lucinda said in a low whisper.

43

BERNADETTE TURNED to follow Lucinda's gaze. Two men were approaching from the trees. They wore black, with something in their hands. These were not hotel staff or maintenance men. Bernadette could see the determined stride of men who meant them harm.

They came up quickly. Stopping only a meter from them. They were locals, brown skinned, dark eyes that darted over the women. One held a gun, the other a machete.

"Give us your money," the one with the gun said.

"We have no money," Bernadette replied. She said it quietly with her hands raised slightly, palms facing out. She wanted to put the men at ease. The 'don't hurt me' posture and also the attack position for Goju Ryu Karate. It would only work if the man came in closer with the gun.

"Jewels, give us your jewels," the man with the gun commanded. He waved the gun at them. In the moonlight it looked to Bernadette like an old 22 caliber. Not as deadly as a 9-millimeter, but it could put a hole in a person just the same.

Lucinda grasped at her necklace. "This has diamond clusters, it's worth over twenty thousand dollars."

"Lucinda, the bullet this man will put in you isn't worth the necklace. Give him the damn thing and he'll leave," Bernadette said.

"Alright, I'll give him the damn thing." Lucinda took her pendant off, throwing it to the man with the gun. He smiled and looked at his friend.

The man with the machete looked the women up and down. "Now take off all your clothes."

"Okay, now he's pissing me off," Bernadette said.

"I thought it wasn't worth the bullet," Lucinda said.

"He doesn't want the clothes, he just a little pervert and wants a peep show."

"I'll give him a peep show," Lucinda said. She lifted her hands up to drop the straps on her dress.

Something flew overhead. It was long. It wriggled. Two snakes wrapped themselves around the men. The men screamed. Throwing the snakes off, they ran for the forest.

Chris came running from the forest. "Are you both okay?"

Bernadette looked at Chris, then down to the snakes wriggling away as fast as they could. They wanted no part of this.

"Nice save. How long have you been watching?" Bernadette asked.

"I came up a few minutes ago. I saw those guys hanging in the trees, so I circled around. When I saw them approach, I could see it was a robbery. The only thing I could think of to help was two rat snakes I saw crawling on the ground. When I heard the guy tell you to take your clothes off, this went beyond a robbery."

"Chris is right," Bernadette said. "The guy with the

machete was going all crazy eyes. I would've had to deal with both of them if Chris hadn't intervened."

Lucinda focused her eyes on Bernadette. "You see what I mean? They sent those men to kill me. I'm grateful you were here to stop them."

Bernadette looked from Chris to Lucinda. "If they'd wanted to kill you, they would have shot us both and taken your diamond pendant. Hired killers kill first, it's kind of their mode of operation as we say in the police world."

"I don't care what you say. I know hired killers when I see them. I'm going to look for my necklace, I think the guy dropped it while he was running away," Lucinda said.

Chris raised his eyebrows. The look he gave Bernadette said it all. Lucinda was a little drunk or a lot crazy.

Lucinda, using a light from her cellphone, walked off into the grass, seemingly unafraid of the other snakes that might be there.

"We might as well help her," Chris said. He turned on the light of his own cell phone to aid in the search.

"I found it," Lucinda yelled out with joy. "That little jerk dropped it right beyond the pool. How about that?" She dropped to her knees and put her handbag on the ground. She got up and came back into the pool area with the necklace in her hands.

Chris nodded to Lucinda. "Great, let's head back to the dining area. Those two might want to come back for a rematch when they realize they were scared off by two rat snakes and not some vipers that could do them serious harm."

They walked back into the restaurant. The people at dinner looked at them with only mild interest. No one had heard anything. Glasses and tableware clinked and clattered as they enjoyed their meal.

"I'm starving, how about you?" Bernadette asked.

"Yeah, hurling snakes and saving damsels in distress always gives me an appetite," Chris said with a deadpan tone. "But don't you think we need to report this to the resort?"

Bernadette put her hand to her head. "Yes, I'm in a bit of a state with having a gun pointed at me and snakes thrown over my head."

They went to the front desk and tried to report the incident to the girl at the front desk. She said the manager was in town that evening, she would phone him, and he would have the police come out the next day to take a statement.

"I guess that's it then. You almost got robbed and possibly raped, and the police might be by in the morning to take your statement. Doesn't that sound like something we did in our own police force?" Chris said.

"Yes, too many times," Bernadette agreed. "So many times, we're too overwhelmed with the wave of cases you can't respond quick enough. I've been on the receiving end of people getting upset when I couldn't report fast enough to a robbery."

They went to their bungalow, showered, and changed. Bernadette checked her phone. Her face went into a frown.

"What is it?" Chris asked.

"I just received a text from Cynthia. They've been looking for Holly Marsden. She left the ship at nine this morning. Marsden said she'd be back for a meeting. She hasn't returned."

"Have they tried to contact her by phone?"

"Her phone goes to voice mail. They've contacted Colombo police and are trying to get the local cell provider to ping her phone," Bernadette said.

"Are they worried about her?"

"According to Cynthia, Holly has never been late for any meeting and always returns phone calls."

"You think your suspect Marsden is making a run for it or someone took her out?" Chris asked.

"Yeah, I do. The dots are aligning from the Cloister Hotel to our ship. Whoever took out Charlotte Bowman might have done the same thing here in Colombo. If Marsden is alive and making a run to the airport, then she might be the killer," Bernadette said as she put her cell phone into her handbag.

They walked out of the bungalow. The night air had a fragrance of flowers. Birds provided a chorus of sound in the jungle. The only thing Bernadette could think about at this moment was the whereabouts of Marsden. She put her phone on vibrate, hoping she'd get an update from Cynthia that evening.

44

THE DINNER PAVILION had no walls. Teak columns supported a pitched roof of thatched palm leaves. A phalanx of fans blew air down on the diners. Small birds rested in the ceiling, flying down to feast on crumbs.

Bernadette could see this place set up for explorers and adventurers to share stories and travels. The tables were set for fours and twos. Some diners had pulled tables together. They joined in noisy laughter over the stories a lady told in Italian.

They found the Redstones deep into martinis with the Braithwaites not far behind. Lucinda looked like she was leading the charge of first to be drunk. With her elbows placed squarely on the table, she was providing a complete version of the exploits by the pool.

Elizabeth saw Bernadette and Chris enter the room. "We wondered when you'd show up. Lucinda's been telling us how you chased those thieves off with snakes. How amazing."

Lucinda leaned into the table. "I was about to show those two boys my titties. Might have taken them by surprise—a damn sight bigger than Ms. Bernadette's here."

Bernadette noticed Lucinda had dropped back into the charade of her accent. Gone was her refined diction by the pool.

Elizabeth smiled at her. "Yes, Lucinda, you've told us that several times tonight, but I believe we can let Chris tell the story as he's the one that scared those two awful men away."

A young lady in a sari came by to take their drink orders. Chris ordered a beer and Bernadette asked for a white wine. The one martini from Lucinda had been enough.

"Not much to tell. I saw those two rat snakes, grabbed them and threw them," Chris said.

"How did you know the snakes weren't venomous?" Nigel asked.

"I saw they had round heads, not flat ones. The flat ones mean you have a venomous snake, the round—you're pretty much okay, except for two banded snakes. But, other than that, you're fine."

Lucinda looked across the table at Chris. "Well, aren't you just one big hunk of cutie pie snake charmer. Don't you think so, Elizabeth?"

Elizabeth looked annoyed. "I don't think those two definitions go together, Lucinda."

"I'll take it as a compliment," Chris said. "As I'm studying to be a wildlife officer back in Canada, the information about snakes comes in handy."

The server brought their drinks and menus.

Elizabeth looked over the menu. "I don't have a clue what to order off this menu. You're the amateur chef, Chris, do you have any suggestions?"

Chris looked up with a grin. "I've been looking at websites for Sri Lankan cuisine. They do southern Indian food like no one else. If you're ready for a little adventure, I'm happy to order."

"Just don't order no stuff that's still wriggling on the plate," Lucinda said. "I saw that in Hong Kong and it made me want to hurl."

"No problem, they cook everything on this menu," Chris said.

The server came over to Chris. He ordered several curried fish dishes with rice, some dahl, which is a bean dish, a jackfruit curry and a few green salads to absorb the heat and the local breads of roti and chapattis.

He turned to Bernadette. "You'll want to switch to beer for dinner, there could be some heat."

"I just hope it doesn't burn twice, if you know what I mean," Lucinda said. She picked up her martini and almost missed her mouth as she took a sip.

Bernadette eyed the table. This felt like a good time to begin a casual conversation to see where it would lead. Nigel seemed like a good place to start.

She sipped her wine, placed it on the table and began slowly, "Nigel, Lucinda tells me you met on Sea Island in Georgia. I've never really heard much about the place. Do you recommend it?"

Nigel lifted his head up from his drink. He stared over at Elizabeth first, then to Fred. He cleared his throat. "It's a nice place, kind of pricey. There's some good golf courses there I've heard, but I never play much so couldn't give my opinion."

"Where would you recommend staying?"

Nigel shot a glance at Elizabeth. She was watching him, as if every word that came from his mouth was being weighed and measured by her.

"Oh, well, there are a lot of places. I expect an Airbnb or

that VRBO website might find you something nice," Nigel said. He looked back at Elizabeth. She threw him a slight nod. He'd done well.

"Oh, really, what about the Cloisters?" Bernadette asked in a low tone.

"The Cloisters?" Nigel asked with a frown. "I'm not sure..."

Lucinda rapped Nigel on the hand. "Oh don't play act, Nigel. I told Bernadette all about the Cloisters. That's how you and I met. You told me how all of you from New Wave went there to have your board meetings and then play golf and get very drunk."

"Oh, the Cloisters—I'm sorry I think I heard you ask about something different. Must be my hearing," Nigel said.

Bernadette could see the disgusted look Elizabeth shot towards Lucinda, then to Nigel. The subject was open. Now she needed to see how far she could push it.

The food arrived and the diners filled their plates with a myriad of delicacies. Bernadette felt famished from her long swim and the events by the pool. She ordered a beer as the curry had some kick that seemed to develop a slow burn in her mouth and unfold into extra heat as it descended her throat. She loved it.

The talk at the table began turning to the food, the differences in curries and heat, and the events of the next day. Bernadette waited until dinner was almost over before she began again.

She dabbed the cloth napkin to her lips and looked at Nigel and Elizabeth. "I wonder if you ran into Holly Marsden on our ship. Did you know she once worked at the Cloister Hotel?"

"Holly... What was the last name?" Nigel asked.

"Marsden," Bernadette replied, taking a sip of her beer.

She looked down at the table as if she wasn't too interested in the answer.

Nigel looked up to the ceiling, then towards Elizabeth. She looked away as if to say he was on his own on this one. "I don't recall that name."

Lucinda broke into a long throaty laugh. "Oh, Nigel, you're such a twit. Holly was the one that always got you guys the good tee times at the golf course. She worked at the front desk, then took over as concierge. You thought she was the total package. I think you told me about five times how smart she was."

Nigel put his glass down. He looked at Lucinda and back to Bernadette. "You must forgive me, I'm getting older and my memory is failing me. Obviously, Lucinda remembers a lot more about my likes and dislikes than I do." He shrugged. "Yes, it seems I knew Holly Marsden. You say she's on our ship? I don't recall seeing her. But then, it seems I don't recall a lot." His face seemed to go into total resignation about either his memory or his lack of tact in putting forth his thoughts.

"We all remember Ms. Marsden from the hotel," Elizabeth said. "She was quite a pleasant Lady. We must give our regards when we get back to the ship."

Bernadette waited a moment to let the conversation hit the lull, the exact pause she wanted. "Holly Marsden is missing from the ship since this morning."

Elizabeth almost raised her hand to her mouth and stopped herself. "Oh, I wonder what could have happened to her? I hope she's alright."

"I received a text from the ship. They have the police searching for her," Bernadette said. She let her eyes wander from Nigel to Fred and then rest on Elizabeth. They all seemed to find something of interest on the table.

Lucinda waved the server over to get another drink and looked at Nigel. "I hope Marsden is okay. She was so nice to me. I find it odd I never ran into her on the ship. She got me hooked up with a Mr. Beaupre, the concierge who sent me all my clients from the hotel."

The server came to the table, and Lucinda ordered another martini. Nigel scowled with his disapproval of her ordering more alcohol but said nothing.

Lucinda leaned forward and whispered, "Now, Mr. Beaupre, he was a character. Dressed in white suits all the time and sat there behind his desk in the hotel's lobby as if he was the lord of all he surveyed. He had a southern accent, but we locals knew he was from Maine. But they loved him all the same. None of us knew his sexual preference. Hell, we didn't care, but we miss him." She wiped away a small tear.

"Did something happen to him?" Chris asked.

"A gator got him on Saint Simon's Island. We heard he was skinny dipping late one night with his friend and, well, no need to fill in the details—he's gone just like that."

The server brought Lucinda a fresh martini, and she lifted it to her lips. "Here's to avoiding the gators." She sipped her drink and began giggling at her own joke.

"I think we should turn in for the night, Lucinda," Nigel said. "We have an early start tomorrow and you'll want some rest for our climb."

"What climb? I ain't doing no climb tomorrow. You think I'm going up a big rock so one of you can throw me off to make it look like an accident? What the hell kind of rube do you take me for?" Lucinda asked. She finished her drink, slamming the glass on the table. Her eyes flashed defiance.

Elizabeth cleared her throat. "Now, Lucinda, you're imagining things, no one here is trying to harm you."

"Really? Is that your story? How do you think George and Ashley would take that? Not very well—because they're both dead. Don't tell me they died by coincidence. None of you believe it either. And don't tell me those two men at the pool was a fluke, hell no, you know it's not true. You're as shit scared as I am. Admit it."

Other diners looked around. The restaurant went quiet.

Elizabeth focused her eyes on Lucinda. "My dear, the reason I asked Bernadette and her husband on this trip is they offered to provide us protection, to look out for us."

"You got guns?" Lucinda asked, turning to Bernadette.

"No," Bernadette replied, "neither of us have a gun or wish to."

"Then what good are you? You expect to find another snake to hurl at somebody that comes after us, is that it?" Lucinda asked, placing her hand on her chin to prop herself up.

"We'll be walking around in broad daylight," Nigel said. "No one tried to approach us at the temple today. You notice they have police everywhere. We'll be fine."

Lucinda pushed herself up from the table. She wobbled, then steadied herself. "Well, I'll be sleeping with one eye open." She threw a one-handed salute to Bernadette and headed for the exit with a walk that weaved from side to side.

Nigel got up. "My apologies, she's been under much stress with the death of Ashley and those two men accosting her tonight. I'll make sure she gets to bed."

Elizabeth watched Nigel hurry out after Lucinda, then turned to Bernadette and Chris. "I doubt if she's going to sleep with one eye open tonight. We must see what kind of shape she's in tomorrow. Again, I apologize for her behavior.

I've covered your hotel bill and our trip. It's the least we can do for what you've been through with our rude companion."

"You didn't have to do that," Bernadette protested.

Elizabeth raised her hand. "No, please, this will make Fred and me feel better about everything we've put you through. This is your honeymoon trip, and it has turned into you being chaperones for us." She dropped her napkin on the table. "Now, if you'll excuse us, Fred and I will turn in for the night. We look forward to our little adventure tomorrow."

Fred stood up, drew back Elizabeth's chair, and they made their way out of the restaurant. Bernadette sat with Chris, nursing their beers as the rest of the diners left the building.

Chris finished his beer and looked at Bernadette. "You want to take a quick spin around the resort to check the security, don't you?"

"You know me too well," Bernadette said with a smile. "We'll call it our evening walk."

They wandered down the path that led from the main reception to the guest huts, then to the front gate. An older man stood guard with a Lee-Enfield Jungle Carbine from World War II. He cradled the gun in his arms while smoking a cigarette. He smiled at them as they walked by.

"Well, there's the extent of the resort's security," Chris said. "If anyone wants to come here by vehicle, they've got it covered. For bad guys who want to walk in out of the forest like they did at the pool, it's open season."

They headed back to their cabin and noticed the lights were on in the Redstone's room.

45

BERNADETTE CHECKED the door of their room. It had an old door lock that a burglar could open with a butter knife. She'd seen many home break-ins where the thief pushed the butter knife into the doorjamb, wiggled it, and defeated the single pin on the doorknob inside of thirty seconds.

She went into the bathroom, found a towel, rolled it up into a rope and placed it under the bottom of the door with a rug in front of it. About as effective as you could get for a MacGyver fix. She smiled, went into the bathroom and slipped off her clothes.

The night felt hot with a humid edge to it. She took her third cool shower of the day and went into the bedroom. Chris was lying there, looking at a brochure of the sights. He instantly noticed her.

"Don't get any ideas, big guy, I'm sleeping nude because it's so damn hot. This air conditioning makes the room feel like a cheap sauna," Bernadette said as she climbed into bed. She threw off all the covers, lying there in the nude to let the ceiling fan cool her.

Chris leaned over with the brochure to fan her. "Does this help?"

"Yes, it does, and you're getting me excited—so stop it."

"Maybe you need to heat up, so then you can cool down," Chris said in a soft voice.

"Oh God, you're such a bastard—a handsome and sexy one, but in this heat, there's no way I'm going to bounce on you. Go to sleep."

She turned the light off and listened to the night sounds. Birds, crickets, and monkeys set up a chorus of sound. The noise seemed to fill her brain. Then, the wall of noise lulled her into slumber until her eyes grew so heavy, she couldn't keep them open.

Strange dreams of men coming out the forest with guns and machetes clouded her subconsciousness. The men wore broad smiles. Then the smiles became evil.

Just as the forest seemed to teem with the evil men—she heard a scream. She bolted upright in bed.

The scream sounded again. All other noises in the night stopped.

Bernadette pounded Chris on the arm. "Wake up, Chris, I heard a scream—it sounded like a woman."

Chris opened his eyes, threw off his covers, and jumped out of bed. He stood in the center of the room, listening. The scream came again.

Chris shook his head and turned to Bernadette. "That's the cry of a devil bird I told you about. The locals say it sounds just like a woman's scream. It's actually an owl."

"And you know all this how?"

"It was the info session on the boat. I mentioned it to you earlier," Chris said. He climbed back into bed and caressed her shoulder. "Now, get some sleep. Try to think of the bird as a serenade to the night."

"To the night of the damned?" Bernadette asked.

The bird screeched again. This time, she could tell it was a bird. She lay there in the dark listening to it. It reminded her of the first time she'd heard a bobcat cry in the wilderness in northern Canada; she'd thought it sounded like a baby crying.

Sometime in the night she fell asleep. She never noticed someone trying to force the door to the room open. The butter knife defeated the lock—but not the rolled-up towel.

46

A BLINDING stream of sunlight hit Bernadette's eyes at six the next morning. They'd forgotten to close the blinds properly the night before. She got out of bed to close them. A policeman was standing outside the bungalow. She realized she was naked. Running to the bathroom, she found her t-shirt and a pair of shorts.

"Chris, we've got company," Bernadette yelled to his still snoring form.

"What's up?" Chris said, rising out of a sound sleep.

"There's a policeman standing outside our door. He must be here for our statement."

Chris looked at his watch on the night table. "Damn, that's early, even by Canadian standards. Give me a minute." He rolled out of bed and headed to the bathroom, did a quick rinse, and was back in two minutes dressed in shorts and t-shirt.

Bernadette went to the door and looked down. The towel had moved. "We had a visitor last night, sweetie."

"What do you mean?"

"I did an improvised door block last night."

Chris stared at the towel, then back to Bernadette. "So glad you're more paranoid than me. Saved our skins."

"We can report this to the police as part of their investigation. The resort might put in some real door locks and get some security," Bernadette said.

The policeman standing at the door was slim and tall with a trim cut mustache. His brown uniform freshly pressed, his boots highly polished, and the AK-47 machine gun he cradled in his arms shone brightly in the sun.

"Good morning, I am Constable Jay Singha. The manager asked me to come by early to take your statement regarding the attempted robbery last night," he said with a slight bow.

Bernadette bowed in return. "Yes, thank you for coming by. I'm Bernadette Callahan, this is my husband Christopher Christakos. I'm in the police force in Canada and my husband was in the force for many years."

"A pleasure to meet fellow officers," Jay Singha said. "I look forward to your observations in your statement. Please, may we meet with the other lady? I will have this done quickly so you may proceed with your vacation."

Bernadette walked down the steps of the bungalow's veranda. She cast a sideways glance to Chris. They'd both assumed they would have to drop into a local police station to make a statement. It would have been more for public duty to let others know there were thieves in the area than anything else.

They walked to Nigel and Lucinda's bungalow and found the door half open. Bernadette could already smell it. The perfume of death—the metallic smell of blood hit her as she climbed the stairs. She'd smelled enough of it in her years in the police force.

With the door open, the humid air had crawled in to

decompose whatever body lay inside. She turned to Chris. They looked at each other, took a deep breath, and pushed the door open.

Nigel lay sprawled across the bed—a gaping hole showed an angry black wound in his head. A small pool of dried blood stained a pillow.

The fan overhead made a ticking sound as it beat the air. The hair on Nigel's head blew slightly around the wound. One of his hands splayed onto the bed, the other across his chest. The television remote lay a short distance from his hand as if, had he'd been able to change the channel, this might not have happened to him.

Constable Jay Sinha stood there in shock. He finally said, "This is most terrible, most terrible. I must call the criminal investigation division at once."

"Yes, please do," Bernadette said. "But we must find his wife, Lucinda. Do you mind if I look in the bathroom, constable? I promise I will touch nothing."

The constable nodded his head in agreement. He wanted nothing to do with the murder scene. Bernadette was fine with his lack of involvement. She wanted to get a quick sense of what happened here. Sometimes first impressions were the best before all the CSI techs roamed over everything and covered the place in fingerprint dust.

She pushed the bathroom door open and found it empty. A full bathtub had a dull gray soap film on it. The tap dripped with a punctuating finality, letting the bather know it was over.

Scanning the floor, she saw no signs of blood. No struggle. Where had Lucinda gone? Bernadette walked out of the room. "There's no sign of Lucinda Braithwaite."

The bungalow next door opened; Elizabeth Redstone stepped out. "What's happening?"

Bernadette walked up to her, putting her hand on her shoulder. "It looks like someone shot Nigel—he's dead. Lucinda isn't in the room. Did you hear anything last night?"

Elizabeth put her hand to her forehead. "Oh my, no. I can't believe it... I didn't hear a thing. I slept with earplugs in because of all the jungle noise. What's happened to Lucinda?"

"We must make a search for her," the constable said. He took out his cell phone and began speaking in the local dialect. He turned back to them. "We will have a complete team from Colombo here in a few hours. Please wait in your room."

"Two hours is a long time, constable. We need to search for Lucinda now. The men who tried to rob us last night might have come back. They came out of the forest before. Maybe that's where they took her," Elizabeth said.

"You are right. Let us go. I will find some others to help us," the constable said.

In ten minutes, several men and women from the hotel were standing around Bernadette and Chris. The constable looked at them. "Where should we begin?"

"I'm thinking we head back towards the pool area," Elizabeth said.

"Why there?" Bernadette asked.

"It's the scene of the crime from last night. You scared off those guys last night. I have a feeling there's a revenge thing going on," Elizabeth said.

A man stood by the pool, skimming leaves with a net. The search team ran by him. The man looked up with mild interest and went back to his work.

They came to the edge of the pool where a thick green lawn disappeared into the dense forest. The leaves were dense. Palm fronds, leaves, and vines produced an almost impregnable wall of green foliage.

Bernadette stopped for a moment, trying to let her eyes adjust to the darkness within the deep jungle.

She saw a flash of white.

"There," Bernadette yelled. "She's in there."

47

FIVE MEN ARRIVED with machetes to hack into the dense undergrowth to get to Lucinda. Bernadette followed behind them as they made a path. Elizabeth and Fred stood by the pool wringing their hands and watching.

Chris picked up a spare machete. With mighty swings he helped them clear the path. In minutes they arrived at Lucinda. She was half naked with a bathrobe wrapped around her waist. Someone had tied her to a tree.

"Whoa, hold up, there's a green pit viper at her feet," Chris said. He cut a branch, put it on the ground, and moved the snake away.

Bernadette put her hand on Lucinda's neck. "No pulse, she's dead. I don't see any bullet wounds or blood. Did the snake kill her?"

Chris watched the green snake slither away. "That's not a big snake. I'm not sure how much venom they carry or how lethal they are, but snakes don't attack someone tied to a tree. You have to step on them to get them to bite."

Bernadette checked out the rope binding Lucinda to the tree. She took a picture of the knot, plus several more of

Lucinda's body. She did it quickly. As Constable Jay Singha arrived, she put the phone away.

"I must preserve this scene for CID, please, if you will return to the pool," the constable asked.

"Yes, constable," Bernadette said. They moved back to the pool where Elizabeth and Fred were waiting.

Elizabeth held her hands to her face. "Is she...?"

"Yes, she's dead. Someone tied her to the tree last night, half naked," Bernadette said.

Fred put his arm around Elizabeth. "It must have been those men from the pool last night—they came back to exact their revenge."

"How awful," Elizabeth said through sobs.

Bernadette backed away from them. She pulled up her phone to scroll through the photos. None of it seemed right to her.

The constable placed police tape around the scene. He walked slowly out of the jungle, looking back several times. Bernadette could see he'd never been involved in a crime scene like this. All rookie police were the same. The textbooks taught officers the procedures of a crime scene. The books never instructed the officers on the feelings that hit them the moment they saw a body.

Bernadette approached the constable. His hand trembled as he lit a cigarette.

"Constable, have there been any tourists murdered in this area before now?" Bernadette asked.

The constable blew a stream of smoke into the air and shook his head. "No, no killings like this. Only minor thefts of property." He put his cigarette out on the ground. "You must speak to CID when they arrive and give them a description of the men from last night. This is a above my skill... my expertise. I'm from the village of Deniyaya, I've seen nothing like this before." He waggled his head and looked away.

The hotel manager, Mr. S.J. Kumari, arrived at the pool. He was a large man in his fifties with a full head of slicked back dark hair. He wore a white shirt that billowed over his black pants and sandals that slapped the paving stones as he walked. His wide face showed a furrow of concern.

He put his hands together, bowed, and apologized to everyone within earshot for this terrible event. His wife arrived at his side. She was a small lady with glasses, dressed in a navy-blue sari and an equally pained expression on her face. It was obvious nothing like this had ever happened at their lodge.

They ushered all the guests into the dining pavilion. Servers brought in tea, coffee, and water. The chef brought out food, placed it on a table, and puttered around to see if the guests were hungry. No one seemed to move.

Bernadette surveyed the room. The Redstones huddled in conversation, sipping tea, and looking forlorn. The other guests sat in stunned silence. Murders can do that to humans, Bernadette thought as she drank her coffee.

They waited in the dining area for over two hours before sirens sounded in the distance. As they grew louder, it became apparent a large convoy of police and army vehicles were on their way. Bernadette counted ten vehicles that included two ambulances and a large truck.

The convoy came to a halt near the pavilion. An imposing figure got out of the lead car. He was tall, dressed in a brown uniform with braids and decorations on his chest. His uniform looked a cross between police and military.

A group of men in SWAT gear jumped out of the back of the truck with AK47 machine guns. They wore helmets and complete protective gear. A man with a large build led them shouting instructions. They lined up in a row, put their guns at their sides and waited.

The decorated figure strode with authority towards the pavilion. Constable Jay Singha rushed out to meet him— stopped in front of him, saluted, and filled him in on the scene. The big man listened, then waved him away and continued his march to the pavilion.

He walked into the pavilion, stopped, put his hands behind his back, and let his gaze move from one side of the dining room to other before coughing slightly and raising his hands.

"I am K.M. Silva, Deputy Inspector General of Police. I will ask every one of you to make a statement of your movements last night and to anything unusual you heard or saw. My men will comb the nearby forest for evidence. We must search all bungalows. No one will leave this place until our investigation is complete. Thank you."

The guests murmured with excitement. Talk of missed tours, buses, and connections rose into a crescendo of sound.

Mr. Kumari stood and raised his hands. "My dear guests, please, the police will try to have you on your way in time to make all of your activities for today." He motioned to the breakfast buffet. "Please have something to eat."

Bernadette watched Inspector Silva speak to a woman who stepped out of a jeep. She wore a blue sari, dark glasses, and carried a medical bag with a small backpack on her back. Obviously, the medical examiner. She walked away towards the bungalows with Constable Jay Singha. She looked all of forty, small and squarish with a slight limp.

As Chris was about to get up to get more coffee,

Bernadette put her hand on his arm. "You want some more coffee?" Chris asked.

"No, I need you to cover for me. These guys will not do interviews soon. The inspector is going to talk to the manager and his wife first, then the guard on duty, then the medical examiner. We'll be an hour before we see someone."

"And you're going to do what?" Chris asked.

"I thought I'd introduce myself to the nice medical examiner and see if I can lend a hand," Bernadette said with a smile.

"Sure," Chris said. "I'll tell them you have a stomach problem and went back to our bungalow for a minute. Don't get arrested for hampering their investigation."

"I wouldn't think of it," Bernadette said as she made her way out of the back of the dining pavilion. The extensive structure had multiple entry points with low stairs leading to the bungalows, pools, and gardens. She chose one furthest away from the police, slipping away without being noticed.

48

BERNADETTE CAUGHT up to the medical examiner. She stood listening to Constable Jay Singha. He spoke rapidly in the native tongue, his hands constantly moving. He finished his story, walking away to the main troop of police.

"Doctor, may I speak with you?" Bernadette asked when the woman noticed her.

She stopped, turned slowly, and lowered her sunglasses. "I am a medical examiner. If you have some ailment, you need to go into town."

"Yes, I know who you are. My name is Detective Bernadette Callahan with the serious crime division in Canada. I knew both of the victims. I wish to offer my help." She put her hands together in the palms touching fashion and bowed her head. "Namaste."

She returned the greeting. "Namaste, Detective Callahan, my name is Doctor Suri Udawatte. I would be happy if you could tell me something of the victims. It will be some time before the inspector will come to me with many questions. You might assist me with answers." She spoke with a lilting English accent.

"Thank you, Doctor Udawatte," Bernadette said. "I will fill you in with anything I can. I was with both of them until they left the dining room at eight last night. Also, wouldn't you rather start with the victim in the forest?"

"No one told me there was one outside. We must get to it first before the animals and the insects do," Dr. Udawatte said. She followed Bernadette as she led her to Lucinda's body.

Lucinda's body looked pitifully sad. Her head lolled downward. The murderers had used the belt of the robe to tie her hands to the tree to keep her upright. Flies buzzed around her face; ants crawled on the white bathrobe.

"When did you find her?" Dr. Udawatte asked.

"This morning at seven. The last time I saw her was at eight last night at dinner. Do you want to know what we ate?" Bernadette asked. She knew medical examiners wanted to know what the last meal was. The autopsy of the stomach contents was a good way of telling death. Food decomposed in the stomach until death. It was the very reason Bernadette never ate before a medical examiner dragged her into a morgue to discuss stomach contents.

"The time of the last meal is sufficient; I will find everything from my autopsy," the doctor said. "Now, let us see what they have done to this poor lady."

She took out a camera, taking pictures of the body in position, then took the robe off. A long slash of purple showed around her waist.

"Is that bruising around her waist?" Bernadette asked.

The doctor inspected the bruise. "This is lividity. It is caused by blood pooling in a restricted area."

Bernadette stood back; she knew what the term lividity was. She'd seen it many times in victims bound up and left for dead by gangs.

"There're no wounds on this victim. Was she in poor health?" the doctor asked.

"She drank like a fish, as we like to say where I come from," Bernadette said. "I think she's thirty-five or forty, but I do not know her medical history."

The doctor only nodded her head, took some notes, and kept examining the body. "You see here on the feet? There's much abrasion of the tissue. But this is strange... I see little blood."

Bernadette walked to Lucinda's corpse, looked down at her legs. The abrasions were obvious. They had dragged her. A small light went off in her head. The two men she'd seen at the pool last night. If they'd wanted to kill Lucinda, why would they bring her here—for revenge? If she was already dead, they needed to get far away from the body.

She walked to the back of the tree and saw a trail. "I'm going to see where this trail leads," she said. The doctor only waved at her. She was pulling out the instrument to check the liver temperature of the corpse, which was always a good sign for Bernadette to leave.

She followed the trail that led towards the bungalows. Turning a bend, she came face to face with a juvenile elephant.

"Hey there, you mind if I just go around you?" Bernadette asked in a quiet voice with her hands by her side. The elephant stopped foraging leaves for a second and stared at her. It raised its trunk as if sensing the air and greeting her at the same time. Then it moved aside.

Bernadette strolled by, put her hands together in the Indian greeting and said, "Namaste, beautiful big fella."

The elephant raised its trunk in her direction, blowing out some air and flapping its ears.

She followed the trail around another bend and found

the back of the bungalows. The Redstones bungalows were on the right, the Braithwaite's were on the left.

She walked back to the doctor and the corpse. Her senses were now in overload. "Doctor, did you see the knot of the bathrobe?"

The doctor looked up at her. "Yes, a sailor's slip knot. I used to sail out of Colombo as a child. Every sailor knows what that is."

Bernadette was going to send the picture to a knot specialist in Canada in the forensics department. Now, there was no need. She looked down at the ground. A plastic evidence bag was lying there with a diamond necklace in it.

"Where did you find this?" Bernadette asked, pointing at the bag on the ground.

"It was in the bathrobe."

"But they stole it from her last night, then she got it back. This tells me this was not a robbery."

The doctor paused for a moment and looked at Bernadette, "You must tell the inspector. Perhaps he will listen to your reasoning. For my purposes, I only look at the dead. This victim died around three this morning. This is all I can surmise from this. Now, if we can go to the bungalow, I wish to see the other victim."

Two policemen put Lucinda's' body in a bag and transported her out of the jungle. The doctor followed Bernadette back to the bungalow with Nigel's body. The doctor got to work on his body doing her examination.

Bernadette walked quietly about the room, trying to not disturb the doctor and do her own investigation. She wondered why they'd never heard a gunshot in the night. Lying in a corner, she found the answer.

Two pillows with burn holes were under a blanket. Bernadette didn't touch them; she could see someone had used them to cover the gun put to Nigel's head. The pillow on top had a hole and scorch marks.

She shook her head and motioned to the doctor. "Looks like the murderers used these as a makeshift sound suppressor."

The doctor limped over, looked at the pillows, then went back to Nigel's body. "Yes, I see some fragments of white fibers around his wound. But there is not much blood as you'd expect from a wound like this. His heart had stopped beating before they shot him."

Bernadette looked up to see the inspector coming towards the bungalow. "I think I'll be going. Perhaps I'll give my report to the inspector later... And if you don't mind telling him I wasn't here..."

Doctor Udawatte raised her hand and smiled. "Not to worry, thank you for your help."

Bernadette went out the back door of the bungalow. She stopped upon seeing a metal object on the ground. It looked like half a roofing nail with a large flat head on it. She put it in her pocket and made her way to the dining pavilion where the police were interviewing the guests. There were only ten bungalows, but that meant twenty interviews as all the rooms were doubly occupied. Police never interviewed two people together.

She slipped into the chair beside Chris. "Did I miss anything?"

He looked over at her. "No, not much. They came by to take names, I told them you'd be back soon and that was twenty minutes ago. What did you find out?"

Bernadette poured herself some water and looked at Chris. "The murders were a setup, using the robbery beforehand as a cover."

"How do you figure that?"

"Elizabeth mentioned on two occasions the killings must have been revenge by the guys who tried to rob us last night. She also suggested we go to the pool to look for Lucinda."

"Yeah, sounds like manipulation of the search. What else did you see?"

"Lucinda's necklace was in her robe. Why wouldn't the robbers take it? And someone tied a sailor slip knot on the robe. Neither of those guys looked like sailors," Bernadette said.

"Do you think the Redstones did it?"

"Yes, but I don't know how," Bernadette said. She looked around the room. The police were interviewing a couple on the other side of the room. A young English couple looked pissed; they'd already said they'd seen and heard nothing and were going to miss their flight back to Manchester. The policeman only wagged his head and wrote Manchester.

Bernadette pulled out her phone and texted to Cynthia, giving her an update on the events.

Cynthia texted back with a '*WTF! Serious?*'

Bernadette sent off emails to both Inspector Lee and Agent Winston of the FBI. There seemed little else she could do. She felt powerless. Her role was that of a cruise ship passenger, not a detective. That pissed her off.

She looked up from her cellphone and over at Chris. "I see this investigation wrapping up in about an hour."

"Why so early?" Chris asked.

"They'll pin it on the robbers from last night. Just my gut feeling."

Shots rang out in the forest.

"What's that?" Elizabeth asked in a voice so loud the entire pavilion heard it.

Bernadette looked in the forest's direction. "I think the

police found the suspects. We'll be back to the ship sooner than I thought."

49

THE POLICE RUSHED off towards the forest. The guests stood up as if they were watching a football match. The hotel manager ran after the police to see what happened. He returned ten minutes later, wiping his face with a handkerchief from the exertion.

"They got the bloody rascals. Killed them both as they tried to flee," the manager said. He clapped his hands as if his team had scored a goal.

The inspector came back smiling. He chatted with the manager for a few minutes and shouted some orders to his policemen. Soldiers dragged two bodies toward a waiting truck. They placed them in body bags once the medical examiner looked them over.

Several policemen stood beside the truck with the bodies to pose for a picture.

Bernadette gave her statement in the next hour. The inspector had no interest in anything she had to say or offered into the insights of the deaths. His men had killed the two offenders.

The police asked Bernadette to identify the bodies of

the men. The police took the body bags off the truck, unzipping them for her to view. She confirmed the dead men were the same ones who'd tried to rob them the previous night.

She signed a document that she could hardly understand that confirmed the identities of the men. The inspector smiled again, bowed with a 'namaste' and jumped into his truck.

The doctor walked by Bernadette and nodded her head. Bernadette could see the resignation in her look. It was over. There was no use in pursuing anything.

Bernadette caught up to her. "Doctor, I hope you won't mind if I ask, did they find the gun on the two men?"

The doctor stopped and turned. "No, they found nothing. The police shot them as they wouldn't stop running. Criminals know that murder of a foreigner is the automatic death penalty. Those men were better off dead in the jungle than rotting in a prison for years before being sentenced to death."

Bernadette pursed her lips. She wanted to say she thought the men might be innocent, but there was no use. The Sri Lankan police had solved their case.

"What will you do with the bodies of the two Americans?" Bernadette asked.

"I will take them to my morgue in Colombo. After I've done my examination, you may have the bodies," Dr. Udawatte said.

"Is it possible to get a report?" Bernadette asked, looking into the doctor's eyes.

The doctor looked down at the ground and back up to Bernadette. "As long as I give you a verbal report. You will receive nothing in writing."

Bernadette nodded and took out a pen and paper. "Here

is my phone number. I need to know the cause of death. You already said the man was dead before the gunshot."

"I don't remember saying that," the doctor protested.

"You said there wasn't much blood from the head wound."

"Yes, I said that. It usually means the heart had stopped beating beforehand."

"I only need to know the cause of death. I promise your words will leave with me when my ship sails out of here," Bernadette said.

"Very well, I will call you in the morning," Dr. Udawatte said. She turned and limped towards her car and stopped. "You know, the Redstones also requested I phone them."

"Why?" Bernadette asked.

"They said they needed to know the exact time of death. Something to do with the insurance in their company," the doctor said. "A strange request, but not uncommon." She turned and got into the back of the car.

50

BERNADETTE AND CHRIS sat in the back of the minibus, the Redstones in the front. Anand was quiet as he drove. There was, as they say, a deathly pall hanging over the passengers. Lucinda and Nigel's bodies were being transported back to Colombo by the police. The bus seemed noticeably emptier without them.

Elizabeth Redstone was busy on her phone talking to someone in the United States to have the bodies of Lucinda and Nigel returned. Her voice filled the bus as she commented on the sad situation and lamented their deaths.

Bernadette tried to tune out Elizabeth's voice as she typed an email to Winston in Washington, D.C. and to Inspector Lee in Singapore. They would need to know the latest events. She finished the emails, put the phone away, and leaned back in the seat.

Chris leaned over to Bernadette. "Does this seem strange to you, how quickly the Redstone's have recovered from the deaths of their so-called friends?"

"Their friends are worth one hundred million dollars to them, but here's the kicker, if Nigel died before Lucinda, his estate goes to her, the Redstones get nothing. But if Lucinda died before Nigel, her estate goes to him. The Redstone's double down. They receive two hundred million."

"That's a big score, what made you think of that?"

"The medical examiner told me the Redstones requested the time of death of both for insurance. But I have a feeling they know already."

"You think they killed them?"

"I have strong suspicions, yes," Bernadette said.

"You want to fill me in or keep it to yourself?" Chris asked.

"The medical examiner said there wasn't much blood from Nigel's head wound. So, he must have died before the gunshot. Two pillows were used as an attempted silencer. But only people who watch old gangster movies think a pillow can silence a gun. It will reduce the sound, but only by a few decibels."

"Then why didn't we hear the gun shot last night?"

"That's an interesting question," Bernadette said looking at Chris. "There was a lot of jungle noise last night, but not enough to mask a gun..."

"Except maybe the cry of the devil bird," Chris added.

Bernadette nodded. "Yes, but how could someone time the gunshot to a bird's cry."

Chris shrugged. "You have the bird's cry recorded on your phone, you plug in a mini Bluetooth speaker, and you shoot the gun and hit the recording at the same time. Seems simple to me."

"That's it. But I'd never be able to get them on this. I'd need more," Bernadette said.

Chris pulled a bottle of water out of the seat and took a drink. "You're sure it's them, even though you had to save them from that island?"

Bernadette closed her eyes, then opened them. "What if that's part of their plan? I mean, maybe they thought the helicopter would make it back to land without having to land on the island. That way they could make it look like they were targets."

"That's kind of elaborate, don't you think?"

"Yeah, it is, but remember these two people stand to gain two hundred million from the deaths of their partners. What better way than two accidental deaths and two of them murdered by a supposed robbery on vacation into the forests of Sri Lanka."

"You don't think the media is going to eat this up? The scrutiny on this will rocket around the world like wildfire. National Enquirer and Oprah Winfrey will probably have a fistfight over who gets to the Redstones for their story."

Bernadette's eyes lit up. "That's it. This story is too bizarre. How could they have ever planned it? These two are electrical engineers. They think they're smarter than anyone else."

"But not smarter than you?" Chris asked with a grin.

Bernadette looked at Chris. "Sweetie, there's something I need to tell you. There's been a few nights I couldn't sleep, and I went down to the cigar lounge."

"The cigar lounge—I didn't know you smoked cigars."

"I did years ago with my grandfather. Anyway, I met an elderly gentleman in the lounge named Bill Loving, a retired Texas Ranger. He told me a story of how he solved a case by going back to the beginning."

"Okay, to the beginning of what?"

"To the beginning of when we met the Redstones. Remember how we became involved with them? We met them at the captain's table, and they invited us on a trip with them. What if everything was a setup?"

"I thought they were being nice. It's also a Canadian thing to do—so what's got your suspicions up?"

"When I did the incident report for ship's security, Cynthia said my being at the scene as a detective gave credibility to the death of Fred Compton. And then again, when I was on the shark line, they had me as a witness to what happened to Ashley. Don't you see? You and I are the best witnesses to the two accidents and to the murders of the Braithwaites."

"But how will you find out who put those two thieves up to their attempted robbery last night?" Chris asked.

Bernadette shook her head. "That's going to be impossible with the thieves dead. But it's the same MO that they did with Charlotte Bowman. Once she'd done her work, they had her killed."

"So, the Redstones had to have someone on the ground here in Sri Lanka to get these men hired, put them in place, then make sure a few of the police would kill these guys."

"Unless they were already dead."

"What did the bodies look like, did you see any flies and maggots all over them?" Chris asked. "That's a sure sign they were killed in advance."

"I only had a quick look at their faces. The soldiers went into the forest, we heard shots, then they found the men."

"Someone must have been superb at setting all this up," Chris said.

"I have a good idea who it is."

Chris looked over at her. "Okay, who is the master planner?"

"It has to be Holly Marsden."

"But she was absent from the ship since yesterday."

"Yeah, perfect to be on land to make sure everything works well. She can now fly back to America when the ship leaves. I'll bet the ship will get a letter of resignation from her saying she had urgent family issues."

They sat in silence as the bus made the journey back to the ship. Bernadette waited until they got closer into Colombo before she checked her phone for cell phone coverage. As they entered the city, she sent more texts to Carla Winston at the FBI in Washington. She put in a request for an FRS on Holly Marsden, a facial recognition search. If Holly Marsden was still in Colombo, the FBI would find her.

The secret was not that well-kept of how the CIA, FBI, and even Canada's Security and Intelligence Agency could tap into worldwide cameras. Only the uninformed thought their rights were being protected.

She sent a text to Cynthia. "We're arriving back early. Do you want to meet with us for a statement or wait for the FBI tomorrow?"

No answer came for fifteen minutes, then Cynthia replied with a text. "I'm off the ship taking care of a few things. Talk soon."

Bernadette put her phone back in her pocket. She felt the nail she'd picked up outside the bungalow and examined it.

"What's that?" Chris asked.

"It's a roofing nail. I found it on the trail behind the bungalow where Nigel was murdered." Bernadette said, handing it to Chris.

Chris looked at it. "It's cut in half."

"I've heard of roofing nails used as firing pins for 3D replica guns. It's the only way to get them to fire a bullet. They make the gun from plastic, but it needs a sawed-off roofing nail to make them work," Bernadette said.

"You think someone used a 3D replica to kill Nigel?" Chris asked.

Bernadette took the nail back from Chris to examine it. "It makes sense. There's only one way to get a gun through the ship's security. It would have to be plastic. They could disguise this roofing nail with a bunch of cufflinks or earrings."

"You still think Elizabeth and Fred are the ones?"

"Pretty much. If this roofing nail was a firing pin for a replica gun, then that about seals it. We'll never be able to convict them unless we find the gun. The police did no GSR testing on Elizabeth or Fred to rule them out as suspects, so this is a walk for them."

The bus pulled up to the pier; they had to drive by a group of media vans and reporters who'd heard about the murder of the ship's passengers. They drove through to the gangway of the ship. Mateo and the captain were there to meet them.

51

THE CAPTAIN STOOD in front of the gangway, hands by his sides, his back ramrod straight. He looked uncomfortably out of his element. Mateo stood beside him. They watched Bernadette, Chris, Fred and Elizabeth step out of the bus.

"I'm sorry for your loss," Mateo said to Elizabeth and Fred. They nodded, making their way onto the ship with a glance in the captain's direction.

Bernadette stopped beside Mateo. "I understand the FBI has taken over this case."

"Yes, Agent Winston contacted me. We'll be turning all of our files over to them. The ship's owners in the U.S. want a complete record of everything we say to them. I hope you'll comply with this," Mateo said.

"I'll do everything I can," Bernadette said. She looked around the gangway. "Is Officer Cynthia McCabe around?"

Mateo shook his head. "I haven't seen her since yesterday morning. I have been tied up in conference calls with corporate security in Fort Lauderdale."

Cynthia came up behind Bernadette. "Hey, looking for me?"

Bernadette whirled around to see Cynthia behind her. "Sorry, didn't see you. Do you have a minute?"

"Sure, I was just checking on our security at the port entrance. We don't want any of those news people getting close to our ship. Corporate would have a fit," Cynthia said.

They walked away from the gangway. "Did you ever find what happened to Marsden?" Bernadette asked.

Cynthia lowered her head then looked back up at Bernadette. "Not a thing. It's like she went into thin air. We thought she might have hit the airport, but nothing. I've called several hotels with no results. We circulated her picture to the local police; they've come back with nothing."

"I'll see if the FBI can put some feelers out for her. They have one hell of a big search engine. They might come up with something," Bernadette said.

"You think she had something to do with the murders, rather than making a run for it? Maybe got scared after what happened to Charlotte Bowman," Cynthia said.

"Look, I shouldn't be telling you this, but I have info from the FBI that Bowman and Marsden knew each other at a hotel frequented by the Comptons, Braithwaites and the Redstones. Four of them are dead. I see a pattern. How about you?"

Cynthia's eyes went wide in disbelief. "You must let Mateo and the captain know."

Bernadette raised her hand. "It's okay, Cynthia, I'll make a full report to the FBI. There's a good chance we might still find Marsden in Colombo. She just might shed some light on this yet. Now, I'm damn tired, I'm heading for my room, a shower, and a beer. We'll talk again."

Cynthia put her hand on Bernadette's arm. "You've been through a hell of an ordeal. I can't thank you enough for helping our ship's crew. This goes a hell of a long way. You've probably saved all our jobs with your work."

Bernadette turned to walk up the gangway. "Don't thank me until I've wrapped this up."

She headed back upstairs to find Chris lying on the lounge chair on the deck. He had his shirt off, a book by his side, and his eyes looked all droopy, like he was about to take a nap.

She sat on the lounge chair and laid a hand on his chest. He opened his eyes and smiled.

"Have a pleasant chat with Cynthia?"

"Uh huh," Bernadette said as her hands made a circling motion on his stomach. She let her fingers roam over his six-pack of abdominal muscles she adored.

He put his hand on hers. "You want to go for some play time before nap time—is that it?"

"Right answer," Bernadette said with a grin. "I love how you get me."

BERNADETTE WOKE UP AT MIDNIGHT, threw on a t-shirt, and went onto the balcony. Stars twinkled behind the fluffy clouds. The city of Colombo was still up, traffic noises, horns, and people sounded in the distance. She didn't know or care what day it was. She knew that tomorrow morning, Carla Winston would arrive. An FBI investigation would be a game changer on this ship.

The problem was, Bernadette had the entire case solved and locked in her mind. She knew the Redstones were guilty. But how would they prove it? Had they committed the perfect crime?

She sat on the deck for an hour, mulling it over. She knew of a way to get them. But would Winston be open to it?

52

BERNADETTE HARDLY SLEPT. Waking at dawn, she made a coffee with the Nespresso maker and watched the city come to life. Chris came onto the deck, wrapping his arms around her.

"You didn't sleep much," Chris said.

"Yeah, it keeps me awake when all the crazy events run around in my head. I try to line them up, then they get all mixed up again. Kind of like playing with a puzzle where you think the pieces fit together, then they don't."

"You think having the FBI coming onboard will help?" Chris asked as he reached for her coffee and took a sip.

"I'm not sure. They have to piece together all the events from Singapore to Port Blair to here. As you said, when you string crimes over distance you make it harder to solve—and how about if I make you a coffee so I can finish mine?"

Chris smiled. "I'll make it myself and order us breakfast. Any word from Winston?"

"Her team of two arrived this morning. She asked me to meet her after she meets with the captain and the head of security. Should be a fun day."

Chris put the pod in the Nespresso maker and hit the button. "After this cruise is over, how about we go hiking into the Rocky Mountains? I hear there's a great place to take pictures of grizzly bears in their natural habit."

"Isn't that dangerous?"

Chris looked up from the coffeemaker. "It would be one hell of a lot safer than this voyage."

"I couldn't agree more," Bernadette said. Her cell phone buzzed. "I got a text from Winston, she's ready to meet with me."

Chris gave her kiss on the cheek. "Enjoy."

BERNADETTE SLIPPED on some casual shorts and top and made her way to the bistro coffee bar. She hadn't seen Winston in over a year. Their relationship had been one of active cases with strange outcomes. But, in the end, Winston always came through.

Winston was wearing a pair of tan slacks and a white blouse with tennis shoes. The outfit didn't scream FBI, which was nice.

"Hey, Winston, your flight okay?"

Winston sat back in her chair and stared up at Bernadette while pulling her sunglasses down. "Any time the government wants to put me in a private jet with big leather reclining seats and excellent food on board, I'm fine with that. And now, here I am, sitting on this luxurious ship sipping gourmet coffee on the other side of the world. Life is fine—there's a murder investigation to work on, but that's the business I'm in."

"You get much from the captain and the chief of security?" Bernadette asked.

Winston shook her head. "Your captain wants this to go

away. He'd like us to wrap the two accidents and attack on the Braithwaites by robbers as unfortunate events."

"That sounds like the captain. If you don't dig too deep into the events, it exonerates him and the ship," Bernadette said.

"What else have you got since I've been on my way here?"

"I think they shot Nigel with a replica gun smuggled on this ship."

"You know who has the gun?"

"Probably the Redstones."

"What kind of evidence do you have?"

Bernadette pulled out the roofing nail. "Found this in back of the Braithwaite's bungalow next to the Redstone's,"

"One hell of a stretch, but I could get a search warrant for that—anything else?"

"Yeah, Lucinda had a necklace in her bathrobe when they found her. The same one the thieves tried to steal. It's got some electronics inside. I want it tested."

"The necklace is where now?"

"The Sri Lankan police headquarters."

Winston stirred her coffee. "Okay, do-able."

"Yes, we need to meet with the Sri Lankan Medical Examiner, she's at police headquarters, then go on a hunt for Marsden."

Winston put her spoon down. "And here I thought I'd get some pool time."

"Does the FBI have any pull in Sri Lanka?" Bernadette asked.

Winston looked around to see if any passengers were nearby. "Actually, we do. When this country had some deadly bombings in 2019, the FBI sent in a counter-terrorism unit. I contacted an agent who was here during that time. He gave me some names we can reach out to."

"How do we play it?" Bernadette asked.

"Simple, we've heard a rumor that the necklace on the victim could be dangerous to the wellbeing of the passengers on the ship. We need to investigate it before we turn it over to the Redstones."

Bernadette smiled over her coffee cup. "Winston, I'm so glad you're here with the power of the American government behind you."

"Uncle Sam is one hell of a powerful man when he's not being screwed around by politicians—you didn't hear me say that," Winston said.

"Nope, mum's the word. Now the next big thing is tracing Marsden."

"We had a hit on the facial recognition data base about four hours ago. She was moving around the city center, then nothing. She's hiding somewhere," Winston said.

"She's waiting for this ship to leave. We sail at six. My guess is she'll be sitting in a bar in a posh hotel with a drink watching us sail away. Tomorrow she gets on a plane, heading for wherever she wants."

"Can we hold her on anything if we find her?"

Bernadette pulled out her phone and accessed her camera. "Here is a picture of a woman walking with Astrid Karlsson, the girl they found dead in the canal in Singapore. I think this woman is Holly Marsden."

"You have to be sure to get a warrant. And the warrant would have to come from Singapore," Winston said.

"You know, our other key, is the woman murdered in India named Charlotte Bowman, who jumped ship after masquerading as Astrid Karlsson. She worked with Marsden."

"Now we're getting warmer," Winston said.

"You know, when I look at this photo, I'm sure it's Marsden," Bernadette said.

"Ah, I thought a minute ago, you said... Oh, I get it."

"Yeah, it's enough to hold her and get her back on this ship. I'll contact Inspector Lee to get a warrant for her arrest as an accessory to the murder of Astrid Karlsson," Bernadette said.

"You know, we probably can't make that charge stick," Winston said.

"All we need to do is to get her in a room and do some sweating. Maybe she'll be able to point us to the Redstones. That's all I'm looking for," Bernadette said. She got on her phone and sent a text to Inspector Lee in Singapore.

"How soon do you think Singapore will get the warrant?" Winston asked.

Bernadette looked at her phone as it buzzed with a text reply. "Lee says he'll have the warrant issued in the next few hours. He'll send it directly to you."

53

THE GOOGLE MAP showed a twelve-minute walk to the Sri Lankan Police Headquarters, but the roads were restricted access. To get there, Winston had to call her FBI people to get clearance. A Sri Lankan police car met them at the pier to drive them there.

"So much for my morning walk," Winston said.

The police car dropped them off at the headquarters' entrance. A high white concrete wall with a double black metal gate and a guard tower looked down on them. They gave their credentials to the guards and waited for the door on the side to open. While they waited, a policeman with a machine gun watched them from a tower on the side of the gate.

"This place is a fortress," Bernadette said.

"They stopped fighting the terrorists in their civil war a few years back. This police force did some serious counter-terrorism. The terrorists paid them many a visit to kill them," Winston said with an eyebrow raised towards the guard tower.

"That would make anyone jumpy. Let's hope we can find something when we get inside."

The door opened, and a policewoman came out in her brown uniform, gave them a greeting of namaste and asked them to follow. They walked into the police compound. Behind the high walls were the high-rise buildings of the complex. An array of security vehicles lined the walls. Police officers walked across the square, going about their business.

Winston hung back with Bernadette as they walked. "I asked to see the medical examiner. The bodies aren't here, but she has all the photos with the reports. From here, we might get some sense of the case and who shot the men in the forest."

They followed the policewoman into myriad long corridors and down some stairs until they arrived at the office of Dr. Suri Udawatte. She wore a green sari and sat hunched over reports on her desk.

The policewoman announced their presence, then took her place outside the door.

Dr. Udawatte put her glasses down. "Please sit down. May I offer you some tea?"

"No thank you, doctor," Winston said.

"I'd love some," Bernadette said, nudging Winston. She knew in her short time in Sri Lanka, it was impolite to refuse tea.

"I will have some, thank you," Winston said, getting the message.

"Officer Neja, tea please," Dr. Udawatte commanded and looked back at the women. "This is the one thing I can get the police to do quickly here." She smiled at her own joke.

"We were hoping you've had time to do an autopsy on the bodies from yesterday," Winston said.

The doctor regarded Winston for a moment. "Normally they would have waited in line. I had five bodies in front of them, but I received a message from on high that the FBI were involved. I assume that is you?"

Winston gave her card to the doctor. "Yes, we received an order yesterday in Washington to delve into this case. Can you tell us anything?"

The doctor pulled the files out while the officer placed the tea on the desk. She looked up, smiled at the officer, nodding at her as she left the office.

"The male victim died of head trauma before the gunshot wound. I did an autopsy of the brain. The bullet shattered the temporal cortex, consistent with a bullet wound, but it had subjected the parietal lobe and the rest of the brain to what I can assume was some kind of electric shock. Quite unusual. I'd normally see this kind of brain damage in an electrical worker."

"And the other victim?" Bernadette asked.

"I determined she died of a heart attack. I can only assume the stress of the robbers returning was too much for her. She was dead before they dragged her to the tree in the forest."

"How do you explain the electric shock to the male victim's brain?" Winston asked.

Dr. Udawatte took off her glasses and pushed the files to the side. "I do not know. My first guess is a taser at full capacity discharged at the head. But a taser sends a pulse with about fifty thousand volts and a few milliamperes. On its standard setting, the pulse cycles for five seconds before shutting off. I can only assume from the evidence in the victim's brain that the robbers did some modifications to a taser."

"Did the police find a taser on the suspects?" Winston asked.

Dr. Udawatte shook her head.

"What about the weapon they used the night they tried to rob Lucinda and me?" Bernadette asked.

The doctor shook her head again. "The suspects must have thrown it away."

"Did you recover the bullet from the male victim?" Bernadette asked.

"Sadly no, it entered through the right temporal lobe and exited through the left. The shot was a through and through. We found no shell casing. Only the powder marks on the pillow. Someone collected both the bullet and the casing."

Bernadette sipped her tea and looked over at Winston. "That's strange behavior for a robbery, don't you think?"

Winston replied. "More the M.O. of contract killers."

Dr. Udawatte shrugged. "I believe you have a saying in North America, 'it is what it is,' I think is how you say it."

"That's the saying alright, and most detectives hate hearing it," Bernadette said.

Winston raised her hand. "I know, I hate hearing it. But that is the report. Now, I made a request to your police department to take possession of the necklace found on the female victim."

The doctor opened her desk drawer and handed an envelope to Winston. "This is the necklace I found on the victim. Although for all its glitter, this is not a valuable piece."

"What do you mean?" Bernadette asked.

"It looks like shoddy workmanship. My uncle was a jeweler who taught me what to look for. This necklace is cubic zirconia instead of diamonds. And It is simple gold plate, not pure gold. The thing is worth maybe a thousand USD."

Winston looked at the necklace. "Not much to die for. But thanks for the information doctor."

"The other issue was the time of death. Did you verify that?" Bernadette asked.

"Yes, this is a contentious issue, I understand. The male victim died at two and the female at three," Dr. Udawatte said.

"Why is this contentious?" Winston asked.

"Elizabeth Redstone telephoned me earlier this morning. When I gave her the same information, she was upset, and asked me to review the information again. I told her my report was final." The doctor waved her hand in the file's direction. "I received a phone call soon after from a lawyer in Colombo telling me a private forensic pathologist has requested to view the bodies and my findings on behalf of Mr. and Mrs. Redstone." She looked down at her wristwatch. "He will be here in a half hour."

"Would you let us know if the pathologist finds anything different from your report?" Winston asked.

Dr. Udawatte looked taken aback. "I'm sure the other doctor's report will go directly to the Redstones' lawyer. This police department has no concern which victim died first. They have determined the perpetrators of the crime and consider the case closed."

Bernadette could feel the tension in the room. There was only one more thing she needed to ask. "Doctor, was the bungalow room where the victims were staying examined for prints of the robbers."

A deep sigh emanated from the doctor as she shook her head. "They called the investigation off once you identified the men they shot in the forest."

"Have you performed an autopsy on those two men yet?" Bernadette asked.

The doctor waved at the stack of files on her desk. "They are on a long list of bodies I need to see. I've had to drop everything to look at the Americans. I might not get them for another week or two."

"I see," Bernadette said. "Well, we've taken up enough of your time. Thank you, doctor."

The policewoman took them back to the waiting police car. They sat in silence as they drove back to the ship. Once back at the dock, they got out of the car and stood on the pier.

"What do you think of this so far?" Winston asked.

Bernadette stared up at the billowing afternoon clouds for a second before turning back to Winston. "If the Redstones murdered the Braithwaites and planned to pin it on the robbers, they did a good job. But there's one problem."

"What's that?"

"If Nigel died before Lucinda, the Redstones are out two hundred million."

"So, that's why they are challenging the autopsy report?"

"Exactly."

"Time of death in an estate means everything, so I'm told. When Nigel died before Lucinda, his estate passed to Lucinda, and his shares in the company insured for one hundred million. And Ashley had put Lucinda in her will, which passed from her estate to Lucinda. So, whoever is in Lucinda's will is in for the best lottery a death can buy," Bernadette said.

"What's our next move?" Winston asked.

"I want to show this to the electrical engineers on our

ship. We're on a pretty high-tech boat, I'm sure someone will have an explanation for the workings of the necklace."

"Sounds good, as long as we stand well back. I don't want to have any jolts like the victims received," Winston said.

54

THEY MADE their way back to the ship, immediately descending the decks towards the engine room. Bernadette remembered seeing the name of the head engineer, Kronis, and the head electrical engineer, Santos, when they were in the cyclone. They ventured below deck with Winston flashing her FBI badge and asking for them. The badge and Winston's no shit demeanor parted the waves for them. They were in front of Kronis and Santos within ten minutes.

Kronis sat at his desk, turning the necklace over in his hands. "Why am I looking at this?"

"The captain said I could reach out to any of the ship's crew to help with our investigation of the accidents and the murders of the passengers," Winston said. "We think they used this necklace to harm people. We need to confirm it."

Kronis looked at Santos standing beside him. "You have any idea how to check this out?"

Santos shook his head. "This is probably above me, but I know someone who should know. Let me get Almira. She has a degree in electronic circuit design." He left the room and appeared with a small young lady dressed in white coveralls wearing a red hajib and safety glasses. She looked all of twenty-five, she listened to Winston before taking the necklace in her hand.

"From the looks of the electronics inside, this device could submit a jolt of some power. Let me take it to the workshop, but first I will order some fruit," Almira said.

"Thanks, we're not hungry," Bernadette said.

Almira smiled. "This is to check the device. I'll need some melons to show what it can do."

They followed her to a small room with a work bench surrounded by an array of electrical instruments. Almira set Lucinda's necklace down, took out a small magnifying glass, hunching over it to examine it.

Almira looked up from the table, "this device has no switch to turn it on. I see a transmitter that would make it function from a signal. I have just the thing in my phone. This is an app called 'Signal,' I'll use it to send a pulse wave to the necklace."

A waiter arrived with a tray of watermelons, cantaloupes and honeydew melons. Almira thanked the waiter and set the melons down on the workbench. She placed the necklace on the cantaloupe.

"Please put these safety glasses on and stand back," Almira commanded.

Bernadette and Winston stood back to the entry of the workshop. They were two meters away. They could see the necklace sitting on the cantaloupe with Almira holding a multimeter handheld device close to it.

"I will activate the necklace, with my phone app and move away quickly," Almira said.

She hit a button on her phone. The necklace hummed— the cantaloupe exploded.

"Wow," Bernadette and Winston exclaimed in unison.

Almira surveyed the carnage of melon on the work-bench. "It seems I set it too high, I'll lower the transmission on the next charge."

She placed a watermelon on the bench, reset her phone, then hit the button. This time the watermelon did not explode, but it cracked in many places as if it had been subject to a minor earthquake from inside.

"How close to the necklace do you have to be to get it to activate?" Winston asked.

"From what I see of the electronics inside, I would say ten meters would do it. Outside that, it may not have an effective charge."

"How deadly is the electrical charge?" Bernadette asked.

"I had my amp meter attached. The first one would have been enough to fracture a brain, the second one would shock a heart. With the right modifications, it could put a heart into shock."

Bernadette looked at the carnage of melons. "You know, I just realized that George Compton and Nigel Braithwaite both wore hearing aids. Could this device be placed in a hearing aid?"

"Absolutely," Almira said. "These electronics act as a transmitter. They could easily work in the smallest of hearing aids or even in glasses."

"That's excellent information," Winston said, taking the necklace back.

"What about using it underwater, how would the neck-lace be activated?" Bernadette asked.

Almira frowned, then said, "underwater complicates it a bit, most radio waves only travel five centimeters. But you could send a timed delay signal that would activate it later."

Bernadette turned to Winston, "that would have worked perfectly for Ashley's death at the shark dive. It was a one tank dive, with one hour or less of air. Whoever sent the signal could have timed it for the assent."

They left the lower levels and walked up the stairs together. Winston held onto the necklace in the same brown envelope she'd received from the doctor. They stopped on the main deck and stepped out to the railing away from other passengers.

"What's your take on this, now that you've seen this little piece of electronics in action?" Winston asked, looking at Bernadette.

Bernadette looked out over the harbor and back to Winston. "I find it hard to fathom, but I see that either Lucinda or Ashley took out George Compton. They were close by. Then it had to be either Charlotte Bowman or maybe Lucinda who activated the necklace on Ashley."

"I thought they were good friends?"

"You know what they say about million-dollar wills, they make the best death sentences for friends and relatives," Bernadette said, looking out into the harbor. "I have a feeling Lucinda was in on the last act. I think they led her to believe she was going to be in on killing Nigel, but the Redstones took her out."

"That doesn't explain her being the last to die. You told me that cost the Redstones two hundred million. I can't imagine they'd engineer all these deaths without a big payoff," Winston said.

Bernadette nodded in agreement. "Yeah, I hear you. I have a feeling they were double crossed. I think we head out to locate Holly Marsden. She knew everyone back in South Carolina. I'll bet she helped in orchestrating this caper."

"I'm with you," Winston said. "I can't wait to hear what she'll say when we throw the evidence at her. I'd like to see if she'll give up Elizabeth and Fred Redstone."

55

THIS SHIP SAILS at 1800 hours, the sign read as they walked back to their rooms at noon. Bernadette let that time settle into her head, then moved on from it.

"I'll meet you back here in thirty minutes," Bernadette said to Winston.

"Okay, I'll tell the agent I came with to watch over the Redstones until we get back—that's if we get back in time to board the ship," Winston said with a raised eyebrow.

"Isn't your fancy private jet still at the airport?" Bernadette asked.

"No, and that's why I'm grabbing my passport and my toothbrush," Winston said.

"The ship's next destination is Kochi, that's only a one-hour flight from Colombo airport. I'll buy the drinks at the airport if we get stranded," Bernadette added with a smile as she headed up the stairs to her room.

She found Chris as he was just about to go out the door. Bernadette let herself collapse into his arms. He kissed her on the forehead.

"Rough morning?" Chris asked.

"Let's just say whoever is playing this game of murder and go hide, that they're winning," Bernadette said as she kissed his neck.

"I was going to head down for some lunch, you want to join me?"

"Ah, bit of a problem with that. I've got to grab my passport—"

"You're thinking you won't make the sailing?"

Bernadette closed her eyes, then opened them. "I'm just covering my options. Winston and I are going to look for Holly Marsden. I have a hunch she's hiding out, waiting for the ship to leave. I don't think she'll appear until just before sailing—that's cutting it close."

"I'll come with you," Chris said.

"But I can't impose on you, this is your vacation too. You'd be stuck in Colombo until we could get a flight to meet the ship in Kochi."

"Not a problem. I'm tired of the rich food on this ship, I could use a night in a regular hotel without a butler asking me if I want the mini-bar filled every hour and I could really get into some Indian street food," Chris said.

"My God, that's why I love you so much. You just can't live the life of the rich and famous. You're a peasant just like me," Bernadette said.

Chris kissed her on the lips. "You got that right. Let me throw a change of underwear and a toothbrush in our daypack for us both and we're out of here."

A half hour later, they met Winston on the main deck. She was standing beside another woman dressed in shorts with a t-shirt that read *Boston Marathon*. She was late twenties with an olive complexion and dark hair and an athletic build.

Winston smiled as they approached. "I see you've

convinced that big hunk of yours to join us." Winston gave
Chris a hug as he joined them. "Going to be hard to have
him blend in with the crowd, but maybe he can hide behind
a food stall."

Chris kissed Winston on the cheek. "Thanks for noticing
how chubby I've become with this cruise ship food."

Winston turned to the woman beside her. "This is
Agent Elana Alverez, she's my assistant on this. I've had her
locked into the security crew doing interviews and
paperwork."

Alverez waved at them both. "Yes, so much fun, on a
classy ship on the far side of the world confined to little
rooms—totally enjoying myself."

"You'll have the place to yourself while we're gone.
Monitor the Redstones and don't fraternize with the staff if
we don't make it back to the ship before it sails," Winston
said.

Alverez ran her hand down her chest. "Me, make googly
eyes at the amazing looking hunky bartenders—you must
be kidding. If you miss the ship, I'll be waiting for you in
Kochi with a great tan and a smile. I hear the crossing to
India is lovely." She patted Winston on the shoulder and
laughed.

Winston looked at the others. "She's only half kidding.
But I know she'll kick anyone's ass who steps out of line
while we're away."

Alverez bunched both her fists. "I have a list and I'm
checking that mother twice. There's a bunch of leads I want
to run down. I have as many suspicions as you do about this
voyage, Detective Callahan."

"What's on your list?" Bernadette asked.

"I'm running checks on this entire crew. After I learned
about the switch of Astrid Karlsson and Charlotte Bowman,

I wondered who else dropped into place for this voyage," Alverez said.

Bernadette turned to Winston. "They must teach new stuff in FBI school these days."

Winston laughed. "No, Alverez comes from the wrong side of everywhere in America. Trusts no one—best damn trait to have as an FBI agent."

Moments later they walked down the gangplank. Cynthia McCabe was on the pier. She looked at her watch and up at them with concern.

"We sail at eighteen hundred hours. You know that, right?" Cynthia said.

Bernadette put her hand on her arm. "Look, we might not make it back in time. We think we can find Holly Marsden and bring her back." She looked around to see if anyone else was around. "I have a feeling she'll be watching the ship leave. I think I can convince her to come back to the ship."

"How will you do that if she doesn't want to?" Cynthia asked.

"I have an offer she won't be able to refuse," Bernadette said with a smile. "If we're not here at sail time, we'll catch the plane to meet the ship in Kochi."

"Be careful in Colombo. I've heard there are some bad dudes in the city preying on tourists—especially after what happened to the Braithwaites," Cynthia said.

"Are you kidding me? I've got Chris and Agent Winston with me," Bernadette said.

Winston looked over at Bernadette with a wink. "I thought you were going to protect me."

"Anyway, we got it covered. I've got your cell number in case we're cutting it close. Maybe the captain will hold the gate for a minute or two," Bernadette said.

Cynthia shook her head. "I have it on good authority that he doesn't like you. He thinks you're bad luck for his ship. If this ship sailed away without you, he'd be doing one of his funny Greek dances on the bridge."

"So nice to feel loved," Bernadette said. "We'd best be off."

They walked to the end of the pier to find a taxi.

"What's our plan?" Chris asked.

"Get lunch in a local Indian restaurant with excellent beer and do a recon of every hotel we think she'd hide in. She won't come out until a few minutes before sailing. We canvas hotels for known sightings of her, then we lay in wait," Bernadette said.

Chris and Winston looked at each other.

"I like the hole in the wall Indian food part with beer. You can fill us in on the rest after that," Chris said.

"Make sure you have only one beer," Bernadette cautioned. "I've got a feeling this afternoon will be busy."

56

THEY FOUND a small Indian restaurant on a side street on the recommendation of the cab driver. With no English and no menu, they pointed at the pictures of food on the wall. Chris did most of the ordering and when the food came it was delicious. Chris ordered them a round of local Lion Beer to go with the food.

Bernadette scooped up the last morsel of curry with her chapati bread, wiped off her hands with a tissue, and grabbed her phone.

"Okay, here's my plan. There are six hotels that meet the criteria of where Holly Marsden can watch the ship leave," Bernadette said as she sipped the last of her beer.

"Why only six?" Chris asked.

"Sightlines of the harbor," Bernadette answered.

"You really think she'll be that predictable?" Winston asked.

"I've tracked wild game for years. No animal I ever tracked would hide without looking to see if their pursuer was gone. I've found humans to be the same," Bernadette said.

"So, our plan to cover six hotels with the three of us is what?" Winston asked.

"We eliminate the other five. They're all about a ten-minute rickshaw ride from here. I've got Holly's picture on my phone. I'm sending it to each of you. We do an old-fashioned police canvas of the other hotels, then focus on the one I think she'll be at."

"You have a favorite in mind?" Chris said.

"Yes, I do," Bernadette said, pulling up a picture on her phone. "It's the Kingsbury Colombo Hotel. It's a five star and listed as fabulous on TripAdvisor."

Winston looked at the picture. "You don't think she'd stay at one of the less expensive ones?" Winston scrolled on her own phone. "What about the Grand Oriental Hotel? It's got a view of the harbor and the ship."

"Yes, it does. I think we check it out, run her picture by the front desk and bellman, but it's only ninety U.S. dollars a night. It's listed as average. Holly comes from the Hyatt Hotel chain and having just come off the ship where she's had to put up with crew quarters, my guess is she'll be treating herself to luxury as she watches the ship sail away."

"it's three fifteen. Let's get moving. I'm sure I can clear two hotels in two hours. Where do we meet?" Chris said.

"Unless you find her at one of the other hotels, I'm betting on the Kingsbury. By far the classiest of the hotels with sightlines. We meet there at five thirty."

"That's a half hour before sailing. You don't think that's cutting it too close?" Winston asked.

"When I hunted prairie dogs as a kid, I poured water down the hole to get them to show themselves. The sound of the ship's horn will be what gets Holly to come out of her hole. Trust me," Bernadette said.

Chris looked at the list. "I got the Metro Port and the

Grand Oriental. I'll grab a rickshaw and report in as I clear them." He got up, walked across the street, and got into a rickshaw.

Winston checked her list and the map on her phone. "The Shangri-La and the Fairway it is for me. I'll check in with you soon." She walked to a rickshaw, got in, and disappeared in a cloud of blue smoke.

Bernadette went to the last rickshaw; she had the Galle Face Hotel on her list before the Kingsbury. As the rickshaw pulled out into the traffic, she had a slight moment of doubt. She'd better be right.

57

THE RICKSHAW MOVED QUICKLY through the traffic and deposited Bernadette at the Galle Face Hotel. The place was enormous. She approached the front desk, showing a picture on her phone, asking if they'd seen Holly Marsden. She explained it was her cousin, but she wasn't sure if it was the Galle Face or the Kingsbury, she was to meet her at.

The hotel staff were helpful. They called over the bellmen and the concierge, they all shook their heads. None of them had seen the lady.

Bernadette walked out of the hotel to stand at the entrance for a moment. She had an odd feeling she'd seen two similar men outside the little restaurant they'd had lunch at. She stared at her phone for a second and waited. Chris sent her a text after he'd cleared the Grand Oriental, Winston texted she'd been to the Shangri-La, and was now heading for the last one on her list.

She looked over toward the taxi line. The two men looked away. That was it. She had a tail. She texted back to Winston and Chris that she had company.

"What are you going to do?" Chris texted.

"See if they follow me. If they do, I think I'm heading for the right hotel," Bernadette texted back.

"Let me know," Chris replied.

Bernadette got into a rickshaw and gave the driver the address of the Kingsbury. He looked at her, and before he got into the cab, he looked behind him.

The rickshaw took off down the street into the heavy traffic. Bernadette took out her phone to pull up a Google map. The rickshaw was on the right main road, then veered off onto a side street.

Bernadette looked into the driver's side mirror—a rickshaw was coming right behind them. She didn't have time to text for help. She'd have to fight her way out of this.

The rickshaw came to an abrupt halt and the driver leapt out and ran. Two men jumped out of the other rickshaw and came toward her. They both had knives and grins on their faces.

Grabbing a seat cushion from the rickshaw, she jumped out to face them.

They were both tall and wiry. The first one moved in quickly to strike. Bernadette blunted his knife blow with the cushion, throwing an elbow into his head then kicking his leg out from under him. His head hit the ground. So did his knife.

She grabbed the knife to face the other man.

His grin disappeared. He hadn't expected this—his partner out cold on the ground—the target armed. Circling her, he threw swipes with the knife.

Bernadette could see the fear in his eyes. She wouldn't be a quick kill and she could tell he'd never been in a real knife fight. Bernadette had trained in knife fighting in karate. The key element—wait for the attacker to move.

She moved backward. Letting him think he frightened

her. He jumped forward, exposing his side. She plunged the knife into his stomach. He screamed.

Backing off—she waited for his next move. If he ran, she'd stop. If he attacked again, she'd finish him.

He clutched his stomach with his left hand. He screamed at her in rage—then lunged.

A fatal mistake. She stepped back from his lunge and hit him on the head with the butt of the knife. He fell to the ground.

A ship's horn sounded from the harbor. Bernadette knew it was the *Orion Explorer*. The first horn was at 1730 to let passengers know they had to be on board in a half hour. Throwing the knife on the ground, she jumped into the rickshaw and put it into gear.

The thing threw up a cloud of blue smoke as she let the throttle go. Pulling out her phone, she called Chris.

"You okay?" Chris asked.

"Yeah, it was a setup. Two guys tried to come after me. I'm certain now it's the Kingsbury. Meet me there."

"I'm on my way. I'll call Winston," Chris said.

Bernadette pushed the throttle on the rickshaw, speeding into traffic. Google maps showed the hotel was ten minutes away.

58

THE RICKSHAW SCREAMED to a halt in front of the Kingsbury. A doorman approached, then stood in awe as a white woman got out of the driver seat. Bernadette ran to the front entrance.

"Sorry, please park it for me. My driver fell ill," Bernadette said.

Brushing by the doorman she hit the doors. Making her way to the lobby, she saw the sign for the rooftop bar.

The only way to get there was the elevator. She found the one heading for the rooftop, hit the button and waited... and waited.

The lights on the floor indicator blinked so slowly it made a visit to a dentist seem fast.

Bernadette took in a deep breath, letting it out slowly. She looked at the figure that appeared on her right. It was Winston.

"You okay?" Winston asked.

"Yeah, I'm fine."

"You've got blood on your shirt."

"Not mine."

"You kill anyone?"

"Lower abdominal knife wound and concussions. Nothing too serious."

"Good."

A figure appeared on Bernadette's left. It was Chris.

"Hey, sweetie. Good to see you. Not my blood—I didn't kill anyone," Bernadette said.

"That's my girl. You hear the ship's horn? How much time do we have?" Chris asked.

"About fifteen minutes," Bernadette said.

The elevator doors opened. A large family dressed in Indian wedding finery got off. They had radiant smiles and many namastes as they departed.

Bernadette, Winston, and Chris got on, punched the button to the top floor, hoping they were the only ones getting on.

The elevator rose a slowly but didn't stop. As they hit the top floor the lights were on, gentle music played, while guests mingled to the sound of a blender mixing drinks from the bar.

Bernadette scanned the room. "I don't see her. Wait, there she is." She spun around to Chris. "Guard this entrance. Make sure she does nothing silly. Winston, you're with me. Let's clip this little bird's wings."

"Great, I've already called us some backup from the Sri Lankan police. They should be here any minute," Winston said.

Holly Marsden was sitting at the bar with a cocktail. She wore a floral dress, looking relaxed and happy. As the *Orion Voyager's* horn sounded yet again, she raised her glass in a toast to wish it a bon voyage.

Bernadette took the seat to the right of her, Winston slid in on the left.

"Hey, Holly, fancy finding you here. Does the bartender make a good Singapore Sling? I'll bet they're killer," Bernadette said.

Holly turned to look at Bernadette, then she turned to look at Winston.

"Yeah, Holly, I brought along some muscle. This is Agent Carla Winston of the FBI. She's kind of interested in your story."

Holly picked up her cocktail. "You should try the Cosmo, it's delicious. You have nothing to hold me on. I left the ship of my own free will. I'm an American citizen. I know my rights."

Winston pulled out her phone. "Yes, you're an American citizen, and there's an arrest warrant from the Singapore Police for you. Seems you were the last person seen with Astrid Karlsson before she died. Also, and here's a big thing, you're directly linked to Charlotte Bowman's murder in Chennai, India, a few days ago. So many things lead to you, Holly. The police in Singapore have listed you as an accessory to murder."

"They have nothing on me. That's a shopping trip from their prosecutors. I'll have my lawyers dismiss it in seconds," Holly said, sipping her drink.

A ship's horn sounded in the distance.

"Well, you'd have to do it from a jail cell in Singapore." Bernadette pulled out her phone and opened the PDF on her phone. "Now here's what's funny. This warrant came from camera footage of you meeting with Astrid outside the dive shop in Singapore. I looked at the tape and I made the ID on you." Bernadette hit the phone link and showed the video to Holly.

Holly's face changed ever so slightly. She took another long sip of her drink. "Means nothing."

"We also placed Charlotte Bowman at your hotel in Singapore. There's a lot to answer for with her. We know you knew her at the Cloister Hotel in Georgia. A prosecutor will have a field day with this." Bernadette said.

The ship's horn sounded again.

Holly finished her drink, pushing it to the barman for a refill. "You should get going. Your ship is leaving."

Bernadette turned her head towards the harbor, then back to Holly. "That's your ship—your salvation, Holly. If I leave this bar for the ship, the Sri Lankan police will arrest you. They have a reciprocal treaty with Singapore for warrants. You'll get sent back to Singapore—but it will take time. Your lawyers will fight it as they grind through your money as you live in a Sri Lankan jail. No, there's no hanging out in a posh hotel like you would in the states. That doesn't exist here. But if you get on the ship, it's American soil, baby. You got options."

The ship's horn sounded—two long blasts.

Holly turned to look at the entrance to the lounge. Two Sri Lankan policemen stood there with their AK47's and steely eyes.

"You're a real bitch, Bernadette Callahan," Holly said.

Bernadette smiled. "Now you're talking my language. Let's get out of here."

59

THEY MADE their way to the lobby. Chris had booked them an Uber while standing guard in the lounge. A large Mercedes sedan waited outside for them. Bernadette and Winston walked on both sides of Holly. They put her in back in the center seat and bracketed her on both sides. Chris got in the front passenger's seat.

"We need to get to the cruise terminal as fast as possible," Chris said to the driver.

The driver smiled. "Yes, of course."

Winston looked behind them to see three SUV's approaching at speed towards the hotel.

"Make that even faster, driver—we've got company," Winston said.

Bernadette turned to Holly. "I'm impressed, Holly. Those two men who tried to stop me were rank amateurs, but it seems you can get new recruits easily."

Holly shrugged. "I have no idea who they are."

The Mercedes driver threw the car into drive, punching the accelerator. The big sedan's back wheels laid a patch of rubber as it roared out of the hotel's front drive. The three SUV's followed in pursuit.

The Uber driver laughed and looked into his review mirror. "They will not catch us. They do not make those silly vehicles for high speed. This is German engineering. You will see the difference."

As they approached an intersection, the driver didn't slow down and threw the big sedan into a sharp turn. The sedan took it with ease, sliding into the turn then correcting as the driver hit the gas to come out of it.

Two of the SUV's didn't make the turn. They came in too fast one went into a store, the other jumped the curb— blowing its tires.

"Hah, there you have it," the driver said. "Superior performance." He turned to look at them.

"Look out," Chris yelled.

An SUV came at them from out of a side street. The driver swerved to miss it.

The cruise terminal was in sight. Winston looked back. The lone SUV veered off as they approached the terminal with the police presence.

The ship's horn sounded, three long blasts.

"She's getting ready to leave. They're clearing the last gangway," Chris said.

Bernadette pulled out her phone and dialed Cynthia.

"Bernie, is that you?" McCabe answered.

"We need you to hold the ship—we're minutes away."

"Sorry, strict captain's orders. We're pulling the gangway now."

"This is bullshit," Winston said. She pulled out her phone and dialed Alverez.

"Alverez here."

"We're five minutes away. Get to the bridge, stop the

damn ship," Winston barked into the phone. "We got Marsden."

"Copy that," Alverez said.

Alverez ran up the stairs to the bridge. Bursting through the crew only doors, she pulled her FBI credentials, holding them over her head.

"Attention. I'm Agent Alverez with the FBI. This ship will hold in position. We are bringing a suspect on board this ship wanted in connection with murders of American citizens. We will charge anyone who moves this ship with obstruction of justice."

The crew went silent. They looked to Captain Prodromou.

The captain put up his hand. "Hold the ship's position." He looked at Alverez. "I don't think I've ever heard a more convincing argument."

Alverez took out her phone. "Winston. You're good. The ship is holding."

"Driver, take us right to the ship," Winston said. She flashed her FBI credentials to the policemen at the gate, who let them through.

"Wow, that actually works, I'm impressed," Bernadette said. "My detective badge might get me into the line at Starbucks back home."

The Mercedes sedan drove up the pier to the ship's gangway. Cynthia McCabe was standing there with Mateo. They got out, Chris paid the driver on his phone and threw in an extra-large tip.

Bernadette approached Cynthia and Mateo. "I'm glad we got through to the captain. He got him to listen to reason. We have Holly Marsden, who the FBI is taking in for questioning."

Mateo looked stunned. "All you had to do was let us

know. We hold the ship all the time for passengers."

Bernadette stared at McCabe who looked down at the ground then got busy with taking down the security checkpoint.

She joined Winston as they walked up the gangway.

"What was that all about?" Winston asked.

"I'm not sure. But I'll need your big FBI search engine to get some answers," Bernadette said.

Winston approached Mateo. "I want you to put Ms. Marsden under lock and key. She has a warrant for her arrest out of Singapore. You got a brig on this ship?"

"We have a separate room we call the cooling off room. Not a true brig, but it will suffice," Mateo said. "She'll be secure there."

"Good," Winston said. She turned to Bernadette. "I'm going to meet with Marsden first, then with the Redstones. Sorry, I can't have you in there. But I'll let you know what she comes up with."

Bernadette nodded. "I can't wait to hear the answers they'll have once we get them talking. Do you mind if I give you a few questions I think should be answered?"

"Sure, I can use anything you have to solve this." Winston said.

60

HOLLY MARSDEN SAT in the room, looking down at her hands. She seemed contemplative and relaxed. A cup of water sat untouched in front of her. Winston sat in a chair on the other side with Alverez.

They'd found a small room used for staff briefings on a lower deck. Winston asked for the smallest room possible, a common tactic to make a suspect sweat and keep the pressure on.

"You want to tell us why you left the ship?" Winston asked Marsden.

Marsden lifted her eyes and looked at Winston and moved her mouth as if to speak, then stopped for a second before saying, "I was in fear for my life."

"From whom?"

"Elizabeth and Fred Redstone—who do you think?" Marsden said, as if the answer was obvious.

"Why would you fear them?"

Marsden drank some water and swallowed hard. "When I heard of Bowman's murder in Chennai, I knew they were taking care of anyone who might have helped them in their project."

"What was the project?"

Marsden rubbed her forehead with her hand. "Before I say anything, I want it on record that I don't have a lawyer present."

"Do you want a lawyer?" Winston asked.

"We're at sea, how's that going to happen?" Marsden asked. "And besides, this may be an American ship, but we are not in America. Anything I say can't be used against me. Are we clear on that?"

"I think we're clear. You came back to the ship with us to save yourself from being arrested by the Sri Lankan police and held for questioning by the Singapore Police," Winston said. "Now, do you want to tell us about your project? And if it leads us to a prosecution of the Redstones, I'm sure a U.S. Prosecutor in Miami will cut you a sweet deal. I just want to solve this case."

"Okay, but remember, I don't have a lawyer," Marsden said in a defiant tone.

Winston nodded her head. "You're right. No judge will allow anything you say to be used against you—so tell me about this project."

Marsden waited a beat, then began, "Elizabeth and Fred told me they wanted to take out their partners."

"You mean kill their partners?" Winston said.

"I never thought they meant it. I thought they wanted to handicap them somehow, to get them off their board or buy them out," Marsden said.

"So, you thought handicap didn't mean murder?" Winston asked.

Marsden shrugged. "Sorry, I've been in the hotel business all my life. I don't understand contract killer for hire."

"But you hired Charlotte Bowman to replace Astrid Karlsson?"

"Yes, I did. She was as close as they come to a match for Astrid. Elizabeth said they needed someone to do some funny business with some diving equipment during the shark feeding. Bowman was a perfect match," Marsden said.

"How did Astrid die?" Winston asked.

"No idea. I met Astrid at the dive shop. Elizabeth Redstone asked me to introduce her. I left them together and came back to the ship with Charlotte Bowman posing as Astrid."

"And what did you think when you heard of Astrid's murder?" Alverez asked.

"Look, I only knew about it at the same time I heard about Bowman's death, when we docked in Colombo. I realized how dangerous those two were. I left the ship."

"Did you know about the necklaces they gave to the ladies and the hearing aids for the men with the special electronics built in?" Winston asked.

Marsden put her head in her hands. "I heard Fred say something about that. I wasn't sure what he meant, but he said he'd built the perfect little 'buzzer,' as he called it. He once said he could buzz someone up to heaven with it. I did not understand what he was talking about."

Winston leaned forward. "Who paid for the Bernadette Callahan and her husband to be on this cruise?"

"Elizabeth saw a story about Callahan solving a case in Ireland. She figured she'd be the perfect one to witness the accidents of her partners. She thought it would be clever if they injured her partners right in front of her..." She looked at Winston and narrowed her eyes. "She thinks she's very smart."

"Was trying to kill them last night at the resort part of the plan?"

Marsden shrugged. "They'd have been collateral damage. Their deaths would have made the Redstones seem even more innocent. You just don't know how cold-blooded those two are."

Winston put her pen down on the notes she was writing. "I think we've heard enough for now. We'll interview Elizabeth and Fred Redstone to see if what you say is true."

"But they'll lie about everything. Don't you see? That's why I ran away. I haven't got a chance around those two. They've got all their money. They'll lawyer up in a heartbeat and leave me twisting in the wind," Marsden said, breaking into sobs.

"If your story has any relevance, I'll make sure you're transported back to American for prosecution. If not, I'll hand you over to the Singapore Police in Kochi." Winston said.

"You can't do that. Bernadette Callahan promised me if I came back to this ship, I'll be prosecuted in America." Marsden said rising up from the table.

Winston shrugged her shoulders. "You have a problem there, Marsden. Bernadette Callahan is a detective with the Canadian police force. She can't offer anything. But here's what I'll offer. You give me what I need, I'll make sure you're prosecuted in America...otherwise, I'll let the Singapore Police exercise their warrant."

Winston got up to leave. "Ms. Marsden, Agent Alverez will take you back to your room. You'll be in protective custody until we reach Kochi."

"Thank you," Marsden said. She dabbed her eyes with a tissue and blew her nose.

Winston walked out of the room to see Bernadette

standing in the hallway. "What? You couldn't hear through the walls? She asked.

"Can you give me some highlights? Bernadette asked.

"Marsden admits to being involved in helping the Redstones orchestrate all the killings. But that's all she'll give us." Winston said. "The Redstones have the greatest motive."

"Yes, but if Lucinda died last, they lost out on two hundred million. Do you think they screwed up the sequence of killing Lucinda and Nigel?" Bernadette asked.

Winston raised an eyebrow. "Murder is not an exact science. Maybe they messed up with that necklace thing you said they have. I'm going to interview them, but I think it's best if you're not in the room. You're too close to all the events."

"You're right. I could use some time with Chris. You can fill me in later. When do you plan to meet them?"

"I asked Alverez to bring them back here after she takes Marsden to her room," Winston said.

Bernadette turned to go and stopped. "See if you can get them to show you the necklace they have in their room. I doubt if they know we've seen how deadly it is."

Bernadette walked down the corridor. She saw Cynthia walking towards her. She stopped, pulled out her radio, listened to it, turned and went back the other way. Bernadette watched her walk away. It looked like Cynthia had avoided her. She'd check that out later.

61

BERNADETTE AND CHRIS decided on a late-night dinner in the Italian bistro again. There was no formal dress, casual attire only, and the dishes were more rustic and less over the top than the fine dining area. And besides, how many times could Bernadette make the black dress look different?

Chris ordered a cioppino that came full of mussels, clams, fennel, garlic and tomatoes with a side of grilled bread. Bernadette chose spinach and ricotta-stuffed pasta shells. After the spicy Indian food, this was a delightful change. Her stomach was feeling a bit off as well. She decided to give it a rest.

The waiter poured them glasses of Chianti and left them alone.

"What do you think the Redstones are telling the FBI?" Chris asked as he dabbed his grilled bread into the cioppino sauce.

Bernadette pushed her glass of wine aside and picked up her Pellegrino, "Well, they've been with them for an hour, I'm sure they've had plenty to say about Marsden's accusations... Oh wait, there's Winston and Alverez coming into the bistro."

"Mind if we join you?" Winston asked as she approached.

Chris stood and motioned for them to sit. "Please do, we wondered how things were going."

"That seems awfully fast," Bernadette said.

Winston and Alverez sat down. The waiter brought them menus and water. Winston sighed as she looked over the menu.

She placed the menu on the table, sipped her water, and looked at Bernadette. "That was the biggest waste of time. They refused to be interviewed separately, then denied everything Marsden said. Claimed it was a fabrication in her mind, and they were being framed by Marsden."

"Were they brave enough to show you the necklace?" Bernadette asked.

"Yep, Fred Redstone took Alverez up to the room, opened the safe, and brought it back to the room. There was nothing in the back of it. No electronics, nothing. They claimed we could search their room if we liked. They stated they didn't see any electrical device in the back of the necklace."

"But I showed it to Fred after Ashley's death. Did you mention that?"

"I did," Winston said.

"Fred Redstone says he doesn't recall any such conversation. He remembers getting the necklace from you when you dropped it by after Ashley's' death. He said he put it in the safe and that's where it's been all this time," Winston said.

"But he looked at the back of it, when I mentioned it had

some electronics in it, he said maybe it was a GPS put in by Nigel," Bernadette said.

"You've got a classic, he said, she said. Did anyone else see the back of the necklace before you gave it to Fred Redstone?"

"Chris glanced at it, but as he's my husband, I doubt if his testimony would carry any weight."

"They've got us on this. And they've refused any further interviews until we get back to the states. They want lawyers present," Winston said. The waiter came by to take their order. "I'll have what the gentleman's having. That looks good. How about you, Alverez?"

"Totally. I love a spicy cioppino, and red wine, lots of it," Alverez replied.

Once they had their wine, Bernadette raised her glass of Pelligrino. "Here's to the Redstones. They've pulled off four murders of their partners. I have to hand it to them, they're good."

"You're going to let them get away with this?" Chris asked.

"Not on your life," Bernadette said. "I'm going after them big time. I suggest you start with McCabe in the morning.

"Why her?" Winston asked.

"Her response to me on return to the ship didn't add up. She said she couldn't hold the ship. Her security chief, Mateo, said it wasn't a problem," Bernadette replied.

ALVEREZ CHIMED IN, "You know, for all my theatrics on the bridge in showing my badge, the ship's captain made no fuss at all. He said to me later, all I had to do was ask."

"There's one other thing. I was attacked on my way to the hotel where Marsden was at. The only person on the ship I told who I was going after was Cynthia McCabe," Bernadette said.

"I thought she was a friend of yours," Chris said.

"We went through basic training together; a lot can happen over the years," Bernadette said. She looked at Winston. "Can you run a search on Cynthia McCabe as well and see what kind of condo she bought on Vancouver Island. That's a pricey place for real estate right now. I didn't think they paid that much on these ships. And I'll give you her cell number to ping her phone. She told me she would be in meetings in Mateo all day. Mateo told me hadn't seen her since yesterday."

Winston said, "I'll put Alverez on it."

"While you're at it, can you find the beneficiaries in Lucinda Braithwaite's will?" Bernadette asked.

Alverez put her wine glass down, took out her phone to make notes. "Anything else?"

"Yeah, I got something," Winston added. "I think we do a check on New Wave Technologies. Find out if there's anything going on in the background."

"I got it," Alverez said, entering the notes into her phone. "I'll hit this right after dinner. I'm sure I'll be able to find the information, and if I can't I have several techies state side that will find it for me. I'll copy you on it as soon as I know."

They finished dinner and went their separate ways. Winston and Alverez headed to their cabin to do research and file reports while Chris and Bernadette went back to their room. They sat on the balcony watching the full moon in the cloudless sky. A small glitter of stars appeared.

Bernadette sipped on a Pellegrino while Chris sat beside her in a deck chair to keep her company.

Chris reached over to massage the back of her neck. "I

know you're worked up over this, but maybe you need to let the FBI handle it now."

"Yes, it's their show. I'm only a witness to make a statement if they need me. But I have a feeling this isn't over."

"What do you mean by that? This looks like a stalemate. They might get Marsden on meeting with Astrid, but as no one can place her at the scene of her death. She'll walk. The same with the Redstones."

Bernadette looked up at the stars. "I have a feeling there's something more. This has all been so meticulously staged to this point. The Redstones disposed of their partners, but Elizabeth messed up with Lucinda's death. I just don't get that."

Chris got off his chair and kissed her on the lips. "I'm turning in for the night, you coming to bed?"

"I will in a minute," Bernadette replied while caressing his face.

She went back into the room, pulled out her laptop, and returned to the lounge chair. There was good Wi-Fi connection on the deck. Hitting the power button, she looked out to sea, waiting for the laptop to power up. A full moon threw a sheen onto the waves. A lone albatross sailed by with its wings spread gliding on air currents of the ship. Bernadette tracked it as if she was a hunter as it headed towards the stern. Something caught her eye.

Was that a small boat following the ship with no running lights on?

62

BERNADETTE'S COMPUTER CAME ON. She checked her emails. There was one from Alverez with some PDF files. She clicked to open and scanned them.

The first one was regarding Cynthia. She'd said she had a mortgage on a condo on Vancouver Island. The condo owned by Cynthia McCabe was a two bedroom, in the toniest area of Victoria, the sale price was 850K with seven hundred per month condo fees. The information claimed Ms. McCabe had a clear title, no debt.

Bernadette raised an eyebrow. "That's one hell of a pad for a police constable turned security officer on a cruise ship. Both Chris and I couldn't afford that on our salaries."

Another file included a note from Alverez that Bernadette might find interesting. Cynthia McCabe hadn't left the police; they had asked her to leave due to 'conduct unbecoming an officer.' The only way she'd have been able to get the job with the cruise ship was if the Royal Canadian Mounted Police sealed her file. She'd worked for a helicopter company on Vancouver Island and then for a forestry company.

"Whatever she did, she got away with it as an officer, and the helicopter company—that's a red flag. She could have sabotaged the Redstone's chopper." Bernadette said out loud

The next PDF was on New Wave Technologies. The offer to purchase the company was being withdrawn. The reason stated was '*unusual accounting practices by the leading directors of the company,*' meaning Fred and Elizabeth Redstone

There was another note about the Internal Revenue Service opening a file on Mr. and Mrs. Redstone. They'd requested a meeting with them. All of their requests so far had been unanswered.

The third PDF was the last will and testament of Lucinda Braithwaite. How the FBI obtained this so fast, she didn't want to ask. Bernadette scrolled past all the legal jargon to the page of beneficiaries. There were only two— Holly and Constance Marsden. She checked the name Constance; she was the twin sister of Holly. A light went off in her head.

She put the laptop down and went to the balcony railing. The boat with no lights was still trailing the ship. It was sitting just off the stern, far enough back to go unnoticed, but it could race to catch up with the ship in a minute if it had to. It looked sleek in the moonlight, all black with low lines and cabin profile.

Bernadette went back into the room. Chris was fast asleep. She decided not to wake him. What if her hunch was just that? She knew what Elizabeth Redstone's next move might be. It seemed crazy even to her—but what if it was real?

She grabbed her phone and cabin key, then pulled on a pair of tennis shoes with a good grip for a wet deck. Closing the door slowly, she took out her phone and dialed Winston.

"It's me," Bernadette said when Winston answered.

"Who else would call me at this hour? What's up?"

"I got a hunch. Can you do a wellness check on the Redstones and on Marsden in her lockdown room?"

"But you're just down the hall from Redstone," Winston said, running a hand over her eyes to focus.

"I have to run aft to the marina. I think someone is about to leave the ship. Meet me there after you do the checks."

"Sure. Where the hell is aft?"

"The rear of the ship. It's a watersports platform on the lower level." Bernadette said.

"Got it. I'll send Alverez to check on the Redstones. I'll check Marsden. We'll be there in five. Don't do any weird shit that'll get you killed. I hate writing reports for cop death —they're lengthy."

"Thanks, Winston."

She put her phone away, running down the stairs to the aft marina deck, which was only a few meters above the water. A person could jump from the ship with ease from there, and it was wide enough to avoid the ship's propellers.

No one else was on the stairs or the passageways as she made her way. An eerie bright light shone through the windows from the outside.

Pushing through the last bulkhead door, she came into the marine deck. It was dark inside. Only a small light shone from a door that opened outward to the sea. She walked carefully up to it.

"Hello Holly, hi Cynthia," Bernadette said.

Holly was pulling on a wet suit. Her head whipped around to see Bernadette in the moonlight. Cynthia stood beside her.

Holly finally opened her mouth "Damn you... how did you...?"

"Know what you might be up to? I'll admit you didn't make it easy. The last will and testament of Lucinda Brathwaite made you and your twin sister, Constance, as beneficiaries. I'll bet there's a suicide note in your room and a safe deposit box with a complete confession of how the Redstones planned all this and used you?"

"You are damn clever, Detective. Cynthia said you'd be right for this job. So sad we didn't take care of you at the resort," Holly said.

"Are you leaving Elizabeth and Fred to take the fall, or have you killed them already?" Bernadette asked.

Holly looked at her diver's watch. "They have about ten more minutes to live. That's the funny thing about heart attacks. Some are quick, some not so much. But you, lady, you're a pain in the ass, you'll be dead before that. Shoot her, Cynthia."

Cynthia looked from Holly to Bernadette. Her hand reached around her back. She pulled out a gun.

Bernadette looked at the weapon. "Ah, I see the replica gun has appeared. Were you hiding it, Cynthia?"

Cynthia pointed the gun at Bernadette. "Does it matter? No one will ever find this gun or your body."

"You're in deep on this, Cynthia. There's no way back if you kill me, whatever Holly has been paying you to help her. I know you also helped hide the security tapes."

"Just shoot her, Cynthia," Holly commanded.

"That's it, Cynthia," Bernadette said. "Holly is about to jump ship. She's going to fake her own death. But you know she leaves no one alive. She had Bowman taken care of— she'll do the same with you. Did she convince you to kill Nigel and Lucinda? Did she do it while you watched? This is different. You have to pull the trigger.

"I don't' know..." Cynthia said. "Look, this is all going

wrong. You shouldn't have come down here, Bernadette." She lowered the gun.

Holly grabbed the gun from Cynthia. "I'm done with this conversation. I've tried to have you killed but you got away. This time, damn it, I'll do it myself."

"Don't do it," Bernadette yelled.

Holly pointed the plastic replica gun and pulled the trigger. It exploded in her hands. She fell to the deck, her body hanging half over the side of the ship.

Bernadette rushed forward. She threw an arm block into Cynthia's shoulder, knocking her to the deck. Grabbing Holly by her shoulders, she pulled her back into the ship before she could fall overboard.

"You're under citizen's arrest," Bernadette yelled at her.

"I need a doctor," Holly moaned.

"I should have let you fall overboard. The sharks would have finished you," Bernadette said.

Winston and Alverez, their guns out, arrived to see both Cynthia and Holly lying on the deck. Holstering them, they came over to stand beside Bernadette.

"This looks like you were right. Ms. Marsden was about to escape with help from Ms. McCabe," Winston said.

"How are the Redstones?" Bernadette asked.

"They're okay. We found the necklace lying on their bed. Alverez deactivated it. That thing was doing one hell of a lot of humming. She threw it in the toilet to shut it off."

63

THE MORNING LIGHT broke over the calm blue sea with a brilliant ray of gold. Bernadette sat on the deck with a cup of tea in her hand, watching the gulls swoop around the ship. They were getting close to Kochi now.

Bernadette had been in an all-night meeting with Winston and Alverez, hearing second hand what the Redstones, Marsden, and Cynthia McCabe had to say. She held her tea in both hands as she stared out to sea.

Chris sat beside her, kissed her on the cheek and sat down. "So, it was all about the money, then?"

Bernadette sipped her tea. "Yeah, an elaborate insurance scam with the players double crossing each other. The Redstones recruited Marsden to help them, she brought in Cynthia McCabe, and then Marsden got greedy. She realized she could manipulate Lucinda and Ashley. She'd convinced Lucinda she was going to kill off the Redstones and leave her with all the money, then give her a cut."

"How did you know Cynthia was at the resort?"

"I had my suspicions about her. When she told me, she was going to be off the ship and Mateo said he hadn't seen her. There was a knot tied around Lucinda, it was a bowline. The medical examiner said it was a sailor's knot. It is, but it's also used in forestry where Cynthia once worked. And she spent time in helicopter maintenance before joining the ship. She must have been the one to sabotage the helicopter to make the Redstone's look innocent."

"Why not let them die on the island?"

"If the Redstone's had died, Nigel and Lucinda would have left the ship. Holly was after Lucinda. The chain of death had to be her being the last to die. That was Marsden's big payout. Remember, she knew every tour the group was booked on. The final act was at Lion Rock. Marsden had figured out how to use the necklace to her advantage."

"I'm sure it surprised the Redstones when they found out how they'd almost met their deaths from a necklace," Chris said.

Bernadette smiled. "They sure were. They couldn't talk fast enough to give the details of how Holly and Cynthia were at the resort to take care of Nigel and Lucinda. But it wasn't done right. Holly and Cynthia claimed the Redstones had a contract out to kill them as soon as their pathologist confirmed that Nigel had died before Lucinda."

"So, they knew they'd been double-crossed?"

"I think the Redstone hired the men chasing us back to the ship. They wanted to kill Marsden. Marsden probably hired the men who tried to stop me getting to her," Bernadette said with a wink.

"Damn, this is complicated," Chris said.

"Big money always does that." Bernadette said.

The phone rang in the room, Chris went to answer it. He listened, then replied, "I understand."

"What's that about?" she asked as he sat next to her.

"Seems our trip is over. Elizabeth Redstone had in fact

paid for our trip, and with the seizing of their assets by the IRS, they canceled all of their credit cards."

"I thought they paid this trip in advance?"

"Ms. Marsden cooked the books on the ship, so they only paid a small deposit to get us on. If we want to continue the voyage, we can give them a credit card to do so."

"How much?"

"I think she said somewhere north of twenty thousand each."

"I think we're getting off the ship—how about you?"

Chris laughed. "Yeah, my thoughts exactly."

64

CHRIS PULLED the bags to the front door. Marcus made sure their bags were taken down. He shook their hands, white gloves on, and wished them well.

They went to the main desk to check out.

A young lady named Meredith presented their last bill. It had a zero balance. "The company has taken care of your bill for solving... the unfortunate circumstances regarding the other passengers," she said with a slight nod.

Bernadette did a quick glance of the bill. "Ah, I should have had some cigars on here from the cigar lounge."

Meredith went to her computer and checked. "No, there's no bill here from the lounge."

Bernadette smiled. "That must have taken care of by Mr. Bill Loving. I'd like to leave a thank you note for him."

Meredith looked puzzled. "Did you say Mr. Bill Loving?"

"Yes, I met him in the cigar lounge a few times."

"I'm sorry, Ms. Callahan, there's no Bill Loving on this ship. And the cigar lounge was closed a day after we left Singapore because of an electrical wiring problem with the air handling system. Passengers were complaining about the smoke coming from it," Meredith said.

Bernadette's face turned a shade of white Chris had never seen before. "You okay?"

"No, not exactly. I think all my conversations with Bill Loving were a dream vision," Bernadette said.

"Isn't that the same thing your grandmother has all the time?" Chris asked.

"Totally the same, and she usually scares the hell out me with them. This one was different—Bill Loving came to me in a familiar place with the scent of cigar smoke. He seemed so much like my grandfather. And the vision he gave me was of going back to the beginning. I met Cynthia McCabe at the start of our cruise. That was my clue."

"You going to ask your grandmother about this later?"

Bernadette shrugged. "Maybe, but this could mean I'm having my own dream visions. I must pay more attention to them."

Captain Prodromou appeared at their side. "I hear you're leaving us at this port. So sad to see you go."

"I thought you'd want to see the back of us," Bernadette said.

The captain leaned forward and smiled. "Are you kidding? The *Orion Voyager* is now big news. You cracked a case of millionaire insurance fraud while on board. Our bookings are up one hundred and fifty percent. The Voyager company is very grateful, that is why we are taking care of your travel arrangements."

"You are?" Bernadette asked.

"Yes, we are," Captain Prodromou said. He looked over at Meredith. "Please arrange for Ms. Callahan and Mr. Christakos to travel first class back to their destination."

"That's most kind and unexpected," Bernadette said.

The captain bowed. "You saved my ass." He looked at Chris, "I'm not sure what the translation is in Greek, but you get my drift."

"Yes, we do, and you're welcome. You're one hell of a captain. Thanks for keeping us afloat out there," Chris said.

Bernadette and Chris walked down the gangway. Alverez and Winston were standing beside a policeman who looked familiar.

Bernadette turned to Chris. "Do you mind taking care of the bags, there's someone I have to meet." She walked up to the policeman, put her hands together and made a small bow. "Inspector Lee, how delightful to see you."

Inspector Lee turned to her. "So, finally I get a chance to meet you. We would never have solved the murder of Astrid Karlsson without your work and determination."

Bernadette shook her head. "I only did what I'm trained to do. I couldn't help following my intuition."

Lee nodded. "In Buddhism we have a saying, 'clear your mind, your heart is trying to tell you something.' You have the genuine gift of intuition. Do not lose that. It will serve you well."

"Thank you, Inspector Lee. I believe we have some things in common."

"Perhaps it is the fault in our stars we are impassioned to serve the truth and justice. But I think we'd rather do this than anything else. I must admit, Detective Callahan, I asked the Singapore Police to let me take custody of the prisoners so I could thank you personally."

He stood back, put his hands together, and bowed low. "On behalf of the Singapore Police and those in both India and Sweden, I give our thanks. You have brought this case to a swift conclusion. We could not have done it without you."

Winston stepped forward, "Inspector Lee, these suspects

are going to be transported directly to the United States. They committed a crime against American citizens on an American owned vessel in international waters. We have jurisdiction. I'm sorry you flew all this way to exercise your warrant."

Lee stepped back and bowed, "I will inform our legal department, I'm sure they will file papers for their extradition once you have charged them."

Bernadette looked at Lee, his face had not changed, there was no sign of the disappointment he must be feeling.

"My apologies, Inspector Lee. You came all this way for nothing." Bernadette said.

"No, not at all. I have had a chance to meet you, Detective Callahan. And I have seen the suspects captured. Sometimes there is no finality in our work, but there is a process. It is good to see that process is working." Lee said with a bow.

Bernadette returned the bow and walked back to Chris. She grabbed her bags from him and walked towards the waiting taxi.

She stopped and looked at Elizabeth and Fred Redstone, Cynthia McCabe and Holly Marsden. They were walking by her towards a police van with Inspector Lee with four Kochi Policeman escorting them.

"None of this will stick you know," McCabe said as she walked by. "I'll be out in no time."

Bernadette smiled. "Cynthia, you forgot your police training. Don't you remember all the criminals you tracked using their cell phones. The FBI tracked yours to the resort. Oh, and I heard they have you at the Quay in Singapore. The prosecutors will have a field day with you. You best start giving up everyone you can to save yourself."

McCabe opened her mouth, then closed it. A policeman moved her forward to the waiting van.

Elizabeth Redstone was escorted by a female police-woman. She stopped in front of Bernadette. "I'll have the best lawyers in the U.S. on my case. Everything I said on the ship will be thrown out."

"Good luck on hiring those lawyers, Elizabeth. I understand they need a large retainer to begin. My sources tell me you're broke." Bernadette turned to Marsden. "Same for you. No insurance company will pay you a dime when you're accused murdering the insurance holder. Kind of a thing with them..."

Marsden and Elizabeth looked down as the police moved them towards the waiting van.

Chris came by her side. "Did that make you feel any better?"

"No, but I like seeing the fear in their eyes when they know they've been caught. But it will never be enough. It doesn't bring back the victims."

THE TRIP back to Canada was uneventful, except for Bernadette's stomach ailment. She'd never had a problem with spicy food before. The first-class flight from Kochi back to Canada was luxurious and comfortable. But it took forty-seven hours with an overnight layover in Delhi. Her stomach didn't settle itself. The airline steward gave Bernadette some antacids that helped, but only for a short time.

By the time they landed in Calgary and made the two-hour drive to their home in Red Deer she was feeling fatigued. Her mind went over everything she'd eaten on the trip. Chris had eaten everything she had, and he was fine.

It took a week for Bernadette to finally make an appointment to see her doctor at the insistence of Chris. Doctor Zoe Murray was in her late twenties, with blonde hair and blue eyes that matched her easy manner. She had a good sense of humor that always made Bernadette at ease on the few times she'd seen her.

Now, as she stared at Bernadette's chart, she cleared her

throat once and looked up at her. "You're pregnant. Congratulations."

Bernadette clutched at her throat, "But I can't be?"

"Why not? I know you're a Catholic, but the immaculate conception was a one-time thing. Unless you're really on to something I should know about." Dr. Murray said with a sly grin.

Bernadette looked down at the floor, "it wasn't in our plans.'

Murray leaned forward and put her hand on Bernadette's, "there's a saying, mankind plans, and God laughs. You're healthy and you're still in your prime, you'll be fine."

THE DRIVE from the doctor's office back to the Royal Canadian Mounted Police detachment was only fifteen minutes. In that time, Bernadette's mind mulled over a multitude of possibilities. Would she stay in the force? Could she ride a desk for nine months? How would they cope with a child and her twelve-hour days? Could she still work the streets as a detective?

By the time she parked her vehicle, she knew the answer. The finality of it would be crystallized the moment she met with her chief of detectives. She found Chief Durham at his desk with his usual mound of papers and his ever-present coffee cup.

"Can I talk to you for a minute?" Bernadette asked, standing at his door.

Durham looked up, "Whoa, you look serious. You usually barge in here and drop in the chair—what's up."

"I just got back from the doctor.'

Durham brushed his hand over his receding hairline, "Are you okay....?"

"I'm pregnant." Bernadette said, throwing the words out as if she'd been given a sentence.

"Oh, thank God. I thought it was something serious. Congratulations." Durham said. "Sit down. You look like you've been charged with something."

'Well, it is serious. You know our force won't let me be involved in anything physical. That means I'll have to be on a desk in the detective unit." Bernadette said as she slid into the chair in front of Durham.

"Nothing wrong with that. They'll miss you on the street, but they could use you for all the research and paperwork."

"I'm wondering if you could put me into cold case work?" Bernadette asked.

Durham pursed his lips. "You want to be dropped in with the M and M boys?"

Bernadette smiled, "yes, McBride and Mankowski. I know they're a bit old school and might resist me coming in, but I think I could do good work on cases that have slipped through the system."

Durham sighed, "old school is putting it mildly with those two. Between you and me, they're misogynistic dinosaurs. They'll hate you the minute you walk in the door. Remember, they got into cold case through a competition. You walk in there because you got a bun in the oven, sorry for the terminology, but that's how they'll see it, and they'll blow a fuse."

"I've faced worse." Bernadette said. "I want to work on the Paradis murders."

Durham shook his head, "oh, so just a simple cold case... I'll take it to the superintendent. Give me to the end of the day."

BERNADETTE SAT on the sofa that evening while Chris made dinner. Sprocket, her big German Shepard lay at her feet. He sensed something was wrong. They usually ran together in the morning, today Bernadette had taken him out for a walk.

Chris came into the living room and sat beside her, "you want to tell me what's up, or do I play twenty questions? You look like you just lost a match in karate."

"I'm pregnant." Bernadette blurted out.

'Okay, that's a surprise." Chris said. He took her hand, " But you know we've always thought we might have kids, now that I'm no longer with the force."

Bernadette put her free hand to her head, 'yes, I know, it's always been in the back of my mind. Now that it's here and the little unsub is growing inside, I'm liking the idea."

"You're calling our unborn baby an unknown subject?"

"What else do I call it? The it? The little egg that could? Unsub seems to work."

Chris caressed her cheek. "I guess it changes our lives."

Bernadette held his hand, "It does in a good way. You'll be an amazing dad, and I'm hoping to be a least a better mother than mine was."

"How about the job? Are you going to go off active cases?"

"That's a yes and no. As you know, I had to tell Durham. The force is adamant that no pregnant officer gets to work the streets or quick react scenarios."

"You'll take a desk job—good for you. I think that's wise."

"I convinced Durham to put me in cold cases. I've got cases I'd love to work. There's some that need investigating to put the heat on." Bernadette said looking into Chris's eyes.

Chris took both her hands in his, "you're going to open the Paradis family murder case?"

"I sure am." Bernadette said arching her eyebrows. She looked down at her tummy and rubbed it. "I want our child to be safe. What happened to the Paradis brothers has always left me with a feeling that an evil lurks in this town that needs to be dealt with."

"Won't that be like knocking over a hornet's nest in this town?"

Bernadette put her hand on her stomach, "sure will. And my little unsub and me will be doing some righteous kicking ass."

Sprocket jumped up from the floor and placed his big paws in her lap. He started to whimper.

"Don't worry big fella, I won't let anyone hurt you." Bernadette said rubbing his head.

"I think Sprocket is worried about you," Chris said.

DEAR READER

I hope you enjoyed the journey I sent Bernadette Callahan on. I went along vicariously as well. Singapore to Dubai was on my bucket list, however, 2020 changed that, so I sent Bernadette instead.

If you enjoyed this book, please leave a review on whichever Amazon site you purchased it from. Reviews are like gold to authors, they help us learn what our readers enjoy, and provide a guide to others.

If you wish to join my list to be informed of my next book, see all of my other works and get a free story, please click on this link below.

www.lylenicholson.com

ACKNOWLEDGMENTS

I would like to thank my beta readers, Stan Shaw, Jeffrey Bush, Patrick Bishop and of course my wife, Tessa.

I'd also like to thank Joe Nahman for his legal advice, Cheryl McKinnon for her insights into the working of the Royal Canadian Mounted police and Tim Gutherie for his technical knowledge.

I'd also like to thank John Appleton for being the last one to glance at the pages to see what I might have missed.

And of course, my heartfelt thank you to Ada Loving, our dear friend who lent me Bill Loving, in name and a mild sketch of his character to come back to life in this book.

ABOUT THE AUTHOR

Lyle Nicholson is the author of eight novels, two novellas and a short story, as well as a contributor of freelance articles to several newspapers and magazines in Canada.

In his former life, he was a bad actor in a Johnny Cash movie, Gospel Road, a disobedient monk in a monastery and a failure in working for others.

He would start his own successful sales agency and retire to write full time in 2011. The many characters and stories that have resided inside his head for years are glad he did.

He lives in Kelowna, British Columbia, Canada with his lovely wife of many years where he indulges in his passion for writing, cooking and fine wines.

If you'd like to contact Lyle Nicholson, please do at lylehn@shaw.ca

ALSO BY LYLE NICHOLSON
THE BERNADETTE CALLAHAN SERIES

Book 1 Polar Bear Dawn

Book 2 Pipeline Killers

Book 3 Climate Killers

Book 4 Caught in the Crossfire

Book 5 Deadly Ancestors

Prequel, Black Wolf Rising

Short Story, Treading Darkness

Stand Alone Fiction

Dolphin Dreams, (Romantic Fantasy)

Misdiagnosis Murder (Cozy Mystery)

Non Fiction

Half Brother Blues (A memoir)